Tinseltown Riff

Shelly Frome

Tinseltown Riff

FIRST SUNBURY PRESS EDITION
Printed in the United States of America
March 2013

Trade Paperback ISBN: 978-1-62006-205-0
Mobipocket format (Kindle) ISBN: 978-1- 62006-206-7
ePub format (Nook) ISBN: 978-1-62006-207-4

Published by:
Sunbury Press
Mechanicsburg, PA
www.sunburypress.com

Mechanicsburg, Pennsylvania   USA

Dedication

For Susan, always, and the magic of the silver screen.

Chapter One

Ben Prine had his first premonition that day as he swung by Olympic Place. Which was odd because he hardly ever had premonitions. Especially not after averting the mad morning rush and pulling into the old familiar cul-de-sac.

At first glance everything was perfectly fine. The adobe-like structures stood as silent as ever, as if the inhabitants were either in hiding or had left for the day. Tightening his focus, he glanced across the street at Aunt June's place, the selfsame burnt-sienna fortress guarded by a maze of cacti he once called home.

No movement there. Nothing untoward going on.

Then why was he so edgy? Was it some kind of emotional memory thing? Because twenty-eight years ago Aunt June's new housekeeper, who couldn't have been more than nineteen, dropped off her three-year-old with the excuse she had some important errand to run and never returned?

Humoring himself, he checked to see if there was a strange car nestled under the hovering agaves as he slid out from behind the wheel. The next camera shot called for a medium close-up of a slim sandy-haired woman scuffing up the drive armed with the news she'd been abducted into white slavery; or was the victim of some horrible accident and only now regained her memory and remembered Ben's birthday.

This notion, of course, was like all hack-writer's notions —*What if? What if? What if?* After all, it was the first rule of the trade. This day can not be like all other days. This was the day something juicy was set in motion.

Stepping away from the borrowed vintage red Prelude, he became increasingly aware of the whoosh of the Santa Ana as it continued to blow in from the desert on this uncommonly hot Labor Day morning. It was a fluke, a faux disturbance that was bound to fade off. Perhaps he could put the jittery feeling down to the fluky wind and his dire need to jumpstart his non-existent career. That's what he told himself.

But it didn't wash. His premonition had no name and could not be explained away. He would just have to let it ride.

Edging past Aunt June's commodious Lincoln Town Car and dodging the cacti, he reached the wrought-iron front door gate and rang the bell. Two latches were immediately released and the inner door gave way a crack.

"A little faster," said Ben. "I'm expecting a call."

The door jerked open, revealing the pinched face, darting eyes and tight wispy hair that belonged to his erstwhile guardian.

"Very funny. As you well know, I'm in an actual hurry," said Aunt June, checking the pendant watch dangling from the chain around her neck. "Unlike you and your Hollywood pipe dreams, I'm off to work." For emphasis, she pointed to her metallic blue pants-suit and matching loafers.

"Well, as it happens, auntie, I just may have something going."

"I'll bet. Did you at least bring back my camera?" She raised an eyebrow as she yanked the oaken door half open and stared back at him through the iron bars. "I've got three new listings: one on Larchmont, one on Genesee, and an apartment building clear over on Serrano. Plus a showing on Plymouth Boulevard. Which means, even in this crap market, I have stuff to post on the website, new stuff to shoot and still make my flight."

"I'll get your camera in a minute. Look, it's almost eight-thirty."

"No kidding. No minute. Move it, please and make sure you got the lens cover."

Humoring her, Ben dashed across the street and snatched the digital camera out of the trunk. He would miss it and its 18-55 mm range and capacity to take sharp evening shots. On a whim, Aunt June had wanted to take quick stills to make her listings seem a lot more impressive. In contrast, Ben had had dubious but desperate uses for this upscale Nikon.

2

He made his way back through the cactus maze, double doors and into the dim alcove. Reflexively, he took a sharp left, plunked the camera down on the desk in his old room, came back and headed straight into the kitchen. He no sooner got to the phone when Aunt June popped her head in and barked a few more snappy orders.

"Hook the camera back up, will you? Which means you'll have to find that cable gizmo which got mixed up in a box headed for the dumpster. Why the box? 'Cause it's filled with your junk. As you might wish to know, I'm putting the house on the market. Selling it for peanuts, cutting my losses and I'm out of here."

"You're kidding?"

"Sorry, don't have time to chat."

"Terrific."

"So, while you're at it, do what you promised. Check out the bars on the windows, hook me back up, take what you want and—"

Racing ahead of herself as always, Aunt June's feisty eyes locked in place. "Hey, that reminds me. What about the birthday?"

What she meant was the arbitrary day they chose to commemorate the last time they'd laid eyes on his biological mother.

"How about when I get back?" Aunt June went on. "Tell you what. We'll do a wrap: have another closing, if you get my drift. Truth is, I've already got an offer. When it comes to rip-offs, shysters can't resist. So, not to put too fine a point on it, if you could just settle on one of the final options."

Ben plopped down on a folding chair facing the ancient wall phone. The final options included any form of work, finding a hard-up girl with money—in short anything guaranteeing Ben was out of her hair. Thus enabling her to close the books on his so-called upbringing.

"It's down to the wire," said Aunt June, standing over him. "You're sacking out at my niece Iris', taking advantage of her good nature. You're tooling around in Mrs. Melnick's tenant's car while he's away. You've been unemployed since God knows when, run out of benefits, can't even afford a cell phone--"

3

"I know, I know. Heading for the dust bin. On the treadmill to oblivion."

"So stop futzing around for rice cakes." (Aunt June could never bring herself to say 'for chrissakes.')

"Look," said Ben, "hard as it is to believe, I've really got a shot."

"Oh, give me a break." Putting a period on this exchange, Aunt June whisked away down the hall.

Ben stared up at the phone for a moment or two, rose and shuffled back into his old room which now served as Aunt June's office. If and when the phone rang, he only had a few feet to go.

With the realization he might never see this place again, he took in the bulletin board, the framed blowup of the Pacific Coast Highway, the calendar with a red check mark for every breakthrough date Ben had failed to meet.

Hunkering down in the far corner, his gaze settled on his old stuff. Call it what you will, time was definitely telescoping on him, everything coming to a head.

He riffled through his first comic strips. All the panels began with a kid in the smog. Sometimes on Sunset Strip, sometimes running down a beach in Malibu, or caught in a house of mirrors on the Santa Monica Pier; sometimes stuck in a ravine or humongous canyon. Then they went blank. Somehow he had to slay the dragon and rescue the maiden. Or do something extraordinary to get his mom back to make up for whatever it was he did or didn't do. And to this day, nothing came of it.

Later on, unable to complete any ideas of his own, he'd appropriated parts of sure-fire cartoons from yesteryear. After those shows were put on hiatus, he'd had a few stints doctoring some failed TV pilots and a few gigs working on movie scripts in development that never saw the light of day. Then nothing. Deluded, wary, but possibly still on the verge *if only* ...

On the verge of what? What was lying in wait for him around the corner? What gantlet would he have to run?

Snapping out of it, he spotted the cable beneath his old binoculars, attached it to the computer tower under the desk, and drifted out into the hall where he ran smack into Aunt June's two-piece matching luggage set.

4

"The windows and skylight," hollered Aunt June from somewhere out back. "Do it all."

"That's a Roger," said Ben, hollering back, his anxiety level holding steady. It was almost nine and no jingle from Gillian, the only real contact he had left.

He yanked out a foot stool and saw to it that the bars over the skylight were securely locked. After all, it wasn't really Aunt June's fault she was paranoid. It had only been a month since she'd heard a car starting up in the middle of the night. With the squeal of tires still ringing in her ears, she sprang out of bed, peered out the kitchen window and noticed her Chrysler sedan was no longer in the drive. No wonder when about to leave this loopy town she relied on Ben to double-check everything. And, unlike Ben, she had a perfectly good reason to be on guard.

Stepping into the living room, treading carefully over the zigzagged blue and yellow Zapotec rug, he checked the other windows, careful not to knock over the Talavera canisters and urns. Having sworn off nubile footloose domestic help like Ben's mom, Aunt June had resorted to matronly Mexican housekeepers. In turn, Ben was forced to pick up a smattering of Spanish in hopes of being fed all those times Aunt June was off on one of her realty toots. In truth, Chicanos were all that had kept him alive.

He checked his watch again and tried harder to stay in the here-and-now.

He returned to the kitchen and wolfed down two of the prepackaged fruit salads. Then he scurried around, double checked the rest of the window locks, pivoted and smacked into Aunt June, her rolling luggage and the large paper sack of oranges she'd plucked from the back yard.

"How about this?" said Aunt June, brushing past him in the hallway. "For starters, keep your eye out for some cheap permanent address. So I don't have to see your mail and wonder what the citation from the Hollywood Community Police Station is all about. Or the overdue bill notices and whatnot. So I don't have to think about any of your goings-on *period*."

Sloughing this off, Ben moved straight back to the sliding glass doors in the rear of the house, secured everything and yanked the drapes shut. Just as June finished arranging the oranges in the refrigerator bin, she poked her head out of the kitchen and snapped, "I see, young man, that box of yours hasn't moved an inch."

Sloughing this off as well, they crisscrossed again.

Finally, the phone rang. Ben let it jangle six times, slipped back into the kitchen, snatched the receiver off its cradle and waited.

"Ben?" said Gillian, breaking the silence. "Listen, I don't have time for this. I know you're there."

"It's nine-twenty."

"I realize that," said Gillian in that condescending tone of hers. He could just picture her giving her chestnut-brown bangs and lacquered do the once-over in the mirror to make sure she was still the frostiest of them all.

"Let's cut the tap dance, okay?" said Ben. "I am, where I've been for some time, at the bottom of your list. Most were either out of town or already committed. Those who were available wanted a little coin up front which let them out, but still left the ones who hadn't picked up their messages. Just now you threw in the towel figuring 'Ben's so hungry he's still waiting desperately for my call'."

This time it was Gillian's turn to leave Ben dangling. After a few beats, she said, "Do you or do you not want to fill-in this morning in front of some wanna-be screenwriters, make a little change and induce me to throw you a bone?"

"A bone?"

"A bone."

"Ah, I see ... Legitimate or illegitimate?"

"It's Hollywood, Benjy."

"That's what I was afraid of."

"Yes or no. I'll need you off and running by eleven."

"Is that clock time or Gillian time?"

"Get in character, pal: the boy next door who gives you no grief."

"I wing it, is that what you're saying? Pretend I'm a player and then—"

"No *and then* unless you come through."

Realizing he was in no position to dicker, Ben gave Gillian a definite, "Okay, you're on."

A second after she hung up on him, he hurried back down the hallway. In the master bedroom that featured duplicates of the framed map, bulletin board and calendar, he caught Aunt June perched on her queen-sized bed, double checking every item in her shoulder bag.

"Tell me this, will you?" she said, squinting over her bifocals. "Why, when you've got two sharp cookies like Iris and me as role models—"

"Right. Admirable Iris massaging yesterday's celebs."

"At least she's solvent. Look, kiddo, I told you, I'm cleaning house and came across your junk. Should've chucked the drawing pads and crayons and put the kibosh on the old movies as well. Played Monopoly with you, got you out on the street."

"Are these misgivings? Sentiments that have never crossed this threshold?"

June pursed her lips, as close as she ever got to an emotional overflow.

"Hey," said Ben, "you didn't put me up for adoption and you gave me room and board."

"Right. But just look at you. Hyper, your sandy hair's thinning, your nice face has some wrinkles, you're thin as a rail."

Scuffing back to his old room, Ben called out, "Don't look now, Miss June, but you're getting a tad motherly."

He secured the window latch, knelt down and noted the copy of Dr. Seuss' *Oh, the Places You'll Go* and the rough sketches for *Rescue Rangers* and *Skateboard Troopers*. Then he leafed through the printouts courtesy of Aunt June's dandy telephoto lens before the Hollywood Police stepped in. Here were stills of helicopters hovering over a roof on Mulholland Drive, and the shattered front door of a duplex over at Pico and Robertson. All taken by crouching under yellow crime-scene tape. Snapping "sneaky-good action shots" for Leo, the mad Russian producer and cousin Iris' current wrestling partner—living proof of how far he'd sunk and how far he was willing to go.

After checking the thermostat, he hoisted the cardboard box as Aunt June scooted past him and dropped her luggage outside the front door. He locked the inside door and the wrought iron screen, hid the keys in the secret spot behind the giant Madagascar and picked up the crumpling box. Weaving unsteadily beyond the cacti in time to catch Aunt June's backside, he shouted, "Saturday," over the flapping lid. "My birthday this year'll be Saturday. That gives me five days."

"Based on what calculation?" said Aunt June, ensconced behind the wheel of her sedan.

"Your own window of opportunity. The length of the annual all-women's realty confab."

"Good call. Gives you enough time to grab any kind of work and hole up on your own."

"Not what I meant."

"Too bad. Anyway you look at it, you got five days. Over and out."

"Whatever. Rest assured the world's most hapless orphan will finally find himself."

Rolling her eyes, Aunt June countered with, "Expect a call from me first thing. I want a progress report. Make good by Saturday or you're out on the street. That comes from me and Iris, straight from the heart."

"Thanks, just what I needed."

Crossing the street, he crammed the box in the trunk of the Prelude. Returning, he performed the same task with Aunt June's luggage, leaned in and offered the customary perfunctory hug as she looked askance at her pendant watch.

"And one last thing," added June, "couldn't help overhearing. They'll be no reconciliations with Miss Gillian on my bed. No possibility of unlocked doors while I'm gone. I mean it, come on now, swear."

Two fingers held in the air and a couple of arm pats did the trick. Just as she was about to turn the ignition key, they both noticed that the faux Santa Ana had kicked up a notch, hot and dry as can be.

"Well now," said Aunt June, "gusts have been a little freaky today. Wonder what it means?"

"Just the proverbial winds of change."

"Change—you said it. Five days, kiddo, and counting. Your dangling days are done."

Chapter Two

Ben was increasingly aware of the Santa Ana as it rattled the jalousies of the hotel's Catalina room. He was also aware of the trickles of sweat seeping into the collar of his button-down oxford. Together both sensations would remain a constant till he proved he could pull this off.

Pausing in hopes the air-conditioning would finally kick in with a reassuring whir, he scanned the sixty or so seated wanna-bes leaning forward in their rattan chairs. He faked another easygoing smile and went on with his sketch of a classic movie plotline. The response was negligible. No light in their eyes, no sign of rapt attention or even interest.

Ben looked over to his far right at Gillian perched by the open window. After all, she was the facilitator, the one who got him into this. But pert, blasé Gillian held her pose and gave him nothing. He was failing; she would toss him no bone, his prospects were nil.

A sweet-faced lady in a lemon pants-suit raised her hand. She pointed out that according to the conference program, participants were to be offered insider tips--*Take-the-guess-out-of-success*, the updated mismatched cops formula and so forth.

Pushing harder, Ben nodded and suggested that classic films were a great guide no matter what the venue. At that point, the whole group grew restless.

"Look," the sweet-faced lady blurted out, "so far, till you showed up, we've been tossed the skinny on *Girly Girls Take Paris* and *Slacker-nerds and the Prom Queen*. So far, we've been reminded that in this economy uncertainty is poison and the letters RE are the ticket--revamp, revisit. So let's move on to what's trending with this recipe. Dangerous-but-fun, we've heard about. Cynical-with-a-heart. So what's new? What've you got for us? Why are we here?"

The spontaneous applause cut through the pervading indifference.

Ben signaled strongly to Gillian. But she remained frozen in her lime-sorbet camisole and matching Capri pants. The whoosh kept rattling the jalousies, fanning her bangs, the only part of her do that wasn't lacquered down.

The attendees began jostling each other, forming a solid block of unease, augmented by the fake Santa Ana and the glare off the mint walls.

Sweet-face stood, pointed an accusatory finger straight at Ben and hollered out, "Where is the insider angle? Come on, let's have it, if you please."

Ben tossed the dry marker from hand to hand and thoughtlessly said, "Right. You're too smart to go down any not-so-good street. And you may not find any you'll want to go down. In that case you'll head straight out of town.'

"Doctor Seuss," Ben said in the sudden stillness. "When in doubt, you can't go wrong with good ol' Doctor Seuss."

This gem was greeted with stone silence.

Ben studied their faces. Most of them were at least in their fifties. And, actually, it was no surprise what he was in for. He'd seen them milling around, tapping away and spreading their fingers on their iPhones. Doubtless spending all their spare time microblogging on Twitter, networking, and scooping up the latest copy of the trades. Also, doubtless, having plunked down hundreds of dollars, champing at the bit at the Hyatt Regency Century Plaza. There they were, about to give a three-minute pitch to junior executives from second-tier production companies. Moreover, they had every tip from *Sure-fire Killer Scenarios* memorized. And the last thing they wanted to do was actually write, let alone listen to Ben talk about classic films.

At the same time, Ben knew this was his own last-ditch pitch. If he couldn't get past these dilettantes, he would wind up driving a night-shift cab to and from LAX, bleary eyed, disheveled, hustling for tips. Remembering this very moment when he blew it all big time.

As the stone-cold stillness shifted to a sense of unified puzzlement and Gillian's cosmetic façade faded from blasé to blank, Ben jumped back in.

"Ideally, I mean," said Ben, winging it. "The lesson from Dr. Seuss is a call to bypass the road well traveled."

The unified puzzlement switched back to unease as the chairs began to squeak.

"Think about it. Every prequel and sequel, every spin on the mismatched cops routine has been kicked around and hung out to dry. But you take another route, leave your comfort zone and go out of your way. Maybe shift gears from mismatched cops to mismatched pair."

Totally reaching now, Ben said, "I mean classic doesn't mean retread. You can still have a blundering rookie who hooks up with a mentor. But does our hero have to be a cop? Does his crusty but benign mentor have to be in uniform and does he have to be crusty and benign?" On a roll, Ben carried on about Dr. Suess's title, *Oh the Places You'll Go*. "Now if that rallying cry isn't apt, I don't know what is."

Agitated murmuring followed by more determined chair-squeaking as though some fuzzy inside information had indeed been leaked.

Sashaying to his side, Gillian added, "Well now, how about that? I mean puh-lease. Take a look at him. Average height, slight build, two eyes, a nose and a mouth. A throwback to the defunct nice guy from MGM. But he just opened the door to the new retro. Right, Benjy?"

"You bet," said Ben, wincing, hating her for calling him that. "Turner Classics meets leading edge."

"Exactly," said Gillian, continuing to affect her best Hollywood hostess tone. "Boy next door latches on to seasoned pro and takes off. Sounds like a plan. Everyone agreed? Terrific. We have to count ourselves lucky that Mr. Prine was available at the last minute. Because he's a busy man, took a few minutes away from his tight schedule and, needless to say, if he keeps playing his cards right, the sky's the limit."

"Yes, ma'am," said Ben, anxious to learn what Gillian had up her sleeve. "Always nice to have those timeless clichés applied to me."

"And what's the key to those timeless clichés? What's always the key?"

Answering her own question, Gillian stepped to the side, erased Ben's notes with a flourish and began listing links that were all over the map. Like unexpected connections between reruns, YouTube and what-have-you.

Her list-making reminded him of the time he found himself in her apartment four blocks north of Hollywood and Vine. The one with the glistening black-and-white décor replete with posted rules of engagement, including the timing and sequence of foreplay. You wanted to keep up with Gillian, you had to get with it, be it sex or projects or, as Sweet-face put it, whatever was trending.

Scribbling away, Gillian noted the wanna-bes' main competition: ninety-five percent of Writers Guild members were unemployed, ever-hungry for any opportunity to take a flyer and do whatever it takes.

Gillian's broad smile and mellow tone belied the way she then uttered, "Those past thirty are especially bad off," aiming the aside solely at Ben.

Undaunted, in no time the bevy of seekers were lapping it up. A portly man in an oversized Disney T-shirt and baggy shorts observed that only an hour ago a woman his age, naked, swaddled only in Saran Wrap, was hawking a video of her love poems. Poised between the two oversized palm fronds fronting the hotel entrance, she'd succeeded in gathering a crowd. "Yes-sir-ree," the portly one chortled, "ready to take a flyer on anything."

Sloughing off this loopy deflection, still dying to find out what Gillian had in mind for him, Ben finally managed to cut the discussion short and announced it was time for lunch. But he'd no sooner left the dais, when he was accosted by a gaggle of leery matrons who questioned him about his credentials and wanted to know exactly how he broke in.

As fast as he could, worrying he was about to lose track of Gillian, he revealed that he spent months watching the mouth movements of Japanese cartoons while supplying the English dialogue. He'd also helped doctor plots for kiddie shows, sitcoms and a few low-budget movies, leaving out the fact that most never got made.

But before he could break away, Sweet-face and the guy in the Disney T-shirt cornered him and asked how any of this actually jibed with *Oh the Places You'll Go*. What kind of success story was this anyway? Then the matrons butted back in. One of them, brandishing a shiny clipboard covered with a jumble of notes, mentioned the movie *Wall Street* and reminded then that Gordon Gekko said, *The most valuable commodity is inside information. If you're not inside, you're outside.* She also crowed that the second Ben let on what he'd really been up to, it was no longer exclusive and anything he had to offer was worthless.

Sweet-face chimed in suggesting that, perhaps, Ben was only a flunky who did odd jobs. After all, who'd ever heard of him? And the best any of them could hope for was to follow suit, volunteer to be a gofer at a production company, latch on to a seasoned pro and worm their way in like Ben.

As they headed off for the lobby kicking this notion around, Ben spotted Gillian by a cooling vent on the far side of the hall. Lying in wait, she now went straight after him, her three-inch heels clacking on the terrazzo floor. How she managed to balance herself--toes tucked into a strand of velvet with no sides or back--was one of the world's great wonders.

"Dr. Suess?" said Gillian, hissing over his right shoulder. "Find some un-loopy road'?"

"Okay okay. But, no matter how you slice it, I put a spin on it which you gobbled up. Why? Because you're relegated to scraping the bottom of the barrel and could really use someone who can wing it with the best of them."

"Oh, really? Well if I struck brain back there, your so-called abilities are bloody useless without a bona fide backup who has actually walked the mean streets and provides me with some bona fide cachet."

"Meaning? Will you goddamn spell it out? What have you got for me and what's the price I have to pay?"

Gillian turned away, obviously weighing the pros and cons of actually letting him in on her latest ploy.

"Come on, let's have it."

When Gillian spun back, her perfect oval face only inches away, he couldn't help noticing that, even when miffed, she appeared freshly packaged. Not to mention everything else in her arsenal that made her so maddeningly self-possessed.

"What are you staring at?" said Gillian.

"Nothing. Talk to me, will you?"

Gillian teetered around in a wide semi-circle and returned to her original square. "All right. Here's the check for your efforts. That ought to cover the repairs on the car you scrounged and leaves only your living expenses and whatever else it takes to survive."

"Speak, dammit, what is the deal?"

She flicked her eyelashes for a few beats and finally came out with it. "This little gig was, of course, just for openers. The real test requires you to leap two hurdles."

"Go on."

"What did you think I meant up there on the dais? Why did I pick you for the topic? Who did you think I was referring to?"

"You don't mean ... ?"

"Bingo. First off, you enlist the services of Pepe, your alleged friend and undercover cop."

The Pepe Gillian was referring to was C.J. Rodriguez. The fact that Pepe was short for Jose and a common Latino nickname was obviously beyond Gillian's sphere of knowledge. So was the fact that his true identity was unknown. All of which didn't make Ben's first hurdle any less problematic.

"Ah," said Ben, doing his own semi-circular turn, "of course. And does this, by any chance, have anything to do with Leo, the gonzo Russian? The very same Leo who conned me into glomming Aunt June's camera and got me to slip past the police barricades the other night to take shots of--?"

"Never mind, never mind. Okay, assuming there truly is a Pepe ..."

"Yes? So? "

"... you, Benjy, will get him on board as a gritty source. Because, pal, you'll be moving way out of your league.

Because the initial question is, How do we get you in the door? With Pepe behind you, we may, God help us, have an outside chance."

"For what?" Ben said as he crammed the check into his shirt pocket. "A fly-by-night indie, a home movie, a shot in the dark? What am I selling out for?"

"At the moment, it's up for grabs."

"Terrific. And what kind of money are we talking? And where do you fit in?"

"First things first, you hear me? What's your schedule like for the next couple of hours?"

Glancing at his watch, Ben hemmed and hawed. It was almost twelve-thirty. He had to admit he was free.

"Fine. You seek out your elusive buddy while I pursue more viable contingencies." With that, Gillian shut off the fluorescent lights, turned sharply and clickety-clacked away.

Before she made it past the louvered doors, Ben hollered, "Suppose, by some weird quirk of fate, he agrees? What then?"

"You'll ring me at my desk by three. If I still have no better option, and against my better judgment, we'll shift into phase two."

"At your desk? On Labor Day? Doesn't Viacom ever sleep?"

A few more clickety-clacks and Ben hollered, "The truth, humor me! Tell me why I'm so blessed?"

"We need a patchwork artist with links to the mean streets. As you've duly noted, with everyone out of town on this absurd weekend, and due to the pressing time frame ..."

"You need a winging-it and grit act pronto."

A quick condescending smirk and Gillian was gone.

For a time, Ben just stood there dawdling. He gazed out at the picture window at the Santa Monica Pier, past the wide sandy beach and swarm of parked cars over to the hazy outline of the boardwalk. He glanced to the left of the Ferris wheel, arcade and roller coaster and fixed on the old-timey carousel. The image of his favorite painted pony came to mind--the silver one with the shimmering green-

and-black saddle blanket. The only one prancing and laughing as if to say, "Come on, kid, let's go for it."

Tossing his lecture notes into his battered briefcase, he moved off. He had a few hunches how to hook up with the mercurial C.J. But the odds of C.J. going along were, at best, a hundred to one.

Outside, the hot breeze turned playful, subsiding into little gusts that meandered through the wide archways of the hotel's portico. The gusts flittered over the gravel of the courtyard and a crumpled leaflet advertising the writers' conference; then picked up a notch around the shiny yellow pebbles and maroon flower petals atop the squat Hedgehog cacti. No worries about the flowers though. They were protected by a network of white knitting needles protruding in all directions.

The gusts drew still for a moment under the pulsing noonday sun. Soon, as if keying on the leaflet, they picked up strength again, lifting the crumpled paper in the air, dropping it and lifting it higher until they pinned it against the jutting spikes.

The premonitions were obviously working overtime. Telling him it was simply a given that his days were numbered and his time was at hand.

Chapter Three

Only a few days before, on a late Friday afternoon, Deke too was on the verge. But he was a wild rover, indifferent about what he might come up against or even what the job was all about. "Bring it on," he said. All that mattered was a chance for a little fun.

As he reached the top of the next rise, he was right where a lanky, rawboned man ought to be. Not still killing time in goddamn Cut Bank helping his old man fence-in a herd of buffalo headed for some meat counter. Truth to tell, the days when the two of them could stand each other were long gone. Nowadays it went like this:

"You home for a while?"

"Not really."

"I could use some help."

"That figures."

And besides, his old man was pushing sixty-five. Hanging around him, you start missing a step. Hanging around anybody or anywhere, you lose your edge.

Taking in the scene, he marked the stretch of dark cloud hanging low overhead. The sky so massive the gray seemed flat and painted, tacked on to a sheet of blue as far as the eye could see. From this vantage point he could look down at the Glacier Park Trading Company by the train stop. Starting with its peaked roof faking a crest in the Rockies, he could easily scan the adjacent Glacier Village Restaurant and jagged flat sign running the length of the building. If his calculations were right, some weasely accountant would slip out of one of these wooden buildings or step off the train. Failing that, the guy was already hunkered down in a rented cabin. Either way, as soon as this little errand was done and dusted, he had the rest of the loose ends to square away.

Walt had hinted the whole job might take him down to Salinas. Which was fine. Walt also hinted it could take him further, a whole 1400 miles, maybe as far as L.A. Which damn well wasn't fine. Deke had always avoided L.A. You head southwest from Vegas onto I-15, you hit the Mojave Preserve, then its Barstow and, before you know it, it's Riverside and you're sinking right into it—the smog, the traffic sprawl, hemmed-in to where it was pure torture working your way out again.

Just the thought of it put a damper on his good mood. Hell of a choice between L.A. and hanging out back in eastern Montana. With its godforsaken squares and rectangles of alfalfa, soybean and wheat. Patches of in-between acres, ochre-colored grasses and then the abandoned line shacks falling apart and empty horse corrals. Plus rusting farm equipment, old tractors with flat tires, a bunch of rotting cars they don't even make anymore: Nash Ramblers, Packards, Hudsons, Desotos and Studebakers. Things you can't get parts for, places too far out for a mechanic to reach; a way of life that went bust. And all the while, his old man muttering, "It ain't so bad." It is, was and always will be so bad. Aside from the in-between acres, Deke too had been lying fallow. And nothing was going to keep him still anymore. Even if it meant goddamn L.A.

Casting his gaze solely on the train station, he waited a while longer. Within minutes, the eastbound special came, passengers got on and off. No sign of the little guy. No sign of him anywhere. From the photos, he was probably in his late thirties, wore horn-rimmed glasses and had a squinty, worrisome look on his face. In other words, he appeared to be exactly like he was: a spooked bookkeeper who'd downloaded some files back in Portland, then lit out for the boonies and figured the trail would go cold. A little weasel who flat-out figured wrong.

Just then, little beeps caught Deke's attention. He plucked up his Levi jacket off the high flat rock, jerked the cell phone out of the top pocket, flipped it open and hit the green icon. Even transmitted through this little gizmo, Walt's rasping drawl was deep and tired. If you didn't know him, you still couldn't help picturing a barrel-chested geezer in suspenders with a walrus mustache and a lot of mileage on him.

"Well?" said Walt, wasting no words.

"I'm on it."

"That's what you said this morning."

"Right."

"So?"

"Two more hours, tops."

Receiving no reply, Deke added, "I'm moving in, what's your problem?"

"My problem?"

"Yeah."

"Contingencies is my problem, Deacon. And time. You hear me?"

"Like I said, two hours."

Walt did another one of his low growls and switched off.

Giving up on the train stop, opting for the cabins, Deke pocketed the cell phone, circled back down, hopped in the rental car and drove another ten miles west.

The stretch of painted gray continued to hold up, still tacked on the waning afternoon sky. After parking on the gravel by the wayside, Deke started walking in a northwesterly direction. In no time, he found himself in the cool of the mountain range, deep inside the thick stands of aspen, pine and cedar that dwarfed everything else and blotted out the horizon.

Though he couldn't smell it yet, he knew the charred timberline was close by where the fires had burned out. Once he came upon the cabin, there'd be nothing to it to flush out the bookkeeper, recover the records and split.

Relying on what was left of the light, he soon came upon a break in the terrain. About a hundred yards across from where he stood, a sheer rock face rose skyward scarred with crevices, slots and slits. It went on far to his left until it diminished into an outcropping of slabs and ledges. All he had to do was follow the ridge, keeping the sheer rock formation in sight till it veered sharply away. At that point he'd be at the gorge where the river ran still just before it churned into rapids. The log cabins would be tucked away on his side of the break. They'd all be empty, vacated by families heading back in time to get the kids squared away for school at the end of the Labor Day weekend. Meaning, all he'd have to do is step inside a vacant bunk and hold out his hand. Not much action, just a little practice, a little warm-up drill.

As traces of the sky began to wash into charcoal and deep blue, Deke easily covered the distance, ambled by the scattering of trees that dotted the rim of the ridge and threaded his way through the low-lying brush and beargrass.

Presently, he heard the water gurgling and took in the scene just as he imagined: his side of the gorge running a few hundred feet lower down a slope with the river humming below. The only thing that surprised him were the hemlocks snapped almost in two, blocking his path. Their tops tugging at the roots as if straining to end it all, plunge over and get swept away. What surprised him more was a rise on the far side where the gorge gave way to a waste-dump of charred and splintered red cedars directly opposite from where the cabins would be.

At that moment he couldn't help but remember the time down in the hot, sticky bowels of Belle Glade, Florida where his old man ran a sugar mill. There they would burn the dried stalks and flush out the critters. Watch them hop and skedaddle till the thick black soil was empty of debris. Like what Walt had in mind for him next probably. More flushing out till the whole job was stripped clean.

Moving on, drifting inside the canopy of gnarled whitebark pine, he passed the first empty cabin and then a second about two hundred yards apart. Past a third cabin closer by, he guessed that even if the bookkeeper decided to run, he would spook him past the pine, down the slope, across the slabs in the river where he'd likely fall in, holding his attache' case up high. And even if he made it to the other side, the climb through the scorched timber would do him in. He'd keel over and that would be that.

Still brushing past the stands of pine, he came upon a fourth cabin. Inklings of twilight glinted off a side window and meshed with the glow of a Coleman lantern.

Bending low till he came within a few feet of the warped back porch, he noticed the backpack and fishing gear-- obviously just purchased after asking some outdoor trader for whatever could be tossed in the trunk of a cab for a camping trip. Knowing diddly about camping or where the fish were running or what bait and tackle he'd need. The little guy was probably sitting there right now, scouring a map, figuring his next move. Maybe even wondering how in hell he could hit a bunch of trailheads and lodges till he made his way across into Canada.

Deke crouched down and watched as a scrawny shape flitted by the window and flitted back. Against the glow of the lantern, the figure looked like a sputtering shadow-puppet.

Deke checked his watch. It was going on six-thirty mountain time with only the afterglow left of daylight. The last thing Deke needed was to waste any more time and wind up traipsing back in the pitch dark. Running into some grizzly cub looking for its mother or worse.

When he glanced back, the flitting figure was gone.

On his feet, keeping low, he skirted around to the log railing, assuming the guy must have flopped down on a chair just inside the back door. But he no sooner reached the edge of the plank steps when something clobbered him in the back. Tripping and twisting around, he threw up his hands just in time to avert the next blow.

"You're trespassing," said the scrawny figure. "I have a receipt. I'm renting this cabin so you'd better clear out."

Regaining his balance, Deke just simply glared at him.

"Ah," said the little guy dropping the chunk of firewood. "I know what you're thinking. Actually, I don't know what you're thinking but let me guess. You're a caretaker or something—sure, that's it. But why did you sneak around? Why didn't you knock?"

Still motionless, it was all Deke could do to keep from losing it then and there.

"Ah," said the little guy once more, clutching his oversized windbreaker, kneading it with both hands. "I've got it. You're with the park service worried about the fires. Boy, you can still smell the soot, can't you? Well, there's no need to worry about me. I am not the type to use a fireplace without observing every safety precaution."

The little guy kept rattling on, as if there was some straw he could grasp if he could talk fast enough.

21

Deke told himself not to throttle him. This was only lost and found. Not worth the effort.

"Right," said Deke as he stepped onto the porch and flung open the screen door.

"Hey, come on," said the little guy, bolting past him through the doorway and fronting him. "Whoever you are, I'm sure we can straighten this out."

"Forget it," said Deke, spotting the attaché case. "It's over."

"Oh, now I get it. I get it. You're the one who's been hounding me."

Deke flipped the latches and spotted the CDs, ledgers and registers. He was about to snap the case shut when he caught the little guy glancing over toward the wall. There atop a knotty pine bureau lay a high-end smartphone and a tri-fold wallet. Noting the ID window and the fully stuffed credit card pockets, Deke tossed both of them in and secured the case.

"No, wait a minute, you can't do this."

"Right."

"Listen to me. That's robbery. Not to mention you're messing with the S.E.C.-- the Securities and Exchange Commission, in case you didn't know it. And that's not the half of it. Do you realize how far this thing goes? You don't, do you? Because if you did, you'd hand that case right back to me and get lost."

"Oh, sure."

Deke shoved him out of the way.

But he countered by rushing past him again, blocking Deke's way out while fumbling for the latch on the screen door.

Deke grabbed a handful of billowy jacket, spun him around and slammed him against the wall. But the second he reached back for the case, the little guy beat him to it and took off.

Hurrying after him, Deke jerked open the screen door, leaped off the porch into the tree shadows, lunged forward and grabbed hold of his sleeve. But it was so loose, he slipped out of it, leaving Deke tripping over his own feet.

Cursing, Deke sprang forward and darted through the overarching stands of pine till he spotted him in the shadowy near distance smacking into a low-lying branch that sent his glasses flying.

Reaching the slope, rushing headlong now, Deke closed in, drawing closer and closer to the darting figure and the running river below. In the back of his mind, he knew you don't scamper down a steep incline of loose soil, rocks and brush and suddenly brake the momentum of a guy weighing at least a hundred and forty pounds. But he did it anyway, lurched at an impossible angle, grabbed hold, hoisted the squirming body and shoved him toward the rock slabs below. The only thing that prevented Deke from inflicting further damage was the wrenching spasm in his lower back.

Ignoring the whimpering cries, he turned around, shambled back up the rocky slope and foraged for the attaché case which he easily located a few yards over in the brush. Clutching his twinging muscles with one hand and the case with the other, he straggled back up the remaining distance. All the while, he barely heard the calls near the river's edge. He also barely heard the tail end of the last-ditch plea:

"Wait a minute. My ankles twisted, maybe busted. You can't just leave me here ... Okay, I downloaded the files, sure. But that's nothing compared to what you've got yourself in for ... I mean, you've really done it now. You hear me?"

"Uh-huh," Deke mumbled to himself, straining as he approached the top of the rise. "Tell me about it."

"I mean, for God's sake! You've got to call somebody. You have to at least do that!"

Deke tried to imagine putting in a call for some paramedics. But the notion didn't take. He could also just hear what would happen if he got Walt in on it:

What you got here, Deacon, is a whole can of worms and I don't know what-all if he survives. Might could finger you for openers. Get hold of government and law enforcement agencies besides. Plus a short circuit with some cartel or what in hell this whole thing's all about. Just goddamn stop and think. There's always consequences, things you don't figure on.

But that was Walt for you. Walt could come up with more worries than an old hen. It was all Deke could do to get back to the car. Back to where he could cross off this first pain-in-the-ass item without getting hogtied with wet-nursing by the river bed and a bunch of lame what-ifs.

He did, however, wonder what Walt would make of the smartphone, wallet and ID as a kind of insurance. But put that possible leverage on hold.

Wincing, paying the fading cries for help no mind, Deke double-backed along the rim of the ridge, the remaining glints of daylight melding with the murky shades of green and gray. The attaché case was almost weightless, but toting it somehow aggravated the jabbing, pulsing pain in his lower back.

Presently, high up, a red-tailed hawk circled by, making swooping shadows against the steep rock face opposite, mocking him, reminding him how clumsy he'd been.

Working his way through the bitter brush, hugging the tree-line, he tried to distract himself with a favorite image. It was an old circus poster over a bar on the outskirts of Cut Bank announcing that the Flying Walenda Brothers were coming to Billings. The caption was: *Life is on the high wire. Everything else is waiting.*

Continuing to disregard the pain, more fun images flashed across his mind. There was a job he'd pulled for Walt outside of Gallup: rifle-toting carjackers, driving semi-trailers, hauling stolen Mercedes headed for Beverly Hills. In his mind's eye, he could still picture the low-slung red adobe shacks ... a blown-up statue of a desperado on the roof of Don Diego's Restaurant, the New-Mex Pottery Co. and Zuni Fetish store. And that's when Deke let loose with 500-gram repeater firecrackers and a torch or two arched in the air landing in the tinder dry clumps of sage and juniper. The carjackers hightailing toward the table-flat mesas, through the smoke and poplars that looked like petrified feathers ... Yes!

As the images of better days came and went, Deke stopped over a dozen times to rest his back. Then pressed the speed-dial on his cell knowing damn well he wouldn't get any reception till he got back to the rental car but trying anyhow.

At one of his rest stops, he reached inside a pocket of his Levi jacket for the little matchboxes. Conceivably, he might have to start a fire to ward off some wild thing if his back caved in. After all, you just never know.

By the time he made it back to the gravel wayside, he was two hours late. He slid behind the wheel, hit the speed-dial again and cut Walt off before he had a chance. "Talk to you later," said Deke.

"Dammit," said Walt, "you'll talk to me now."

"I got the goods, I'm comin' in."

"Oh, yeah? Maybe I don't want you comin' in till I hear what happened. What's the fallout, how was it left? And don't tell me it was, 'Sorry for the inconvenience, mister, won't happen again.'"

Dismissing all thoughts of the racked-up accountant, Deke said, "Look, Walt, I've had it."

"Don't give me that. The problem, honcho, is spillage. Spillage here, spillage there, maybe could be all the way down the coast. Now give it to me. How did it go?"

Deke hit the ignition, shoved the case under the dash and said, "I shut it down on this end, Walt. And like I said, I'm comin' in."

Deke left the rental car at the Enterprise lot in West Glacier and managed to catch the night train with a few minutes to spare. But he got no rest, only dozed off once in the half-sleeper. The rocking motion kept aggravating his back and soon he was at it again, taking stock.

He was pushing forty. Which meant sloughing off what just happened and staying on top of his game. Especially if he wound up in goddamn L.A. and had to take on some flaky Angelinos.

Chapter Four

Still holding his own on that same blustery Monday, Ben spotted a Chevy pickup. It was parked far behind the endless rows of shiny sports cars clogging the beachfront; the only item of note the fact that it was dusty, ancient and out of place. But to someone like Ben, it was another sign, perhaps prompting him to slip away with some migratory workers or just plain toss in the towel while he had the chance.

Girding himself and shrugging off this latest cop-out, he moved on. The hot sand sifted into his loafers, the hurly burly of the Pier greeted his eyes and ears a scant few hundred yards to his left. But he had no time to muse over the carousel, nor the Playland Arcade and the Rollercoaster with its screeching passengers at the farthest end. At this point it was all as amorphous as the signs, omens and the dusty old truck.

The offshore wind began to pick up again, blowing off the land out to sea. As he focused solely on the water, he noticed the rolling beach-break, one swell catching up with another forming a low, long line. His gaze took in the little kids flopping on their boogie boards directly ahead, barreling through the froth and scurrying towards him onto the sandbank. At a distance beyond the kids, a gaggle of Chicano teens were splashing and dunking each other.

Shielding his eyes from the glare, he finally caught sight of a figure in a wet suit far to his right, paddling out on his stomach toward the surfing area. In the haze it was hard to tell exactly, but the surfer appeared to be shifting position and sitting up as a new wave crested. Then he stood when the wave broke, dropped down the open wave face, lodged himself somewhere in the hollow of the wall of water, disappeared in a rush of foam and reappeared momentarily further out.

Another wait; more minutes passed. Ben scanned the surfing area again. Finally, a second figure appeared closer by, as if accepting the challenge. He was clad only in white swimming trunks, knees bent, crouching low on a spear-shaped board. For a time, the wind seemed to blow harder, holding up the swells and freezing them in place.

Grinning, Ben glanced back in the direction of the borrowed Prelude but realized he no longer had a camera. It was doubtless clutched in Aunt June's hands as she snapped away at a new listing, while here a true photo op was going to waste.

In that same moment, he thought he heard something. Though the sound mingled with the myriad of other noises, the grinding gears made him wince. Obviously, it had to be the old pickup. Scanning the line of vehicles, he could barely make out the outline of the weathered tarp covering the truck-bed as it lurched away. How he managed to hear the gear shifts or catch the fleeting outline of a tarp cover and why he even bothered to notice was beyond him.

Turning around, he again caught sight of the sinewy form that belonged to C.J. Rodriguez, drawing even closer, banking off the wave's lip, in the pocket, cutting back and slicing across. Before the cresting whitewater fell on top of him, C.J. went the guy in the wet suit one better and flung his arms out wide, the haze glinting off his straggly black hair.

It was a goofy move, greeted by wild applause from the splashing Chicano teens. This, apparently, was his current mood. And this is what Ben would have to contend with if he had any hope of getting him to play back-up.

Instantly, there C.J. was, on his belly like the kids, paddling in Ben's direction through the little breakers until he emerged. He flashed that toothy smile of his as his tangerine surfboard trailed by his ankle like a spent fish. The gang of Chicanos rushed forward and surrounded him, slapped his palms and dispersed, yelping the chorus to some hit Latino tune.

"So, payaso," said C.J., calling over as he tugged on the Velcro lash circling his foot. "You found me, huh? What for? I think I don't want to know."

Payaso was short for clown. It also meant C.J. was definitely in a quirky mood.

"Talk to me, man. What's the story?"

Ben studied C.J.'s broad face and his set of white teeth that were a hair too large for his mouth, causing the left side of his grin to swerve upward when he was in this taunting mode. Coupled with the cocky way he was swinging his shoulders, the message was clear. Ben was in for a bit of horseplay, provided he could stick it out.

Standing directly in front of him now, raising his voice over the din of the Pier and the kids shrieking in the background, Ben offered an offhanded hint as to what he was after. C.J. raised an eyebrow and began easing his stiff muscles.

Twisting and holding it for about twenty counts, C.J. kept up his end of the conversation. He remarked about some previews flashing up on the TV screens at Ben's pseudo-cousin Iris' gym the other day while he was working out on the punching bag. As usual, C.J. noted how dumb most police shows were, the old ones and the new ones as well. And that went for the movies too. Scoffing at this particular promo, he pointed out that "no self-respecting cop would let some muchacha distraido tag along on a stakeout."

Ben agreed, still without a clue what C.J. actually did on his Hollywood beat amidst the swarming tourists. While undercover, his bailiwick could be organized crime, homicide, all manner of theft and swindling. It could be anything and everything.

"Oye, carnal," C.J. said, bending over, touching his toes. "Carnal" was short for dude and signaled today's horseplay would include put-downs and a little sparring. "When you going to ditch that nice schoolboy outfit? What is that shirt, what are those payaso khaki pants? Where is the tan, man?"

"I lost it."

"You never had it. Swim, do something before you get sin vida—muerto. Use Iris' gym; three times a week, not once in the blue moon."

"Uh-huh."

"Work out, not just under her sheets."

"Look, I use the spare room, okay?"

"Sure, sure," said C.J. straightening up, shadow boxing and then landing a soft left jab to Ben's shoulder. "Dame un tiempo."

"Give you a break? Give *me* a damn break." Ben held out his palms, warding off a few blows to his face as C.J. kept pulling his punches.

"Listen, you tell me she is not a real cousin, so what is the matter with you? No lead in the pencil? Lo siento."

Reluctantly taking the cue and teasing him back, Ben said, "Hey, just 'cause your mom worked some cantina doesn't mean everybody's hot to trot."

C.J. feinted with his right and grazed Ben's ribcage with a left.

"No te atrevaz a llamar mi madre una puta," said C.J. faking a couple of left hooks and just missing with a roundhouse right.

His palms stinging trying to protect his face, Ben shuffled backwards toward the parked cars, amazed at the number of youngsters gathering round C.J., egging him on.

"Hey, cool it down. I did not call her a hooker. I was only ..."

Another roundhouse right and a practice left and right cross as Ben continued to peddle backwards.

Flinching, Ben yelled out, "What are you, getting serious? Brilliant. This is what I get."

"For what?" said C.J. dancing around on the balls of his feet, dodging and weaving.

"How about helping you with your English so you wouldn't sound so damn stupid?"

"Oh, yes?" said C.J., peppering Ben's hands again with a barrage of left jabs.

"And showing you the ropes around your ..." Ben was about to say "Hollywood beat" but cut himself short.

C.J. dropped his hands and stopped moving. "Okay. And I show you how to defend yourself and what happens? Oye, cabron, you hold up your palms and back away. What is going to happen to you? Ai, Chihuahua!"

"I don't know. That's the whole point."

With the Chicanos crowding out the little kids and patting C.J. on his back, C.J. announced that he promised his banda de locos, his crazy teen gang, some beginning surfing lessons and would be right back. "Better in the water than drive-by shootings, si? Then you tell me what it is you came for."

The teens followed C.J., still patting away. The little kids drifted off and returned to their parents and their boogie boards. One scrawny Chicano, no more than thirteen, lingered.

As Ben rubbed his ribcage, the scrawny one cupped his hands over his mouth and yelled, "Yo, gringo, yo extranjero. You know something?"

Ben shook his head.

The kid held up his baggy bathing suit with his left hand and shot a boney fist in the air. "You just lucky he took pity on you. You go to our barrio, we got real stuff for you. We pop your eye out and take your maldito money."

"Forget it. Estoy bromeando. We were just kidding."

In response, the kid rattled off a barrage of freshly minted curses. Ben replied that apparently C.J.'s acts of civility as a role model weren't paying any dividends, an observation that went completely over the kid's head.

Shuffling his feet, glancing back at his friends as they began calling his name, the boy shouted, "You can not tame us. You can not hide behind your Mercedes and your flojo beach houses. We rule. Los cobras rule!"

"Great tag line, kid," Ben shouted as he ran back to his compadres, holding up his shorts with both hands.

For a few minutes, C.J. was in the midst of the bunch, chiding the skinny kid, then simmering down and demonstrating how to paddle out to meet the waves. A few tried to emulate him but gradually lost interest, falling back on their own water sports, dunking each other with complete abandon.

At this point, the odds of getting through, let alone hop-scotching to the next phase of his mission impossible, was getting more remote by the second. And for no apparent reason, the slight pummeling and the bony kid's threats had unnerved him. Like another prompt of what was yet to come. He wished he could shut off these portents of doom, but it was just one of those days where there was nothing you could do.

Shortly, C.J. reappeared, shaking his head, dragging his surfboard, a thick white beach towel draped over his shoulder, a red sweat band around his forehead. With his shoulder-length hair now stiffening from the salt water, he looked like an extra in some B flick about Cochise and his renegade Apaches.

Again for no reason, Ben thought about the pickup truck. He told himself he had to damn well cut this out and face the inevitable as C.J. moved to his side.

In silence, Ben walked C.J. back through the sea of cars to his metallic blue Mustang and waited while he secured the surfboard to the roof-rack and slipped on a loud Hawaiian shirt. Despite himself, Ben scanned the area for a closer view of the dusty truck. Perhaps it had stalled and was still around. But there was no sign of it.

The pair of them still mute, Ben followed C.J. up to the boardwalk. Going against the shuffling throngs, they headed for the park, Ben continuing to trail a few steps behind.

The stroll ended as C.J. flopped on a vacant bench on the rim of the expanse of grass that fronted the paved walkway. He leaned his head back catching the shade provided by the towering date palms. Moments later, breaking the silence, he said, "I ever tell you 'bout my father?"

Sitting next to him, Ben said, "Nope."

"He was the one in the cantina, not my mother. One arm. A cornet player ... silver, you know? with a sweet tone fantastico."

Another silence.

"So, amigo? And your father?"

Ben shrugged.

"Your mother? You say nothing. Like you come from outer space."

Ben shrugged again.

"An orphan? Plus still no woman to make love with, plus—"

"Never mind. That is not my immediate problem."

"Then what is it on your mind?"

Two overly endowed women wiggled by, clad in leather thongs designed to reveal as much skin as possible. A petite blond followed in their wake wearing a hot-pink tutu and matching halter, meandering like a lost bareback rider.

A guy strolling by with stringy hair, a cascade of silver earrings circling his left ear and a ratty backpack, shook Ben out of it. He checked his watch again and stood up. He noted the makeshift tents peeking out here and there from the far side of the rows of palms. The homeless were out there, panhandling, girding their loins and securing their shelters in case the wind gusts kept it up for another night. Clearly indicating that, given this economy and to hell with the stupid signs and portents, Ben was this close to joining them.

"Que tranza?" said C.J. looking up. "You going to talk to me? Si or no?"

As succinctly as possible, Ben mentioned Gillian's proposal, causing C.J. to spring up. "What are you saying to me? What are you asking?"

"A token gesture."

"In English, por favor."

"A phone number. Just in case."

"In case you what?"

"Get in over my head ... some facts or police procedures I need to know."

"Por que?"

"To give me some leverage. To impress the producers. Otherwise--oh, forget it. Forget I asked."

Before he took two steps away, C.J. was on top of him, spinning him around. "You that bad off? What they done to you?"

"Blown the whistle, called my bluff. It's now or never, that's the deal."

Shaking his shaggy head, C.J. said, "I tell you, somewhere they do good pictures, you know? Find these people. Enough of this merde."

Ben didn't respond. How could he? As a hack jobbed-in from time to time to do patchwork on throwaway ventures, this was make or break. But how could he explain that? Every time he'd broached the subject, C.J. had rolled his eyes and come up with the same advice. So what was the use?

Picking up on Ben's deep funk, C.J. quit trying. Reverting to his swaggering norm, he snapped his fingers, slapped his fist into his palm and did it again for good measure. Pressing a finger into Ben's chest, he said, "No fancy-lens camera at crime scenes or your distraido brain where it does not belong."

"Okay."

"Levantate!"

"I'll do that. I will look sharp and stay on top of my every move."

"Exactamente. You swear?"

Ben swore, claiming he was so alert today, his head was splitting.

Still pushing it, C.J. said, "And you go nowhere near a police station. What you get from me comes from the sky. En secreto. Get it?"

"Got it."

"Good."

Plucking a blank card from his shirt pocket, C.J. scribbled the number of the Farmer's Daughter Motel on Fairfax and a name: Chula.

"Night shift again?"

"Si."

"She'll deliver a message and get back to me."

C.J. rubbed his knuckles on Ben's forehead. "This time it comes to something or you are quits. Finito! Comprende?"

"Absolutely. You got it."

Breaking another awkward pause, Ben said, "Well well, a chance to connect with the fabled Chula. This *is* a coup."

"Too many words, carnal. Always too many stories, too many words."

"I know, I know."

C.J. moved on. Back to his banda de locos perhaps, or off on another escapade as an undercover Zorro.

Chalking up this first task, Ben headed over the crosswalk going with the flow. He deliberately made his way down to the car park, keeping his fluttering notions to a minimum, making sure he didn't get ahead of himself. Brushing by any number of parents, little kids and wavering boogie boards, he keyed on the familiar dullish red surface of the borrowed Prelude.

Pulling out just as deliberately, he tooled onto Ocean Avenue, past Colorado, swerved onto the ramp and merged with the skewing muscle cars barreling down the Santa Monica Freeway; all the while wondering where he could find a phone in time to catch Gillian at her desk at Viacom.

He pressed on and weaved in and out of the speed lanes, grateful that the clutch was no longer slipping. Finally holding steady in a center lane, he eased up on the gas and tried to take stock of his situation. But the grinding noise made by that old pickup crossed his mind again and kept clouding his thoughts. Which totally made no sense, save for the fact that this sign wasn't abstract. It was somehow, by some stretch of the imagination, synchronistic.

Focusing harder, he realized that since they had cancelled his cell phone service and there was no time to go all the way back to cousin Iris' place, his best bet was the Hollywood Costume & Memorabilia store on La Cienega. In a pinch, the manager, a wannabe sci-fi writer, would let him use his cubby hole behind the 1950s movie stills.

Minutes later, Gillian kept barking into the receiver, pressing him for a definite answer. "Out with it, Benjamin. Did you hook up with el mysterioso? Is he on board, yes or no?"

"Yes," said Ben. "But he is to remain anonymous. Available to me when in dire straits."

An almost inaudible "hmm?" and an interminable stillness before she finally said, "All right. I'll spin that to a 'at your beck and call.' Give me a few minutes, I'll set something up."

"An actual few minutes?"

"Oh, puh-lease. What's your number?"

After they both rang off, Ben occupied his time perusing the faded posters tacked on the walls, like the one for *The Day the Earth Stood Still*. This was the oldie that featured a dignified alien who came down to earth to issue a warning about nuclear warfare. But was pleased to learn that everyone on this planet wanted peace and tranquility. A premise far removed from life as we've known it and any pop mayhem Gillian was pushing nowadays.

True to her word this time, Gillian rang him right back. "You're on. She'll see you anytime between four and five."

"Who will see me?"

After Gillian filled him in employing her usual cryptic style and was about to cut him off, Ben said, "Hold it. As much as I am champing at the bit, are you asking me to believe she will see me right now? That it's actually come down to me and a mystery sidekick?"

"Highly competent back-up."

"Right. A grade-A Sancho Panza."

"I'm waiting, Benjy. Take it or leave it."

"Fine. I will go in blind."

"And you will comply."

"And I will comply."

Satisfied, Gillian gave him the unlisted address in Laurel Canyon and advised him that if, by some miracle, she gave him a thumbs-up, the rest would fall into place. Predictably, before Ben could say another word, he was left with a sharp click and a dial tone.

Dutifully thanking the would-be sci-fi writer for the use of his sanctuary, Ben wandered back out into the blustery haze. While talking himself into this dubious chance of a lifetime—which, as far as he knew, hinged on a ditsy rock star--he could swear he saw the phantom green pickup cruising past the next intersection.

He also sensed that the wind gusts were shifting direction. On some whimsical wayward course independent of anyone's calculations.

Chapter Five

When Angelique flounced onto her sun porch, practically naked save for a frilly pink-paisley skirt that barely covered the tops of her thighs, Ben knew he was supposed to react. Turn red, leer, cover his eyes, bolt from the premises—something. But he just stood there. All he saw was a body-builder Barbie. Even her breasts seemed manufactured, the result of so many reps on a Strive body-part enhancer, plus quarts of cousin Iris' Protein/Power Cooler.

"Ooh," said Angelique, feigning innocence. "You're here."

"Yup," said Ben, trying to appear nonchalant and competent. "As requested, right on time."

"Oh, golly. How embarrassing."

"Oh?"

A fake pause, eying him, putting on her own act as well. "Guess I should slip on something a bit less revealing."

"Whatever you say."

"Okay. No peeking."

"You bet."

Before easing back through the bamboo curtain, she gave him what he assumed was one of her patented glances: lowering her smoky eyes and pursing her pouty lips, belying the fact that her ingénue years were a distant memory. She waited again for a more heated response. Still covering up a sense of unease, Ben could give her nothing but a wave of his hand.

To any casual Hollywood observer, a slender sandy-haired thirty-something had just flunked the test. The shot of Angelique's moves alongside a lasciviously responsive Ben surely would've boosted his cachet among his hapless associates alone. Those, that is, who were hobnobbing at today's coffee klatch on Fairfax at the Farmer's Market across from the Screen Writers Guild. Be that as it may, it wouldn't dawn on his fellow hacks that something else was off-kilter on this loopy day. Doubtless, they'd be so taken in, they wouldn't have noticed the scene while cruising up the Hollywood Hills and winding around Laurel Canyon. They wouldn't have sensed that no other rock stars were wailing on their keyboards; no pool parties were vying for billing as most outrageous. Moreover, under the overcast sky and fickle wind-gusts, all the hidden villas were silent. No motor bikes had caromed past Ben as he ascended. Even the weekend foragers, scouring through the wood ferns, needle grass and chaparral, hadn't materialized out of the gullies and ravines. This was not Laurel Canyon as advertised. No matter how he tried to remain focused, this was Ben's special omen-generator working on overtime.

Amplifying this notion, a shift into second and a sharp turn up Angelique's hidden drive became a walled-in s-shaped slalom run. At the top, the turnaround was blocked by a silver Jag with Vegas plates, perfectly positioned to make the downward spiral, leaving Ben with the prospect of exiting backwards. After managing to crank up the hand brake as tightly as possible, he'd slid out and found the high wooden gate ajar, opening onto a long, narrow azure pool. At the far end he'd spotted a scrawny form lying on a chaise lounge like the discarded dregs of a failed debauch. The eyes were covered by opaque sun goggles resting on a beak of a nose, a huge orange towel covered most of the rest. The sun porch opposite ran the entire length of the pool. As for what lay beyond the sun porch, there was the bamboo curtain Angelique had just slipped through and, like everything else, anybody's guess. Anyway you looked at it, Ben needed to keep his eye on a quick exit. Anyway you looked at it, today's edginess was more than justified.

He waited a while longer for Angelique's return. He paced around the sun porch and glanced back. The scrawny form with the beak didn't stir. He peered through the rolled-up bamboo shades that separated him from whatever was lying there, over to the opening in the gate, praying that no one would pull up behind the Prelude, blocking off his only avenue of escape.

Just then, Angelique reappeared and murmured, "How about this?"

Glancing back, Ben positioned himself so he could respond to her and keep apprised of the prone, goggled thing from Vegas.

Still naked from the waist up, she clutched a yellow Lycra top with slashes on the side as if she'd just been in a knife fight, two silky tube tops, a nylon bomber jacket, a polka dot halter, and a florescent pink button-down with the shirttails tied in a knot. "Which one? Which one?" she squealed.

"The button-down. Look—"

"Hey, come on. You can at least gape at my bod and take in my porcelain complexion and tousled wispy locks. Wanna know the secret? My hair's really light brown, but after lots of sun and a douse of platinum and gold, it gets this bold-blond glow. But it's no good if the sun is gonna hide like this."

"Granted. It's tough, I understand. But if you could put something on and we could get on with this …"

"Another secret for you. I get a lot of facials. A skinline by Nicholas Perricone plus my hair and nails done every week. And a massage and body scrub for sheer indulgence."

"That's terrific. But—"

"I'm giving you clues, dammit. I'm clueing you in."

"Really? I'm sorry, I hadn't noticed."

Angelique's Barbie face went blank for a second. "Hey, what gives? The other seven came on strong. Said how they could … re … re …"

"Revive? Revitalize? Revamp?"

"That's the one. Revamp my image by repositioning me within the right tailored vehicle." She uttered this statement slowly, like memorized patter she'd been rehearsing all day. "Revamp not ditch it," she went on, a little faster this time. "They each also hit on me and wanted to jump on my bones."

"Well, that's guys for you."

"Two were women."

"Exactly. Listen--"

"Hold it."

Angelique went blank again, gazing past Ben over to the pool. Then, staring Ben in the face, she said, "Has Ray moved at all?"

"Must have," said Ben, assuming Ray was the creature from Vegas. "His head is now facing this way."

"Oh, rats, better hurry. I'll choose one of these tops. Which'll give you two minutes to ready your pitch."

"My pitch?"

"Oh, get off it," said Angelique. "I am in trans ..."

"Transition?"

"Yeah. The cutesy-hot shtick has obviously had it. And that's despite what those studio bimbos have been blowing in my ear."

Dropping her act entirely, Angelique's features suddenly hardened. "It's a bitch running on two speeds, you know? Skin-revealing casual to red carpet. Sleazy duds by day, flash and glitter at night. And even then, half the time who the hell knows if you've got it right. I have got to jack it into gear!"

Still having no idea how to get in and out of this as fast as possibly, all Ben could mutter was, "Like I said, must be tough."

She nodded, said, "You got it," and let out a weary sigh. "Hey, you want one of Iris's smoothies? Soy yogurt, fiber infusion, chopped fruit and protein powder. Before, she gets here, I mean."

"Iris?"

"Of course. Get with it. Like everything's gotta click, you follow?"

"Great. Let's skip the two minute breaks and get down to it. Just keep holding the tops up."

"Yeah, fast but not that fast. I gotta be dressed for it."

Again she was gone. As the wind gusts fluttered through the palm fronds, Ben stepped out onto the pink cement rimming the pool. He checked out motionless Ray and peered again through the gate at the Prelude. Going over his exit strategy, he'd have to slip into reverse gear, head twisted toward the rear window, glide down the serpentine run and hope to God he didn't smack into Iris and get completely boxed in.. With luck, he'd finally get something going with Angelique and hightail it. In short, following the first rule of this business, he'd jump in with a hook, spring back and hope he scored enough points to keep the ball rolling.

Off the top of his head, he began to come up with a recipe that might zip him past this hurdle.

Once again the bamboo curtain rustled. Angelique plopped down on the edge of a white leather recliner. Her chosen top was the tackiest of the lot, the yellow floral with the slashed slits still covering up next to nothing.

Ben stepped back onto the porch as she fumbled for a stick of gum, lit a cigarette, took a deep drag and said, "Okay, shoot. And remember Gillian gave her word it wouldn't be ditsy. And none of that stuff with me playing some sleaze has-been. Check out the monitors at Iris' gym with me in my glory. You get my drift?"

"No worries. We'll capitalize on today's tough times, hankering for the good ol' days of 'You go, girl,' 'Breakin' out' and 'Catch me if you can.'"

Ben didn't know if these were song titles or what, but he was on a roll and didn't want to give Angelique any time to think.

"In other words," Ben went on as Angelique tossed the gum wrapper aside, "chicks want to be the Angie of old--do anything and take it all back. Let's simply call it *Retro Now*."

Angelique winced, sucked in more smoke, held it and blew it out through her nose. "That was um ..."

"Too brusk?"

"Yeah. Like you see right through me."

"See a way to appease our target audience, you mean. They want to do it and, like I said, take it all back."

(Ben also had no idea what he meant by "do it" or "our target audience" but keep on going.) "Call it Angie rides again: fearless, cruising the back streets, darting in the shadows, shaking off the denizens of the underworld."

"Hey, let's leave Ray out of this."

Thrown for a second, Ben countered with, "Look, I'm just throwing out some ingredients. You told Gillian you wanted it streetwise with backup, well you got it. Got an underpinning. Working title, *Angie's Run*—whatever."

"*Angie* ... The Rolling Stones ... me in the same league, I like it, I like it."

"No no, not rock videos or any of that stuff. That's out of *my* league. Okay? You've got to keep that in mind."

"Okay, I got it, all right already."

"Great. So, what do you say we leave it at that? I mean, with you under the gun, Ray about to wake up, Iris on her way, and my car parked--"

"It was the tour that did it," said Angelique, sitting up, puffing away. "I always hit 'em with this killer pose and listened to 'em scream. But this time they checked me out when I put on my pouty face, flashed some thigh and cocked my head. *Nothing.* Like they were waiting for the headliner. Like they didn't realize it was me. I broke into my jiggly moves, my backup dancers offering maximum booty-shaking sizzle, the screen blazing with meteor showers, the band pumping and blasting. But the teenies barely shook it. Even when I tossed them scented tattoos."

She coughed, puffed faster and sprang to her feet. "Then my voice went off key and the reviews hammered me."

"I hear you, I get it."

"That was at the Arena a few weeks ago. So, when the same thing happened up in Monterey and Ray told me when you can't cut it the burial is permanent-- in an unmarked grave, he said--I ditched the rest of the tour and went ballistic."

"Honest, believe me, you don't have to go on."

Prancing around, the cigarette turned into a pointer. "So ... I mean, like Gillian said, with you being so hungry and having been around the block, and all the others out of town or putting me on, more after my bod than repackaging my brand ... you could maybe crank me up a second coming. With the backup of this machismo guy Pepe."

"Absolutely," said Ben, wondering how Gillian latched on to C.J.'s nickname.

"'Cause, like Iris my personal trainer says, how you manage to keep going with the handwriting on the wall is beyond belief."

41

"Is it ever. Well then, can we call it quits for now? Okay? Are we done?"

Squashing the cigarette on the terrazzo with her gladiator sandals, Angelique said, "The pressure, it goddamn gets to you, know what I mean? Drives you outta your skull."

Ben held up his hands in surrender, pivoting, stepping away.

Just then Ray began to stir. Ben caught sight of a hand emerging under the beach towel, fishing around, retrieving the blue-tinted goggles and slipping them back on his wedge of a face. There was a wheeze, then a yawn as the scrawny bare arms reached up to the overcast sky, collapsed and crossed over his chest.

"Oh, screw," said Angelique. "Ray's coming to and look at the time." She made this last observation without benefit of a watch, disappeared through the strands of bamboo and returned with a folder under her arm and a fistful of business cards.

"Got so antsy, just had them made with a big smiley face. Can you stand it?"

Dropping half the cards, she pulled out a printout and pointed a lacquered fingernail at the bottom of the page. "I mean, it all figures. The latest test marketing report: 'No mileage left on the tease and predator thing ... needs a complete makeover ... new venue, new media, something more hard-edge.' That's, of course, where you and Pepe come in. Exactly what you've been going on about. Like a miracle. Like you knew all along."

"Well, what can I say? Nice meeting you, it's been great."

"Plus," said Angelique, trying to hold him in place, "right after the Monterey bust--talk about fate or what's in the stars and stuff--Ray's got this thing going. Before it tanked in Portland, I mean. But Ray says he's on it. But then Ray gets here early, way before she gets here to put her own little spin on it. I mean, it's all too frickin' much. Am I right or am I right?"

"Before who gets here? Somebody besides Iris?"

"Never mind. That's not your lookout. And forget I let on about Ray. Oh, I am so whacked, I can't tell you."

Angelique bent down, picked up a couple of her business cards, shoved them in Ben's shirt pocket, rushed past him, studied Ray's fagged-out form, rushed back, grabbed Ben by the elbow and began escorting him out.

"You'll have to finagle with Leo," she jabbered on, like she was on amphetamines.

"Leo? The mad Russian? The blowhard from Odessa?"

"Watch it. And don't let Iris hear you say that. Besides being her sex partner, he's the producer, dummy."

"The producer? You're kidding."

"Look, whatever it is, he's gonna produce it. You want this gig, you better be on time."

"For what?"

"A meeting at the Polo Lounge. I just set it up for six."

"Six? You mean in just a couple of hours?"

"That's it. So move it." She flicked her tousled hair back in the direction of the pool. "Damn damn damn, he's getting up."

"Hold it," said Ben. "Leo, Ray, somebody else about to arrive—how far does this thing go?"

"Never you mind. What did I tell you? Stick to what you do, that's all."

By this time they were next to the old Prelude which was still doing its damnedest to grip the asphalt.

"And don't blow it," said Angelique, darting away.

She stopped at the gate and announced to no one in particular, "She's late and Ray's early. Oh, gimme a break, will ya?" Wringing her hands, Angelique took a couple of glances down the drive, whirled around and disappeared behind the gate.

In turn, Ben slipped behind the wheel and gunned the motor to make sure it didn't stall. He shifted into neutral, wary of freeing the hand brake. He calculated if he could ease down the drive and avoid smacking against the walls, he'd be home free.

All set, he released the hand brake. Looking back, with his right arm snug against the top of the passenger seat, his left hand gripping the steering wheel, he began to roll down the slope; all the while jamming and releasing the break pedal, turning the wheel, straining his eyes trying to make out some landmark other than the blur of curving pink. Then his foot started slipping off the pedal, the car picked up speed as his steering became erratic, the tires squealed, the weight of the Prelude fighting him off till the gantlet ended with a blast of a horn, a full-throated screech of the brakes, a jerk forward and a thud.

The Prelude stalled as he jerked up the hand break and spun out from behind the wheel. The first thing that greeted his eyes was the caved-in front bumper and toothy grill of an old green Chevy pickup.

Chapter Six

The truck door squeaked open. A willowy figure slowly emerged and stood on the running board. Backlit by the hazy sunlight, in Ben's eyes she seemed caught in a time warp, like a sweet maiden from an old pastoral movie. She wore bib overalls, a checkered blouse rolled up at the sleeves and tennis shoes. But that didn't diminish Ben's first impression. Her hair was a warm honey-blonde, loose and wind blown; her features on the delicate side, her lips soft and full. If it weren't for the high cheekbones, sunburn and absence of any hard muscle tone, some might say, in a pinch she could also pass for Angelique's kid sister. Except that her eyes were wider, searching and pale blue. And when she finally spoke, regardless of her feisty tone, his first impression remained fixed in his mind.

"I don't believe it," said the maiden, jumping off the running board. She eyed the dented front bumper and grill, all the while rubbing the back of her neck.

"Me neither," said Ben, hurrying over to her. "Are you hurt? Maybe you should see a doctor? Maybe we should call somebody?"

"Report the accident, you mean?"

"No no. It's not good, I know. But not that bad. Not that bad at all. What I meant was ..."

"No insurance, right?"

"Look, what I'm saying is, the important thing is to maybe get you seen. Unless, of course--"

"Unless, of course, I'm just a little shaken up. Then it's no big deal. And since you have no insurance, that's no big deal either. As long as you can buy me off."

"I didn't say that."

"And what were you doing backing down anyways? You outta your mind?"

When he told her about the silver Jag blocking the turnaround, she immediately stopped rubbing her neck, scampered past him partway up the drive, and rushed back. "Vegas plates?"

"That's the one."

"Don't tell me. Just don't tell me."

"All right, I won't. Now about your condition ..."

"Uh-huh. Let's see some I.D."

"What do you mean?"

"You don't think you're gonna get away with this?"

"No no. Of course not."

"Then who are you and what are you doing here?"

He fished in his shirt pocket and handed her one of Angelique's smiley cards.

"Ah," she said, eyeing the card more intently than her dented bumper and grill. "Still cute, still all pink curlicues."

Ben plucked out a second card, glanced at it, put it back and said, "Well now, how about that? The old movie studio that's out of business."

"Out of business?" said the maiden, absentmindedly tapping the hood of the pickup.

"Unoccupied but I see that's about to change."

The address under the smiley face and *Starshine* logo was the Avalon Studios on Van Ness, tucked away a few blocks south of Melrose and the teeming world of Paramount. Word had it that it was vacant since yet another takeover after the previous two ventures had tanked. Hence, fueling Angelique's anxiety to latch on quick for whatever the project-to-be. Hence the impending meeting with Leo. A meeting that would never take place if Ben didn't come to terms with the maiden right here and now.

Breaking the silence, Ben said, "Listen, if you're really okay, we'd better disengage before Iris comes barreling up and we'll have another fender-bender."

Ben responded to her raised eyebrow by announcing that Iris was Angelique's personal trainer and, in a manner of speaking, his cousin.

"I don't know, man. I mean, this is all too much."

"Tell me about it."

"Tell me about this movie studio?" said the maiden, her blue eyes as wide as ever.

"Doubtless the subject of a meeting I have to attend right now. Which will mean money for any damages, a doctor's appointment if necessary and all manner of sundry things."

"Broke, huh? I knew it. And from the way you're jerking me around, this probably isn't even your car."

Not giving Ben any chance to continue his do-si-do, she insisted that he write his name and home phone on the back of the card. Without thinking, he scribbled away and added Iris' number.

"Hey, if you're lying to me ..."

"Not me, ask anybody. I kid you not, which, in this town, is unheard of and a huge failing."

She scooted partway up the drive again, spotted something and rushed back down. "I'll be in touch, gotta think this through. But if you're diddling with me, I'll find you, I swear. Later, okay?"

Ben asked again if she was sure she was all right. He also asked where she was staying just in case. She gave him a funny look, hopped back behind the wheel and worked the choke till the motor coughed, sputtered and caught hold. Shortly, all that remained was a fleeting shot of a weathered tarp, flapping behind the cab window and tied down over the truck bed partially covering the rear plates.

All the while, he thought he heard an odd sound coming from under the tarp. But he quickly put it out of his mind. He also dismissed the fact that at first she was headed up the drive and now she was gone. He told himself all this discombobulating would have to go on the back burner. No one's mind, no matter how facile, could possibly take it all in.

Trying his damnedest to make the best of it, he drove off repeating an old mantra:

"This time. By God this time I am truly on the verge."

Chapter Seven

Hours later he repeated the mantra. After all, here he was ensconced at a choice patio table at the Polo Lounge. Shafts of a vermilion sunset were glinting through the overarching Brazilian pepper tree, the hot winds had dissipated, the temperature was around a comfortable seventy degrees and Leo was about to enter and foot the bill. In short, no matter how maddening Leo could be, it was not inconceivable that Ben did indeed have a foot in the door.

It was now ten after six. Ben's waiter, who resembled a proto mannequin, came by again sporting a white double-breasted jacket with gold buttons, ducked under a branch and deftly missed the jutting wires that held the pepper tree in place. Without missing a beat, he replaced Ben's frozen margarita with a second. The drink was Ben's attempt to slow down his thinking and keep plying his mind with a positive spin.

However, try as he may, one notion kept slipping in. No one can back down a serpentine driveway, smack into a phantom old Chevy pickup and just slough it off as another pointer. If nothing else, it certainly called for a second drink.

Sipping a bit faster, wondering what was keeping Leo, he checked out the scattering of wrought-iron chairs, sea-green pillows and bamboo umbrella stands. Gazing here and there, he noted a few recognizable high profile players and watched them chatting away, tossing out industry tidbits in and around the pink stucco alcoves.

Killing more time, he zeroed in closer by and began to eavesdrop. It seems the four women at the table directly behind him were beside themselves. They had been shopping all over Rodeo Drive the past few days and had even swung by Beverly Drive for the diamond sale at

Fourteen Carats. Presently, they were at a total loss. The woman with the clipped British accent suggested they re-engage the croupier from that Vegas gaming table while their husbands scouted locations in "some ungodly patch of Baja." Unfortunately, no one was keen on the idea. The Brit kept exclaiming, "What to do, ladies? What to do?"

Ben chuckled at this mindless diversion as the second margarita began to kick in. So many out of work, so many on the brink, and now these ladies suffering the slings and arrows of impending boredom.

But back to his own situation. Perhaps he actually could tap Leo for an advance, resolve the little fender-bender in some amicable way and, in turn, find a secluded haven inside the Avalon Studios and the land of the second chance. Then rationalize the omens and put them irrevocably aside.

Halfway through this margarita daydream, Leo burst into view. Barreling through the glass entry, he jostled past the gold-buttoned mannequin who teetered in his wake. After making a grand plea for forgiveness to no one in particular, Leo smoothed the remaining gray hairs along his temples. In the fading sunlight, Leo's bald dome seemed shinier than usual, as if bronzed and glazed for a festive occasion.

Shambling like the proverbial Russia bear, he spotted Ben right off, stepped down onto the patio and made a beeline. After giving Ben a ferocious hug, he reached back and yanked up a wrought iron chair with no regard for the lady Brit who was using it as an arm rest. By some miracle, she kept her balance and gave Leo a flinty look.

"Is beautiful, Ben," said Leo, ignoring Ms. Brit, drawing his chair closer. "You, me, Iris and Gillian. Is like family. All brought about by me, I am telling you with no bull."

"All brought about by capitalizing on some offhand remark, you mean. Something you heard at the gym and passed on to Gillian."

"You're saying please?"

"Who," Ben went on, "among other things, used it to hawk her screenwriters' conference for idle wannabes."

"Again, you will please repeat?"

With the aid of the margaritas, feeling no inhibitions whatsoever, Ben declared, "Doubtless, this whole thing was instigated by you after learning that down-and-out rock star Angelique was looking for some streetwise venue. Then learning that Gillian was looking for a way to both keep her Secrets-of-Screenwriting gigs going and her development projects percolating. Hazarding a guess, and at the risk of repeating myself, I'll bet, like always, you overheard something and jumped at it."

"Oh, you're meaning muscle man with long hair at Iris' gym. Mexican fellow who has cachet maybe."

"Aha. And says who?"

"Iris tells me he signs in as Pepe. You know him maybe. So I figure he has cachet because someone else at gym tell me someone else tells him this Pepe is undercover. And person who tells him knows somebody at big studio who says what is going on under the covers is new crime stories but like old and so is going to be hot."

"And how, pray tell, does this retro brainstorm connect with conning me to glom Aunt June's super camera? Glom it and zoom-in past police barricades? How, in the whirl of your gonzo schemes, does this all add up?"

"Fits positively like hand in glove, I am telling you. Pictures you take show Angelique this is insider person she is talking to. Person who has access and penetrates like movie camera, like seeing-eye dog, like Cossack who travels anywhere, what you need, where you want to go. So Angelique finally is saying to me ..."

Fumbling for a slip of paper in his out-of-style cubavera jacket, Leo proudly stated, "And I am quoting here, 'Wow, this Leo sure gets around.'"

"Terrific. And as a direct result, I am now on the L.A.P.D. nuisance list."

"But worth it, I am telling you with no bull. Is price you pay when you strike hot iron. And what we got, I am swearing to you, is hot irons in fire for sure. Empty studio with cop movies sets, everything connecting."

Leo shook Ben's arm with all his might, released his grip and signaled to the waiter for the usual, which was a double Belvedere Polish vodka on the rocks. This was followed by a disparaging look on Leo's part, signaling that

he was unsure about Ben's preppy attire. To be with-it,
this new venture called for California-black duds like Leo's.
But then, in typical Leo fashion, his meaty features shifted
a tad to uncertainty.

"Mistake?" said Leo. "My getup, deep charcoal and
shiny, is no longer in? You're not telling me?"

"Haven't said a word."

"Exactly. I'm talking face you are giving me. Better we
table this, yes? Until I am taking more soundings."

"Gladly."

But it was obvious Leo wasn't about to table anything.
Just as Ben was up against it the day his unemployment
insurance ran out, Leo was more than a bit anxious about
his prospects. Otherwise why was he running around
putting so much stock in Angelique's *Starshine
Productions*?

Pulling himself together as the vodka appeared as if by
magic, Leo downed it, spotted someone in the opposite
corner and slapped Ben on the back. "I see power brokers I
must greet. You understand, old timer that you are. But I
am returning spit-spot, we are getting show on the road
before you can say okeydoke. All right, dude? Yes!"

True to his word, Leo's table-hopping and shmoozing
seemed to be going well and took up less than five minutes.
Which bolstered Ben's hopes somewhat and indicated
there may be more to Leo than hot air. To be fair, it was
highly possible that Leo did indeed grow up in Odessa on
the Black Sea, ran a theater, had a hand in some fledgling
movie and entertainment operations in Bucharest,
Budapest, Belgrade and Istanbul. It was even possible that
he once played the panpipe in a gypsy band throughout
Romania. Leo was that mercurial as evidenced by his
grappling with the Hollywood scene, not to mention his
alleged feats of sexual prowess with Iris. The problem was
always the problem: any Tinseltown venture, no matter
how promising, was a crap shoot.

The gold-buttoned mannequin reappeared. Ben ordered
another drink and an entrée seconds before Leo barged
back through the pink alcoves.

"Leo," said Ben, just as Leo alighted with an exuberant
sigh, "Can we nail this down?"

Leo ordered another double vodka and told Ben to leave everything for now on that selfsame table.

Pressing on, Ben said, "As it happens, I just had a little accident—very minor—but I will need some additional coin. And some tangible reassurance. Are there really bona fide, legitimate backers in place?"

Leo, who was waving at people again and only half listening, countered with, "No worries. You got agent, someone you must fork over percentage?"

"Not exactly."

"So, I'm telling you, no worries, dude."

"You're telling me nothing."

"Oh?" said Leo, getting a little miffed. "You getting serious, making life no pleasure in this cockamamie world?"

"In a business where everybody lies ..."

"I am lying?" said Leo, rising, reaching up to the fading sky and jostling Ms. Brit yet again.

"I didn't say that."

Leo sat back down, moved his chair in even closer and lowered his mellifluous voice and soulful eyes as if about to reveal Russian state secrets. "Listen to me and listen good. I get tourist visa from U.S. embassy in Odessa. Is good for six months. Extension is good twice, no more. Assurances, you want, I give you assurances. Immigration office expect me back spit-spot."

"So? What are you telling me? You're over the limit? You're in trouble?"

"So," said Leo, "I don't know if is from God for my Slavic soul or drop in from sky or around the corner or what have you for breakfast. Gift horse does not everyday look in my mouth. Angelique is climbing walls, front money almost in place Thursday, not in place Friday, comes back in place yesterday but not all."

"Translation please? And what are the odds?"

Leo waved at a few up-and-coming starlets in flimsy attire making a mock sweeping entrance. After another conspiratorial look, Leo lowered his voice another decibel.

"Question, dude, which is always question. Can be marketed, no or yes with hot outlet like race horse ahead of pack? Is right now in Gillian's lap. With maximize exposure? Is also in Gillian's lap but cooking up storm on the stove. Making banker in Budapest jumping to loan money against presale of foreign rights. I know business, business knows me. Is on my head, not yours. Is golden rule writer is last to know. So what is your problem?"

As always, Ben had no idea how these things got bankrolled. He could have brought up dubious Ray from Vegas and something gone wrong in Portland and tried to link it with the floating front money. But all he could muster was, "Bottom line? Money in my pocket is my immediate problem."

"You give, you get. I get from you, everybody gets. I become specialist, do work not everybody can do, am needed in this town of tinsel. Cash money man writes letter of support, I am fulltime employee and not deported. Everything is okeydoke. We are joined at hip. So, tomorrow, in studio, you are starting from storyboards like cartoon. From beginning you begin, on way to road to happy ending. For story, for family—you, me, Iris, Gillian. My hand to God."

"Hold it. Let me get this straight. Are you telling me, starting tomorrow, I just walk in there, into the defunct Avalon Studios and wing it? And then I somehow get paid?"

"Yes, yes, yes. Bring estimate from garage, crayons, what-have-you-got," said Leo rising to his full height. "Avalon Studios, first thing. Time is depending on tonight with Iris."

"Oh, no," said Ben, as Leo's immediate plans came into focus. "Come on, Leo. Not the sexual gymnastics. I desperately need some sleep."

"Sleep you will get. Tonight you go to movies, remember? Was all arranged."

It was true. In all the madness, Ben had forgotten. "How many rounds? How many timeouts? How long till I can crawl into the back room and crash?"

By this time everyone was looking up, including the four jaded women and the gold-buttoned mannequin. Unfazed, hovering over his audience, Leo announced, "Is not sex. Is world going round, is celebration, is ritual. And is over truly by eleven."

Ms. Brit turned around in her chair, looked Leo in the eye and muttered, "There is nothing so disheartening as a cheery Russian."

Still totally disregarding her, Leo said, "Dinner and movie, what could be better for you? No microwave. Drinks, food on me. Then, tomorrow you create with fever."

Ben could have corrected him and said "fervor" but why bother? Correcting C.J. Rodriguez's English was at least fruitful.

A smack on Ben's back and Leo bolted out of sight. The mango infused seafood dish that followed managed to make a difference. That, coupled with the third margarita and the stylings of a jazz pianist who began tinkering with old Cole Porter melodies.

A short while later and another margarita for good measure, Ben scuffed out of the Polo Lounge into the twilight afterglow and found himself grinning. Unaccustomed to a good meal and nothing more bracing than an occasional Heinekens, he was feeling no pain and had only an old Cary Grant flick remaining on the night's agenda. At this point he had put everything on hold, including any thoughts as to Ray's true identity: causing Angelique to become skittish; causing the maiden to turn back and run.

Just in case, he cast his gaze high and low. All was still, not a smidge of a warning sign.

Again he reminded himself (with Angelique, Leo and Gillian seconding the motion), it was all out of his hands. You have your niche, you stick to it. Ever since he was a kid, it was always the same: *Find something to do, Benjy, there's a good boy. Got business to attend to. Real estate, out of your league.* Everything in this factory town was compartmentalized. Especially *business that had to be tended to*, including Aunt June's hawking of alluring property for well-heeled clients like Ms. Brit and company. Which went a long way to explain why Ben was so fragmented. Keenly aware that things were happening in Vegas and East L.A. but shutting his eyes. Cautious yet eager, lost yet hopeful.

Reaching for some more reinforcement, he turned to the words of an old college professor:

"It's simple physics, Mr. Prine. Think about it. Couple any endeavor with external fluctuations and there is no telling what will happen. And since external fluctuations are a given, any endeavor, especially in your field, is a random proposition."

Right, Ben told himself, reveling in the comfort of his margarita-saturated brain. Absolutely. It's all a bunch of quarks--up, down and backwards ... moving here, moving there, moving everywhere. I mean, hey, there's no telling.

He spent the next few minutes repeating this new mantra. Shrugging everything off, being quite offhand about it.

Then trying a lot harder; trying to repeat "Hey, there's no telling, kiddo" with a little more conviction.

Chapter Eight

As morning came on two days before, Deke found himself in the observation car following the course of the Columbia River. The lean woman in the green jump suit to his right was still carrying on about the fluky wind gusts. The flukiness, the woman declared, was the reason there were no kite-surfers flying backwards or landing nose down, flipping over, re-launching or some such thing. That was also why there were only a few tiny fishing craft wending their way for Deke to enjoy. As if Deke gave a damn about any of this small talk. As if he didn't have enough on his plate.

On the other hand, Walt always told him it was good that folks naturally took up with him. It was useful, one of his pluses. Deke had the kind of lantern jaw and all-purpose face anybody could use as a sounding board without fear of response. People would open up and, thirty minutes later, couldn't recall exactly who it was they'd been talking to. When it came to nosing around and disappearing into the woodwork, Deke's cool, flat style couldn't be beat.

His shortcomings, as Walt always pointed out, were another matter. He was also a liability, what with his wild side always percolating underneath. Judging from what just happened with the nerdy bookkeeper, that was a topic Deke would have to sidestep. And the thing with his back was only a glitch: what came of hurrying, Walt bugging him and loose terrain high up on the rimrock. Since Deke had no use for fathers in the first place, he'd just shake it off at the noon meeting. Like he'd always shook Walt off as far back as the time Walt was running security for his old man at the sugar plant down in the Glades. And as he'd shook Walt off for the past fifteen years in Vegas. And as he'd keep shaking him off till Deke came up with his own sweet plan.

In the meantime, he let the lean woman jabber away. He nodded, rested his palm firmly on the attaché case by his side, and tried to ease the tension in his lower back by breathing through it. Like on the TV exercise show he'd seen in a motel room the other night.

But the breathing didn't do diddly. Truth to tell, something was still eating at him. The way things were going, after laying fallow the past month, he *had* lost a step or two and would have to watch himself.

Mulling things over, he recalled that the Outfit out of Chicago had its finger in casinos and anything you could name in Vegas. Loose ends were Walt's lookout and Deke was on standby if something got out of hand in Vegas. So why had the Outfit dispatched Walt to Portland? That and the run-in with the little guy and the funny way Walt was talking meant Deke really had been out of touch. Meant he was going to have to keep a sharp eye and have something up his sleeve just in case.

Which was why, first chance he got, he examined the contents of the attaché case real close. He first made double sure he had the key item: the purple memory stick shaped like a thick piece of chewing gum with the word Sony on it and XC 2TB. He'd heard Walt mention about a file transfer which meant the thing was some kind of memory card. A record that proved some phony company was cooking the books, under investigation by the Feds like the little guy said. Then there was the little guy's tri-fold wallet and his smartphone. At the time Deke wasn't sure why he swiped them but now it was starting to hit him. The plastic window showed his name was Elton Frick. The driver's license, CPA and other plastic cards showed he had a lot of connections, and so did the numbers on his speed-dial. In some way, possession of this stuff gave Deke an edge. A bargaining chip, maybe. Especially if Frick survived and was found crawling around miles-long 500-foot-deep Lake McDonald and didn't fall in. Or managed to crawl back up to the cabin to wait it out. In any case, Frick would be too spooked to finger him; and Deke had the wallet and all in case Walt or the Outfit tried to stiff him.

Or in case Deke wanted to stick it to the Outfit after not only tracking Frick down and recovering this incriminating stuff, but also maybe tracking down the whole scam from start to finish.

What he'd lost in the bargain was the fun he'd always had. This new feeling-his-age crap sure as hell was getting him down. But, still and all, the chance of being on top of the game instead of winding up on the skids like guys everywhere was one hell of a sight better.

And so he eased back and let the sights come and go as the train rolled on: the gray sheen of the water approaching the Dalles and the Wishram station stop; the gouges of beige and deep chocolate brown across the way as if some giant had chipped out hunks of basalt. Pretty soon, the Columbia opened wide, the foothills of the Cascades glowed green, covered with thick Douglas fir and stands of skinny poplar. In the distance, the silvery Bridge of the Gods spanned over the Columbia so hikers could scamper across the Pacific Trail into Oregon.

But the sight of a bridge with no railings got Deke to feeling testy again. Losing a step, sure, but still as cocky as they come. Still the same rambler who, up till lately, hung loose around Cold Creek till Walt beeped him back down to Sin City or wherever.

Snapping out of it again, he noticed the seat next to him was empty. The lean woman might've said, "Nice talking to you." He couldn't really say.

Trudging back to his berth, he noticed the paper and pulp mills cropping up outside his narrow window, then the rows of tract houses followed by ones with second-story wooden balconies. In short order, traffic lights popped out along with eighteen-wheel rigs, rectangular high-rises and the green 5-South-to-Portland sign. The commercial craft and pleasure boats that clogged the Willamette came into view and clinched the deal. Deke was going to have to get himself set.

Less than twenty minutes later, he emerged from the cozy Portland train station and hailed a cab. While hanging onto the attaché case and making sure Frick's billfold and smartphone were still secure in his travel bag, little spasms continued circling around his lower back. At this point he longed to meet up with Walt and have it out then and there. Smack up against something hard instead of more of this dos-a-dos.

Still antsy, he hopped a MAX downtown to Pioneer Square. The mix of fruity people on the glass-paneled light-rail system got to him immediately. It was Saturday, everybody's day off. But did deadbeats in whacked-out T-shirts and sandals have to keep piling on, stop after stop? A few, okay, but there were bunches of them carrying green and white placards all starting with the word *Save*: "Save the Trees ... Save the Streams ... Save the Trails ..."

He tried the breathing thing again and waited for the deadbeats to scramble off before he exited at the Square. Echoing his impatience, the MAX trundled on away from him, headed due west like some jangled kiddie trolley.

Almost instantly, sunshine streamed down as the sky switched from gray to deep blue. An old lady yelled at the metal ticket machine, punching the rows of buttons, begging a senior all-day rail pass to drop in the slot. The ticket machine ignored her.

Moving away from the tracks, Deke tried to get his bearings. A file of brick steps led down to a piazza of pavers flanked by tall concrete shafts. Down below, a milling crowd suddenly looked up at a copper forecaster in the opposite corner that seemed to be going beserk: tolling bells, then whistling as pieces of jagged metal shot out from all directions. The tree huggers with the *Save* placards chanted the predictions: "Temperature, seventy-five ... humidity, forty-seven percent ... clear and sunny!"

Next, a pear-shaped bearded guy braced himself against the forecasting machine and jerked a floppy bible out of his knapsack. "You're all fornicators!" he yelled down at the top of his lungs. Some of the crowd jeered. Most of the people turned away and went back to what they were doing: yammering, messing around, working on their sun tans and the like.

"You better change your ways and I don't mean perhaps," the guy went on, pitching his raspy voice a notch higher. "I am warning you. Today is the day. Jesus ain't gonna wait much longer. You got a chance. It counts most on a bright sunny day when it seems you can get away with anything. But you can't. The dark angel's gonna snare you and cut you down."

In a way, Deke was glad he'd stuck around for a second, glad for the reminder. Nothing was going to snare him and cut him down no matter what he was about to run into.

Chapter Nine

Deke finally came upon the rust-colored Roman frontage of the Hotel Vintage Plaza. He was late. Walt was bound to be in even a worse mood. But no matter. The sooner Deke got it over with, the sooner he'd be able to get a bead on where in hell this was all headed and get the drop on them all.

"You know what I think?" said Walt, leaning back on the wine-colored sofa. "I think you done it on purpose. Gave him so much slack he was bound to reach the empty log cabins so's you could have yourself a good ol' time. Serves you right about your damn back."

Deke could've kept up the lie about the loose terrain. But he was more than sick and tired of Walt's badgering. So he cut him off with, "How do I finish it, Walt? What's the damn tie-in?"

"With what?"

"Don't hand me that. What's the tie-in with the bookkeeper outta the picture?"

"Out of the picture is he?"

"Right. With him spooked and you got the goods."

"Outta the picture and spooked. Is that what I'm supposed to believe?"

Walt pulled on his red suspenders and leaned forward. He shook his full head of white hair and then leaned back hard, just missing the bottom of the gilt frame rimming the dumb painting of tiny birds perched on dainty wine glasses. He folded his thick arms and shook his head a second time as if Deke was still that lanky fool kid down in the Glades.

"Somebody put a trace on him, did you know that? Like he's some kinda missing person. How come? I'll tell you how come. Fallout and spillage is how I read it. And if so, if

61

that's how it plays out, it ain't gonna be just some twisted back you got comin'. Handwriting will be on the wall and you're gettin' a little long in the tooth to hightail yourself out of it. So, you gonna talk to me while we still got time?"

"Don't push it, Walt."

"Oh, yeah? Since when? Since when ain't there a question mark after every damn thing you done?"

That did it. Deke tossed the attaché case at the wood-paneling right next to Walt's head.

Catching it just in time, Walt scrunched up his bushy brow. He set the case down on the coffee table between them and flipped the latches. Reaching inside, he grabbed a ledger and waved it around. "Okay, we'll drop it for now. But it ain't finished, not by a long shot. You hear? Not till mister bookkeeper is salted away. Now where were we?"

"A tie-in. You want me to run this down all the way, you got to at least give me a tie-in."

"Why?"

"So I know what the hell I'm doing."

Walt thought about it long and hard. "Okay, I can give you this much. A point man for the Outfit set up some entertainment company here doing whatever the hell they do up and down the coast."

Leaning over opposite Walt on the matching vevety sofa, Deke took a few sips of black coffee and set the cup on the burgundy side table. "So?"

" So, he overreached himself, his cover got blown and he had to split."

"How come?"

Again Walt gave Deke a look and held back a while. Finally he said, "Since when are you interested in whys and wherefores? What is goin' on here?"

"Since when do I have to track something down that's not a one-shot? So why did the point man take off? How did his cover get blown?"

"'Cause he still had to file a 10K with the S.E.C., that's how come. Have an audit and such."

"So?"

"So," said Walt, "the CPA spots a red flag, downloads the data and says he's gonna expose the point man and every goddanm thing else he's in cahoots with. Are we clear now? Are we through?"

"Spots what red flag?"

"The goddamn dummy operation. Humongous expenses, no payroll checks and a high volume of money comin' into a company going bust."

"So where *was* the money coming from?"

"That's it, Deacon. It's bad enough worrying about the spillage after one of your one-shots. But I sure as hell ain't gonna add to what you're capable of if you start figuring and putting your nose in too."

With that, Walt tossed the ledger back in the case, set the case by his side on the cushion, poured himself another tumbler of dark ale and drained it dry.

As the pain from the strained ligaments in Deke's lower back started in again, Deke gulped down some more black coffee and said, "You're telling me one blown dummy operation's bled into another. Leaking maybe all the way down the coast 'cause the point man dropped the ball twice. And this time it's liable to all come apart."

Leaning forward once more, Walt spelled it out as if he was talking to a flunky who was this close to getting sacked.

"Look, I don't know what's come over you, but you'd best get with the program. What's really goin' down is none of your friggin' business. It's the Outfit's business. What're they payin' me for? What they're always payin' me for. For damage control, to find somethin'—guys who've been stiffing them, goods, information--whatever. So I don't worry my head none about no big picture. I don't worry about nothin' long as there's no screw-ups on this end that gets them down on my ass. Which brings us back to square one. Is there a screw-up I don't know about? Is this CPA really spooked, it's only you with a twisted back, and we can just goddamn get on with it?"

Still fighting off the twitching pain, Deke stretched out his long legs. The gold antique clock in the corner announced it was one-thirty. The dark wood paneling and the plump winy-red chairs made him feel he was caught inside some tycoon's bedchamber. But he kept cooling it down, kept playing the game. "I told you, Walt. No worries."

"And I told you, since when?" said Walt, his raspy twang really getting on Deke's nerves. "It don't figure it was nice and tidy and I can just cross it off the list. It brings to mind the time you rode the clutch on your old man's Jeep, stripped the gears and blew the head gasket ramroddin' it to hell and gone. And then, when your ol' man called you out on it, you shrugged him off. Then got in trouble with some backwoods slut. And shrugged that off too."

"Can we just get on with it?"

"Fine. Since you're so all-fired anxious for the bottom line, here it is."

Walt reached over to the side table and took a long pull on another tumbler of dark ale. "I have had it, the Outfit's had it, you've had it. Even if the bookkeeper's on ice and you do good on this last leg. On this end, it's strictly electronic surveillance from now on. Legit corporations still on their feet who want to make sure of who, if anybody, they're hirin'. Background checks, deleted e-mails pulled from hard drives; scourin' databases and the like. Get me a team of hackers, changing the name to Great Western Risk Management. Nothin' anybody can connect me with. Nothin'."

"Well now," said Deke, realizing he might have known.

"Look, at the moment I need a tracker to wrap this up. I can't use no ex cops or P.I.'s 'cause anybody in on this botched operation can spot one a mile away. Bottom line, we need the skinny on what's going on with the leak in the pipeline. First stop, Salinas and something to do with farm workers and a clunker. And if anybody knows about crops, pickers and clunkers it's you. But with you damn near useless 'cause of your back, maybe you'd rather pack it in right here and now."

Walt reached over for a handful of mixed nuts, washed them down with the rest of the ale and slammed the bottle down on the side table so hard the vase full of gladiolas jumped to the side.

"So what's it gonna be, Deacon? If it's yes, you ain't gettin' nothin' but expenses till everything—and I am mean every thing—is goddamn swept clean. No holes in the flow, no more fallout and no questions about what this is all about."

Just then, the waitress with the clown-like face came scurrying in, swept away the bottles, cup and silver pot, set them on a tray and promised to replace them with more of the same. Halting in mid-sentence, she stood still with a frozen grin like some windup toy whose batteries were shot. She came back to life the second Walt tossed a few bills on her tray.

"Ooh," said the girl. "Your steaks. Your meal. Righty-o. Don't go away. Be right back."

She backed off past the built-in bookshelves lined with identical leather-bound volumes and cooed, "Have fun."

Deke held his ground, still taking in Walt's little bombshell. In the meantime, Walt simmered down and rambled on about how Deke might be able to parlay this into some kind of career move. Maybe find work in the shipping and trucking business. Keep things moving along. Something less of a strain. Still deflecting, he told Deke that while he'd excused himself a few minutes ago to see to a little business, for old times sake, he'd also made arrangements for a chiropractor in a suite on the fourth floor. Plus a gal who did a great massage and threw in other gratuities as well.

"I'm sayin', great room service they got here," said Walt, attempting to ease the tension. "The more I find out about this town, the more I am starting to appreciate it. At least twenty-five degrees cooler than Vegas, a lot greener, Mount Hood lookin' down at you and they got somethin' called grass and rain. All I need is a replacement for the naked bimbos shakin' it on the table tops at the Tabu, makin' the colored lights go round. And the strippers playin' water volleyball. But hell, in this economy, you can't have it all."

As if Deke had resigned himself to Walt's terms, Walt went on about arrangements in the hotel's men's shop for Deke's new suit with all the trimmings. "You'll need it soon as you hit L.A. And I'll eat this coffee table if the trail don't lead you straight there. Oh yeah, there's nothin' like that exec look. They'll figure you for some hotshot producer and sell their mother on the off chance you're their ticket to the moon."

Walt chuckled over that one, Deke kept glaring at him. They sat like that, neither one speaking for a while. Walt shoved more mixed nuts in his mouth, guzzled another ale and kept wiping his walrus mustache with the back of his hand.

"Oh," said Walt, "one more thing. Been in touch with our screw-up point man. He's putting a good face on it, like it's nothin'. Even asked for you special. The suit was his idea. Goes with your style, he said. Now ain't that a kick in the head?"

"Come on," Walt said in the icy stillness. "What the hell's it gonna be? Look, I'm easing you in and out. All you have to do is go along till you plug the hole. You'll be on a leash but still have plenty of slack."

"And what if the hole can't be plugged?"

"I don't think I heard that."

No sooner had Walt raised his bushy eyebrows for emphasis, when the clown-girl was back with a whirl. She wheeled in her serving cart, whisked everything off the coffee table, plunked down their order and snatched off the silver covers, revealing the steaming plates of rib-eyed steaks and side dishes.

"Whoops," she said. "Forgot the extra ales. They are icy cold, set to go with frosty mugs this time. Be right back."

She exited as fast as her bandy legs could carry her. Walt set to work slicing up his meat into tiny bite-sized cubes. Deke guessed it was some kind of ulcer, what you got for being a testy bastard all these years. It was no secret that Walt had no friends or love life to speak of. Not ever.

"Here's to home cookin'," said Walt, taking a careful bite of steak and chewing it slowly.

The girl returned and set the frosty mugs and open bottles of ale on the side table.

"Whoops," she said, "Whoops again. Did I do this wrong? Can you manage? I should've got some tablecloths, huh? And the coffee table is kinda low and—"

"It's dandy," said Walt. "Just give us some time and space, okay, hon?"

The girl didn't like Walt's "hon" or his wayward hand patting her backside. But she registered a forced smile anyways. "You sure? It's no trouble. I could—"

"Leave us now, hon," said Walt, beckoning to Deke to fill him a frosty mug to the brim. "We'll be fine."

The girl looked at Deke for a cue. Deke nodded. She scooted off as Deke poured the thick ale while Walt gave the girl a horny grin.

"Here's to cuttin' our losses," said Walt.

Deke continued to give Walt nothing. As he saw it, his only choice was to keep playing along till he was ready to make his move. Which figured to be some time between tomorrow and the day after.

Walt wiped the foam off his mustache. Then he squinted, knitting the furrows on his mottled forehead, making the folds by his pug nose even more pronounced. "If it ain't askin' too much, I'd appreciate some kinda response. At least let on how you feel about headin' for the last roundup."

For an answer, Deke snatched a serrated blade and tore into his steak.

Chapter Ten

For a pittance, you could take in an old flick at the Hollywood Forever Cemetery on any given Monday evening. As this crazy Labor Day drew to a close, Ben looked upon this outing as a continuing escape hatch as he drifted among the other film buffs setting up their folding beach chairs and blankets. Here he could kick back and enjoy one of his favorites projected on the wall of Rudolph Valentino's mausoleum, with the tops of spindly palms lazing over the shadowy images. It was Ben's cup of tea. An homage to movieland's past. A fitting way to comfort those nearby stars of yesteryear, gone but close by and not forgotten.

However, despite the lingering buzz from the margaritas and the promise of mindless diversion, the low-key anxiety threatened to slip in again. As he eased behind a hibiscus hedge and sat on the carpet of grass, he rationalized that besides unwinding, he was also killing time in a productive way. Re-appreciating narrative film technique till Leo and Iris went to the mat for the last time. Honing his storytelling skills for his stint at the Avalon Studios and the big day tomorrow. Besides, there really was nothing left for him to do except sit back, watch the film, wend his way to Iris' and go to bed. Give his body and overworked brain a reprieve.

And so, at a still tipsy remove, he took in the restless opening credits of Hitchcock's *North by Northwest* punctuated by Bernard Herrmann's agitated score. However, unlike all the others—bobbing their heads in front of him, tittering and chuckling like the cynics they were—Ben began to get drawn in.

Which made no sense. Besides being half-sloshed and out of it, he knew the film inside and out. It was just a romantic spy chase from the fifties: Cary Grant in too-too-sunny Technicolor. There was no realism, no way whatsoever of taking it to heart. And certainly not while surrounded by people knowingly nudging their companions.

Trying another tack, pretending he was back in class at Southern Cal, he affected a nod in sync with the trio of cronies seated on a blanket to his immediate right. He recalled that Hitchcock wanted to do a chase across the faces of Mount Rushmore. Lehman, the screenwriter, wanted to do a frothy "movie/movie" featuring a cardboard Madison Avenue type. Hitchcock insisted on the chase. Giving way, Lehman added a double-agent love interest and a bogus manhunt forcing Cary Grant to hop a train to Chicago. Thereby concocting a getaway north by northwest to the top of a fake Mount Rushmore. There Grant hung by his fingers with one hand as a ghoulish baddie crunched his knuckles with the heel of a boot and, simultaneously, the double-duty heroine dangled over the precipice clutching Cary's other hand.

Still nodding away like a seasoned pro, Ben took in the sequence as an equally tipsy Grant skidded out of control down the Coast Highway. His car almost but not quite skittering off the cliff edge and plunging into the churning Pacific on a road that was supposed to be Glen Cove, Long Island.

What a hoot.

But, try as he may, his old nemesis began creeping in. The scene kept reminding him of careening down Angelique's driveway and smacking into the girl's truck. And a subsequent scene, as Grant attempted to escape by sneaking aboard a train, reminded him of the time he himself attempted to leave LaLaLand for a job interview for a kiddie show out of the selfsame Chicago. As if the stifling heat of L.A.'s Union Station wasn't bad enough, along with the hyper kids climbing the walls, the footrace to the coach cars had literally done him in. The hissing steam from the idling engines choked him. The screams of parents who'd lost track of their kids, the barricade of baggage handlers' carts piled high plus the throng jostling for position only added to the melee. Out of nowhere, a heavyset guy with a shaved head rammed him against a sleeper car, stripped him of his train tickets and shoved him into the mob.

And what was Aunt June's response?

"What is that, a joke? You looking for sympathy? Try closing a two-story multi-million dollar teak-and-concrete job on Carbon Beach. Try putting something on the line for once, instead of sneaking out of town or always doing a number on me."

Turning away from the flickers on the mausoleum wall, even in his grogginess he knew she was right. He *was* doing a number, a Cary Grant—talking himself into it while secretly looking for a way out. Anything to let himself off the hook.

And that hook wasn't planted by Aunt June. That hook was planted the moment his mother left him with the Dr. Seuss book. The ribbon of candy-cane roads on the cover led up to a dancing boy on top of a high peak, the words "Oh, the Places You'll Go!" floating overhead. In his kiddie brain, his mother would only return once he reached the top. Every year since, the words inside the cover worked on him. *And will you succeed? Yes! You will, indeed! 98 and ¾ percent guaranteed.* And not a day had gone by when someone didn't say, "How's it going, Ben? What're you up to? Gonna snatch that brass ring?"

As for this nutty last chance, he had to take it on. Chuck the mind games, the I-damn-well-can but How-can-I-possibly? underneath. His little kid's hang-up aside, there was no way he could let everybody down.

After the roll of the final credits and the cheerful, whistling applause, he was greeted by the trio of jobless cronies from the stomping ground at the Farmers Market.

"Hey, buddy boy," said the loudest of the three, the one in the baggy pants with the perpetual grin. "What a goof. Can you imagine?"

Ben wanted to say, "You bet," but let it go.

"So," said the one in the Lakers T-shirt, "how's it going?"

The quieter one of the bunch sheepishly piped in with, "Yeah, Ben. What're you up to? Gonna snatch that brass ring?"

Chapter Eleven

A few miles due east of Fairfax on Beverly Boulevard, Iris' house stood like a cinder-block sentinel. Like Iris herself, it was tan and resilient, impervious to everything. Twenty years ago, in lieu of a front yard and conventional living room, Iris had the builder erect an outsized fitness room. As an afterthought, a narrow hallway was tacked on with a tiny kitchen to the right, a den to the left, and two bedrooms at the rear. The smaller bedroom, next to a sliver of driveway, was filled with Iris' junk and a cot and presently provided Ben with temporary sleeping quarters. The larger room next to the bathroom, smack up against the constant traffic flow, served as Iris' boudoir. Thus Iris' idea of a heavenly retreat continued to sit on the noisiest corner lot in captivity.

It was here that Ben made his final pit stop at a few minutes past eleven. He doused the headlights and backed up a few yards away from the front curb in case Iris was still up and at it. Knowing Iris, if she spotted the condition of the back bumper of the borrowed Prelude, she would be off and running at the mouth.

So far so good. Iris's abode and the neighbors' houses, set back and hidden by thick foliage, were quiet and dark. No one out and about save for the hum and roar of the traffic as it simultaneously headed east and west at the crossroad.

A click of the latch key and it was only fourteen strides across the padded floor, a short shoeless trek down the narrow hallway, a shift to the right and, at last, to bed.

But, alas, no such luck. Less than two seconds after he squeezed the front door shut, Iris was on top of him.

"Whoa," said Ben, holding up his hands in mock surrender. "Relax, it's just me."

Iris stood her ground in her terry-cloth shorty pajamas, rubbing her chopped ash-blond hair with a towel, training her beady eyes on him as if still unsure whether he was friend or foe.

"Okay, Iris, I give. Did Leo run out on you after you'd pinned him for the umpteenth time? Or was it the other way around?"

"Knock it off. How was the retro flick in the old cemetery? Filling your head with retro rot while I'm left holding the bag?"

"Okay, come on, come on. What is it?"

"Besides the fact that June gave me a jingle, interrupting the action, telling me to keep an eye out and make sure you were squared away by Saturday? Out of my hair, that is, and everybody else's."

"Yes, besides that."

"It was the other calls, is what it was, and the stupid answering machine. So, okay, one interruption was good, namely June's news about your fake birthday this year. Reminding me of our tough love pact and that you are outta here."

"We've covered that. Who else called?"

"Angelique, that's who else. Pulling her hair out even after I had given her a full workout, mixed her a mango stabilizer and left her place smiling. Which, by the time I got off the phone with her, was as good for Leo and me as a cold shower. And then we got the girl. Which totally put a damper on it. Which I don't want to go into, or your qualms about healthy sex between two robust, middle-aged people. Which is putting me in the mood for a mango stabilizer myself before I too lose it and really let off some steam."

"What girl?"

"Right," said Iris, slapping him with the towel as if they were locker room buddies, and bounding away into the kitchen. "Don't get me started. I cranked the ring tone from alarm to tinkle and am unplugging the damn thing for the rest of the night."

"What girl?" Ben asked even louder, traipsing into the kitchen as the juicer went into high gear.

But it was no use. Amidst the hum of the air-conditioner over the sink, the grinding juicer and the traffic noise which managed to insinuate itself through the louvered windows, Iris was in the throes of peeling, fending off slimy glop and measuring assorted powders and herbs.

For answers, Ben resorted to the answering machine in the den directly across. The news from Angelique only reiterated most of what Ben already knew: "I'm still like so antsy ... besides everything else, somebody was supposed to show who didn't. And that Ben, that sorta cousin of yours. Cute, sharp in a way like I said, but I don't know ... I just don't know. A little nosy if you catch my drift. Oh well, talk at you later."

In sharp contrast to Angelique's sputtering patter, the maiden in the Chevy pickup was perky and direct. The message she left was that Ben was in no way getting off easy. Among her issues was the fact she needed a place to hole up. She ended with, "So, buddy, if you are finally home, you can count on seeing my face. And I don't mean perhaps."

Too beat to react, Ben put the messages on the back burner. Even the insistent tinkling sound that followed seemed remote and distant. Absentmindedly, he picked up the receiver. "Sorry, we are closed for the night."

"Hey! Que esta pasando aqui?"

"C.J.?"

"Who else?"

"What do you mean, 'What's going on?'"

"Soy serio, payaso."

"Okay, you're serious. Cut the put-downs, give it to me in English and make it short."

From the scuffling sounds and echoes on the other end, Ben guessed that C.J. was at the Hollywood station. After he calmed down a bit, Ben learned that he had just intercepted some goofy message. Ben asked him to speak slowly and clearly trying to both keep from drifting off and make out what he was driving at.

"Idiota dispatcher," said C.J. "Who can read his gringo handwriting, you know? But it sounds like you. I tell you to call Chula at the motel if you want me. Ese foe el trato!"

"I know that was the deal. Are you going to tell me or not?"

"Hey, you don't got to take a tone with me because they know I know you. You are on the nuisance file. No me hagas esas jaladas."

"Hold it," said Ben, becoming more alert. "You're the one jerking me around."

"Oh, yes? If it's not you, then what payaso made the call?"

"What call? Spell it out right now or I'm hanging up."

C.J.'s husky voice faded off as he shouted at someone. A tarty voice shrieked right back. This went on for a while until, as mercurial as ever, C.J. came back on the line laughing. "The hooker we dragged in, she says bad things but likes my chest and big muscles. Only the long hair, she says, it has to go. Dame un tiempo."

"Give *me* a break, you mean. How old will I be till you read me the stupid message?"

There were more scuffing noises. Then the words came haltingly over the line as if C.J. were decrypting a secret code. "'Evil enterprise ... coming your way ... the audit proves it ... start looking for—'"

"What audit? What is this, a joke?"

"Ay, Chihuahua, there is more. About the Rockies ... crippled ... high fever ... no I.D., somebody got to believe me."

"Listen carefully. I don't know who this guy is or what you're talking about."

"Es la verdad? You did not send this?"

"No. Es la verdad."

Ben heard a groan on the other end and sounds of a scuffle.

"Okay okay, it is late," said C.J. "I jump the gun maybe. Nuisance call is passed around, so loco, so Hollywood, guys in the squad remember you and give to me. So maybe —"

"No maybe. You jumped the gun and owe me an apology."

"Si, lo siento. It happens stations in Frisco and Vegas get this too. Maybe it is a promo."

"Calling police stations?"

"Why not? Enough times then it gets on the news, you know?"

74

"Nobody in Hollywood is that desperate."

"Everybody in Hollywood is that desperate. Especially you, pendejo."

"Oh, that's cute. Another put-down. Are we through?"

"Si, si. Hey, you still got a birthday coming up, que no? What you say I buy you drinks?"

"Great."

"Bueno, got to go. Tranquilazate."

"Not me, *you* take it easy." It crossed Ben's mind to ask C.J. about an uninsured motorist in a borrowed car smacking into somebody's old truck, but it could wait. Everything could wait.

Returning to the hallway, he was greeted by a frothing beaker of Iris's mango glop.

"Down the hatch, buster. You are so outta shape, it's pathetic."

"Gotcha." Ben knew the only hope of hitting the sack was to obey orders.

"Who was that?" said Iris as she disconnected the phone.

"Nobody, nothing."

"At this time of night?"

"It's L.A. Only health freaks know it's late." Ben downed the slippery liquid, wiped his lips, handed her back the beaker and prayed he wouldn't throw up. "Can we say goodnight now?"

"Look at me, Benjamin."

Ben did as he was told and peered down. As seen through his watery eyes, Iris' combative face seemed almost benign.

"I promised ol' June," Iris barked, "that I would make sure you got your act together. Which is a no-brainer, what with Leo needing you to do the same and me dying to have this place all to myself again."

"Understood, Iris. Say it again and we'll dance to it. Just post the drill on the frig. I will commit it to memory at first light."

"Damn straight you will."

With that, Iris marched back into the kitchen, tossed the beaker in the sink, whisked by him and, for emphasis, slammed her bedroom door. Traipsing down the hall, too

75

out of it to do more than take off his shoes and unbutton his shirt, Ben shifted past the two racks of barbells and flopped onto the cot.

In the dream, nothing worked, nothing fit. He got out an easel and tried to sketch a simple storyboard opening, but the panels turned into pictures of a crippled accountant dangling from a ridge, and the sheets of paper transformed into a ledger and then a ledge. Somebody stood above him crunching his knuckles with the heel of his boot; then a dangling maiden by his side was yelling at him while clutching his hand for dear life.

The scene dissolved as he rushed here and there in the pitch dark searching for the Prelude but couldn't find it anywhere. The traffic whizzed by him when he spotted her again wearing the same bib overalls. But there was no way of crossing over as the cars reached the speed of light and his legs were as heavy as the weights at Iris's gym.

She reappeared as a silhouette far off in the distance. "Let's see some I.D. Let's see it from both you and the accountant."

All at once there was nothing but a cutting room floor. At his feet were strips of film; directly ahead, a blank mausoleum wall. He shouted over the wall, insisting that the maiden and accountant didn't belong in this movie and he had the outtakes to prove it. He bent down but all he could find was a toy box filled with crayons, binoculars and an oversized copy of Dr. Seuss' *Oh, The Places You'll Go.* The binocular lenses were shattered. The wind whipped by and rustled the tops of the spindly palms. Ben cocked his head and heard something whistling down the canyon closing in on him.

Startled, Ben sat straight up in bed. Sighing, dog-tired and unable to take it any more, he scrunched back down, rolled over and hugged the pillow. Reaching for the most benign imagery possible, he started counting mellow, sweet-natured sheep. Which, in practically no time, began to do the trick.

Just before he dozed off again, the counting brought back fuzzy images of accountants and C.J.'s call. Which showed how much police departments knew. Accountants were just bookkeepers. Theirs was a simple balancing act. The reason you'd always find them at a remove--cool, calm and collected.

Yes sir, no tension, no mayhem, no conundrums. Cool, calm and collected; that was the key.

Chapter Twelve

The day before, Deke was seated uncomfortably on a Southwest flight to Oakland. It wasn't just the dark suit and new shoes that cramped his style. It was everything, including his stiff back.

For openers, they told him at the check-in counter that the first seats on the plane were roomy, perfect for a long-legged fella like him. They didn't tell him that the whole time he'd be facing a plump, moon-faced mom and her thirteen-year-old moon-faced son and sixteen-year-old moon-faced daughter. He'd never seen a threesome so bubbly in his life. Without asking, the bunch of them—sometimes taking turns, sometimes talking all at once—told him crap he didn't want to hear. They were from Spokane, clad in sparkling Spokane sweatshirts—in-your-face commemorations of the son's exploits at first base in the Little League regional championship. After a play-by-play of the final inning, mom skipped over to the girl's triumphs on the swim team while the girl, at the same time, turned red and kept tugging at her short pleated skirt. Then mom switched to the wonders of the folks, schools and community get-togethers back home.

Then it was, Was the gentleman going all the way to Disneyland? No, only to Oakland. But afterwards, on to L.A.? Maybe. First time? Not exactly. Well, let me tell you all about Disneyland and the sights you absolutely don't want to miss.

As if mom jabbering away wasn't bad enough, the shapely flight attendants wore khaki shorts and matching loose blouses, and kept making dumb remarks up and down the aisles and over the intercom. It started with, "We've got good news and bad news." And then moved on to groaners like, "Hope you brought some flotation devices with you 'cause we're fresh out. Just kidding, folks." And,

"If you're hungry, too bad. What did you expect from a no frills airline?" After each bonehead announcement, one of the attendants would wiggle by, pick Deke out especially and say, "Hey, darlin', having fun yet?"

At this point, Deke figured his new outfit made him look rigid and uptight. Which was the same reaction he got from the hooker and massage gal in Portland. She took one look at him in his new duds and told him he was going to be a real challenge. But neither she nor the muscle-relaxer pills Walt foisted on him hardly made a dent. They both mainly served as reminders he'd better not twist or make any sudden moves. Any way you looked at it, ever since that run-in with Elton Frick, ever since he'd scrambled after that nerd accountant, he'd been hamstrung.

Forcing himself to concentrate and shut off the yakking Disney-brained three, he closed his eyes and tried again to sort it out. Just as he'd done before boarding while shuffling the cards in Frick's wallet:

As things stood, two things went off the rails. First, Frick was about to blow the whistle on the pop touring company the Outfit was using as a front. Now that Deke had recovered the memory stick and as long as Frick was out of the picture, that problem was scratched. But the Outfit's point man screwed up again leaving a bigger hole— this one in the pipeline; what the Outfit was really running under the Fed's nose. Meaning, as far as Walt and the Outfit were concerned, intercepting that missing stash patched the hole and marked the end of the line for Deke. As far as Deke was concerned, sticking it to Walt and the Outfit and keeping the missing stash all to himself would put him in the catbird seat for the first time and for a long time to come.

And that's as far as Deke could get with it. The yakking and flirty interruptions from the flight attendants made any thoughts about what it might take and what he'd run into almost impossible.

Eventually, the Disney-brained three said their cutesy goodbyes but, as usual, he barely acknowledged it.

Afterwards, at the terminal, two more muscle-relaxers enabled him to get the new, soft-grain luggage off the conveyor belt in Oakland in time to meet up with his contact. The guy was twenty-something, baby-faced, wore a black tank top with a shimmering crimson logo that read *Starshine* over his silver cargo pants.

After letting on that his name was Tyler, he snatched Deke's luggage and told him to follow close. Holding on to his carry-on bag, Deke nodded as Tyler dumped Deke's suitcases in the trunk of an electric blue Lincoln town car waiting at the pickup curb and told Deke to hop in the back.

Shortly it turned out that Deke had two disposable clowns to deal with. The driver, who introduced himself as Seb, had on a duplicate getup, his head and neck shaved smooth, accented by a stubbled pasty face. To top it off, he had four silver studs lodged in his earlobe and a set of blood-red Starshine tattoos plastered over both flabby arms.

As Deke shifted around in the roomy interior, he realized that either Seb was on something or had a screw loose. As a duo, Tyler tried to play it brainy while Seb kept breaking into some lame, rhyming patter as he headed the Lincoln south toward Salinas.

While barreling down a clogged freeway, air-conditioning blasting, tinted windows up so Deke could barely make out where he was, Deke reckoned his only recourse was to eke out whatever information he could before cutting loose.

"I hear all you fellas from Starshine are about the same age."

"More or less," said Tyler, turning his smooth face in Deke's direction.

"Less is more," Seb chimed in. "Over thirty you hit the floor, like a wasted--"

"Shut it," said Tyler. "Stick to your driving."

"Like you're the boss, chief Crazy Horse, and I don't give a toss."

Tyler shook his head and shrugged in apology. "Pay him no mind, man. He drives pretty good. That's about it."

"Yeah," said Seb, switching lanes and then swerving back to the center. "Enjoy the ride as I drive with pride."

"Could've saved you boys the trouble", Deke said, after a few minutes of dead air. "Don't know what you heard, but my back's fine. I could've rented a car."

"Not the point," said Tyler, still facing him. "We got to tighten things up. Orders from above."

"From above with a shove."

Breaking in and out of his routine, Seb added. "I told Tyler here we should've cut and run. But oh no, Tyler says the man with the plan, the punster-funster's gonna take on Hollywood. Oh yeah, big whoop. Put his finger in the dike and shoot the moon."

Tyler slapped Seb's flabby arm and told him to keep his eyes on the road.

Deke let another few minutes go by before slipping in another prod. "Seems you boys got yourselves a bookkeeping problem."

"Well," said Tyler, "you know how it is. Hard to keep accounts of all the spin-offs and stuff. And, like any business, you got to retool sometimes. Who knows? Probably some little misunderstanding or bump in the road."

"Yeah," Seb shouted, gunning it past two eighteen-wheel rigs and barely swerving back in time, "no worries. We got airhead Angelique in gear but never worry, never fear."

Tyler slapped him hard this time. "Shut it, Seb, and just freakin' drive."

"Sure thing," said Seb, jabbing a finger at the review mirror. "Dis me in front of our over-the-hill dude here so's he can dis me too."

Deke reached out and squeezed the back of Seb's neck. "Like Tyler said, you'd best stick to your driving."

It was silent after that for a good long stretch. Deke passed the time making out highway signs indicating how many miles on U.S. 101 before Hayward, Fremont and San Jose.

It was outside San Jose that he'd had it with the hazy sky and the dullness of the landscape. What ranges he could make out weren't ranges at all. They were squashed down, lumpy and brown, more like a string of sand piles. Nowhere near the jutting rimrock that carried you up to the Bitterroots, Rockies and Cascades. Nothing like Mount Charleston, Red Rock or the Valley of Fire out of Vegas. These coast ranges were for weekend picnickers.

Heading toward Morgan Hill, Deke started in again. "So, the only lead you got is a Town & Country wagon with an artichoke pasted on it. And you figure it's a company car from Salinas."

"We know it's a company car," said Tyler, looking back at him grinning. "Besides, we checked from Monterey up the coast and back. Nothing. It's either stowed away somewheres at its home base or headed south."

"With the missing cargo."

"Come again?" said Tyler, playing it coy.

"Vital to your retooling plan ..."

"Say what?"

"... that's sprung a leak."

"Whatever."

"Don't be rude, mister dude," muttered Seb. "You're just a hound till the lost is found."

Whacking Seb hard across the neck to save Deke the trouble, Tyler said, "Look, man, all you have to do is help us find the station wagon. We'll take it from there."

"In or around Salinas, is that it?"

"Yeah, Salinas," said Seb, taking his hands off the steering wheel in fake rapture. "The salad bowl of the world. Green gold, they call it—fresh lettuce, broccoli and such. Stick with us, lame old bro, and maybe you'll learn something."

"Uh-huh," said Deke. "Just making sure."

It was just as Deke thought. These two knew next to nothing. A company wagon with an artichoke stamped on it had to hail from Castroville. Deke had forgotten more about harvesting crops from coast to coast than these jokers would pick up in a lifetime. Which meant he'd be ditching them in Prunedale about thirty-five minutes short of where they were heading. Which meant they could keep the fancy luggage. The sooner he was shed of both it and them the better.

Approaching Prunedale, his excuse was that he had to relieve himself and he hadn't a bite to eat since an early morning black coffee and pastry in Portland. He timed it so that Seb had to pull over at a spot where 101 became El Camino Real. Which, as luck would have it, featured a roadside diner with a sun-bleached "Open on Sunday" sign plastered across a plate-glass window.

Without missing a beat, Deke headed for the restrooms in the back as Seb, still looking for some way to get even, called after him. "There are salt marshes along the Salinas River, bro. And shacks where the migratory workers stay. But I'll be glad to fill you in on all that stuff. Yeah, old man, I'm generous that way."

Deke glanced past the counter and spotted the back door under the wheezing air-conditioner. Another glance to the front of the place and he caught sight of Seb seated at a booth studying a plastic-coated menu. It was mid afternoon. No other customers. No sign of Tyler either.

Deke bypassed the restroom, crossed to the kitchen, brushed by the short-order cook and waitress who seemed too bored to notice. He exited and found himself hedged in by a tall wire fence that rimmed the perimeter of the building. Stepping over to the near side of the building, he peered around the corner. The traffic zipped by in the haze of dry heat. Tyler's back was to him, standing by the trunk of the Lincoln facing the traffic.

Deke walked back into the kitchen and looked around till he spied some rubber gloves and a can of oven cleaner on a nearby shelf. The bold red letters on the can warned that the product was of industrial strength, required the use of those gloves and, in case of contact with the skin, would cause severe burning. In addition, inhalation of the fumes without proper ventilation would cause respiratory problems. Deke grabbed the can and gloves and slipped out and around to the side of the building.

Soon Tyler shuffled out of sight. Then returned to the trunk of the car, possibly unsure whether or not Deke was going to try to get his hands on the luggage and split.

Deke waited till Tyler gave up on his guard duty and reentered the diner. Wasting no more time, Deke reached inside the back seat of the limo for his carry-on, hurried around to the dashboard, sprayed the steering wheel and the inside of the windshield till it was thick with yellow foam; sprayed the outside of the glass for good measure, tossed the gloves and can and took off down the road.

In no time, he was well off 101 and El Camino Real. But the funny thing was, even over the whisking sound of traffic, he could hear screaming and yelling. Proving that the warning on the oven cleaner label was accurate. And Seb simply got what was coming.

Picking up his pace, he thought about how far behind he was in the game. Not much, he reckoned judging by the laidback way Tyler and Seb were acting. It also dawned on him that Walt knew Deke would put up with those two for only so long. That he would use them and, soon as possible, take off.

He started to wonder if he'd underestimated Walt. He also wondered who the other players were and what, if any, obstacle they might pose.

Chapter Thirteen

As Iris warbled the Southern Cal Trojans' fight song in the shower, Ben gulped the last sips of iced Kenya AA. After a good night's sleep, the advent of a sparkling new day and an accountant's outlook still fresh in his mind, Ben was good to go. Accountants had their balancing act; Ben had his. The juggler was his spiritual ancestor. Juggling was his stock in trade. His task was clear.

Tossing the remnants of a Go-lean blueberry waffle into the bin, he was about to head out the front door when the phone rang. He snatched up the receiver in case it was another snag. Luckily it was only a long distance call from Aunt June applying a little more pressure.

"Relax," said Ben, "rest assured. When engaging in any venture, one must be orderly. Keep everything in its proper place. Maintaining a keen sense of balance is the watchword for today."

Taken aback, Aunt June said, "Venture? What kind of venture?"

"Strictly business, ma'am. Just as you prescribed."

"Am I hearing right?"

"Indeed. Now if you'll excuse me, I happen to be on a very tight schedule."

"Wait a minute. This is a little hard for me to believe. A business venture with who?"

When Ben mentioned Leo's name, June began to back off. When he added that Iris was on his back to meet the deadline, June became ecstatic.

"I like it, I like it. When Iris dropped the hint, I naturally took it with a grain of salt. But considering the pressure Leo is under and the fact that you are as close to vagrancy as you can get ... I mean, if you could really swing it, parting ways will not be sweet sorrow."

"Meaning?"

"Like you said. No time for small talk."

"Come on, Auntie, out with it."

"Well, as I forget to mention, I have this great chance to hook up with Pacific Realty. But this fella wants to make sure I'm unencumbered."

"He? I thought it was an all-gals conference? And you were off men for life?"

"Yeah, well, what can I say? The guys happen to be having their own realty thing next door and—never mind."

"Great. So now you can tell this dreamboat—"

"Ted."

"Tell Ted you threw the gauntlet, I snatched it up and am literally off and running to solvency."

"Terrific. So, we're clear on this? No backsliding?"

"Not if you get off the phone and quit hampering me."

"Absolutely. Tell you what. From here on I'll check in with Iris and let her keep on your tail. In the meantime, I'll tell Ted it's looking good. They'll be no strings back in L.A."

"Sweet, Auntie."

"Oh, come on now, we've got your birthday coming up. This time we'll have something to celebrate."

"Really sweet."

"Don't give me that. First we gave you till you were twenty-one. Then twenty-five. Then we pushed it to thirty. You are three years overdue! Besides, you admitted you owe me."

As always, Aunt June wasted no time with coddling goodbyes. By the same token, Ben hurried out of the house. It was the day after Labor Day, a normal workday even by Hollywood standards and he really did have a tight agenda. It crossed his mind to put in for another cell phone, but that errand was way at the bottom of his list. At the moment, he didn't have a second to spare.

Turning the ignition key of the still-trusty Prelude, letting the cylinders idle, he checked his watch. It was eight-thirty, right on schedule. He would drop off the car for an estimate on the crunched tail lights. Then swing by the Farmers Daughter Motel and hand Chula a query for C.J. to estimate his possible culpability vis-a-vis the little accident with the maiden's old pickup. Next, he would skip over to Iris' gym and work out while boning up on the latest schlock on the video monitors. After that, armed and apprised of the viewing habits of Angelique's target audience, he would hit the Avalon Studios for his power meeting with Leo and Gillian.

While heading out, he kept in mind last night's message on Iris' answering machine. The maiden's housing needs, little threats and whatnot held fifth place on his agenda and would be attended to as soon as he got the chance.

As it happened, his trip to the Honda dealership took up very little time. However, the cost of replacing the tail lights and, it seemed, the rear bumper as well was only a tad less than outrageous. The real issue was dropping the car off and getting it done in time before Oliver, the owner and Ben's old hapless agent, returned from the orchid festival in South Florida. So much for task number one.

At step two, the surly albino manning the desk at the Farmers Daughter Motel informed Ben that Chula would not be in before four and it was against policy to pass along personal notes. When asked, "Whose policy?" the reply was a snide, "You got a problem with that? Somebody told you this was a community bulletin board or somethin'?"

Shrugging off the second glitch of the day, bypassing the usual parking problems, Ben left the car in the motel lot next to the empty pool and hurried down Fairfax to Iris' gym. A quick change in the locker room, a dash to the right with pop-rock blaring over the loudspeakers competing with the whirr of the fans, he barely managed to beat out a chubby matron for the only unoccupied treadmill. He pressed the speed button on the digital control board till it hit the brisk walk mode, grabbed the remote and began hitting the channels. The images and the subtitles informed him what in the world was going on.

Less than a minute after, a bronzed Amazon in her early twenties hopped on the treadmill beside him the second it became vacant frustrating the matron once again. Simultaneously, the bronzed one clicked her remote, revved the speed button to full throttle and began pounding the revolving belt.

As luck would have it, while tapping his own remote, Ben found three MTV channels. At the same time, (thanks no doubt to Iris) a brace of monitors over to his left and to the far right was looping old Angelique videos. With her younger buff form on full display, these gems showed her bouncing around a pink Styrofoam stage set, laboring to transform from airhead to predator. Taken together, the MTV shows Ben was perusing directly in front, the pulsating images of Angelique's former self to the right and left, and the blaring pop-rock over the hidden speakers would have to do in order to stay on schedule.

Checking his watch, Ben soon discovered that none of the MTV scenes lasted more than two to three minutes. Adding to this apparent regard for attention deficit disorder, the Amazon next to him was watching a soap which also couldn't hold a scene for more than a minute or two as she continued to pound away on the revolving tread as though doubling the pop-rock beat.

Focusing as best he could, the first show Ben keyed on was about a twenty-something who only wanted to "be okay" and clear up a misunderstanding. It seemed her fellow plain-Jane roommates accused her of being mean. In the next shot, she announced she would settle for "an okay nice job" in an "okay part of town" with "some okay nice guys" who would tell her she was "really okay."

A second show featured footloose singles ensconced in a beachfront condo who were "looking to be doing something that feels like me." And "to stop being polite and get real." At the moment, this involved a pair of heavily muscled beach boys dickering over whether or not to hold back. The object of their dilemma was a cute Latina lazing nearby on a straw hammock.

Switching to the third channel he found a wide-eyed brunette who was starting up a band and was excited because they were "beginning to vibe" over her new song entitled *I'm a little mixed up in my head*.

Refusing to give up, Ben scanned a dozen more channels until he came upon a young women apparently praying to herself as she scaled a rock wall on a show called *Really Real* replete with standard-issue types like a slutty girl, a sweet one and a racially ambiguous one.

For relief, Ben glanced over at the soap the Amazon was glued to. All he could gather before the next instant break was that a jilted night nurse was stalking a doctor with a syringe.

"Oh, give me a break," Ben pleaded.

Without missing a beat, the Amazon jerked her head and gave Ben a quizzical look.

Shrugging, Ben wanted to tell her to hang in there because surely, no matter what venue Gillian had in mind, Ben could come up with something a lot less mindless. But he kept the thought to himself as she jerked her head right back to the soap, continued to pound away and gave the night nurse a thumbs up as she stuck the needle in.

Finished with this cursory research, just as he was about to hit the cool-down button, Iris' muscled forearm reached over and pressed the accelerator. With her beige jumpsuit and chopped hair pressing in on him, she shouted over the blaring speakers, "Go for it and then get with it. You're due at the studio in forty minutes."

"No kidding," said Ben, trying to sneak the speed indicator back down.

"Come on, Benjamin, at least jog. Get in shape, shape rules. How many times I've told you?"

"Too many." Ben hit the stop button and hopped off.

"Just looking out for you," said Iris, grabbing a towel and wiping off the machine's jutting handles.

"You mean Leo," said Ben, drifting over to the water-cooler.

"You bet your ass. Guess what happens if this deal with Angelique tanks. Guess what your life's gonna be worth."

Before Ben could answer, two nubile teens on the adjacent step machines and the grunting Amazon had all shifted their focus to Iris' jabbing finger as if checking out a new reality show.

Impervious to the scene she was making, Iris followed him to the men's locker room door. "Hey, I'm talkin' here. Don't get dreamy on us, for God's sake."

"Will you please, kindly, back off?"

"No way. I am officially in Leo's corner, Angelique's coach and June's proxy."

In what passed for a display of affection, Iris reached up, mussed Ben's hair and tweaked his cheek.

As he watched her stride off in that jaunty way of hers, Ben couldn't help noticing the close-up on the nearest monitor. There again was the marked resemblance between the old Angelique and the maiden in the vintage pickup.

As for Ben's next and primary destination, for the most part the Avalon Studios were a well-kept secret. Only people in the business knew that somewhere south of the sprawling empire of Paramount/Viacom stood a miniature production facility down Van Ness and around a sleepy corner on Clinton. And few people recalled that in its heyday, as movies segued from silent to talkies, it was called *Famous Studios.* From there it went through name changes like *Prudential Pictures* and *Allied Producers.* Later on in the 1940s, it was known as *Cimarron* and, later still, the logo changes included *Phoenix, Odyssey, Galaxy* and a host of others until it settled in as a production facility rental.

Remnants of the old days still littered the back lot, like the set pieces for an outer space TV series and what was left of a generic Western town. Recently, just before the latest failed venture, the three airplane-hanger-sized sound stages were employed for a yet another short-lived shopworn TV cop series; the selfsame show featuring a distracting sexpot "muchacha distraido" C.J. discredited for Leo's edification. Ostensibly as a result of this fiasco and subsequent bankruptcy, the studio gate was now manned by a guy shaped like a beanpole with a goofy drawl to match. Ben expected a skeleton crew till the new operation got up to speed, but this was ridiculous.

"Hold on," said the beanpole as Ben jammed on the brakes just past the metal barricade.

"Why? What's the problem?" said Ben, switching off the engine.

"Just hold on, is all. I'm Lester, who are you?"

Ben sent the electric window sliding down and said, "Ben Prine. I'm expected."

Drawing closer, Lester's flame-red hair glinted in the sunlight, his sliver of a face pale in comparison. Leaning down, Lester said, "Then maybe you can tell me what's goin' on?"

"What do you mean?"

"There was supposed to be four of us. I report and find the other three opted for some theme park somewheres. And a little while ago, this Russian comes by and says not to worry, he'll be right back. I mean, hell, how do I know who to let in? Am I supposed to man this whole thing by myself? And for how long? And who pays me? What is this, some kinda hustle?"

Lester ran back to his glass-plated station, ducked inside and scampered out holding up an air rifle. "This is all I got. For guard duty and such."

Smirking and changing his tone, Lester added, "But hell, since this place has an old western set and all, which is the only reason I took the job ..." For emphasis, he peered through the front sight. "Pretty neat though, huh? Oak wood stock—butt and forearm. Blueing, steel cocking lever, gravity fed. Just like Steve McQueen ridin' shotgun next to Yul Brynner in *The Magnificent Seven*. That old movie is my favorite."

Ben didn't have the heart to tell him McQueen's gun had a pump action. And he didn't have the patience to put up with him a second longer. "I'll take up your concerns with Leo. See you in a bit."

"Not so fast. You still ain't told me who you are. And what, if anything, this new operation's got goin' for it?"

"Desperation."

"Come again?"

"The Russian has to make it work. He has no choice."

"Oh?" Lester cranked the lever of his air rifle, aimed at the flat rooftop of the nearest sound stage and said, "Okay, that's more like it. Maybe I jumped the gun. Get it?"

"Uh-huh. Where do I park?"

"Just a sec." Lester ambled back to his station and reappeared with a handful of printouts and notes. Shouting over to Ben, he said, "Office building's locked. So is soundstage one and two, plus the screening rooms, editing, media, grip, electrical, hydraulic lifts, carpentry and set building, tank stage, café, plus—"

"Then what *is* operational?"

"Everything else I guess. Which don't leave a helluva lot except soundstage three, writer's bungalow, what's left of the western town and—"

"Never mind. I get it." Ben put the Prelude in gear. Lester banged on the trunk.

"One last thing," said Lester, returning to Ben's side. "Got this here note from some gal from Paramount."

"Gillian."

"That's the one. Says for you to check it all out and she'll give you the skinny during her break."

Ben drove on, passing the cylindrical office building and media center and the brace of main sound stages. Following his nose and his memory, he took a left and cruised down a narrow alleyway flanked by the tech support buildings and post production site and the vast sound stage two. He hung a right in front of the pink stucco café with its matching tile roof and open veranda; then parked in the shade of a stand of ficus trees whose multiple trunks bundled together like swollen tubes.

There, in the stillness, he reminded himself if he was going to pull off this juggling act, if he was truly going to keep all the balls in the air, he'd have to make sure nothing got scrambled.

Along these same lines, Ray from Vegas belonged in a completely separate box. So did the girl in the old truck and Leo's one-big-happy-family promo.

It was bad enough he knew next to nothing about crossovers streaming in cyber space. Or what they were currently throwing in the mix including anything Gillian may have in mind. His newfound accountant mindset not withstanding, as everyone had made abundantly clear, he had no recourse but to play it as it lays while avoiding any more deflections.

Thus, following Gillian's directive till she and Leo returned, Ben doubled back around the corner and walked up the tech alley to the side entrance of soundstage three. Inside the huge dimly lit cavern, he meandered in and out of the warren of police offices, holding cells, interrogation rooms and the like; each furnished with every detail down to the log book and roster sheet on the desk sergeant's counter.

He glanced up at the second tier of motel room facades, shabby interiors doubling as hideouts and stakeout blinds and a cutout of a sniper's lair. Rimming the walls, encircling the entire cop world, he found fire-escapes, spiral staircases, spider-covered attics, back alleys and various clichés of Halloween Hollywood including a rusted wrought-iron gate encircling a number of open graves.

Leaving the soundstage and returning to the locked café, he gave the back lot and the rest of the area a quick once-over. Diagonally across from the ficus trees and his parked car was the salmon-colored writer's bungalow. Fanning out and away from the bungalow was a cut-rate moonwalk replete with craters, fragments of a shattered space ship and simulations of a windswept barren outcropping. Ruffled-leafed banana plants and rubber trees and a sea of palm fronds fought for purchase and were succeeding in their quest to conquer outer space.

On the other side of the bungalow, in the opposite direction, he took in Lester's beloved western town, complete with hitching posts, raised planked sidewalks, livery stable and corral. A cursory inspection revealed that all but the livery stable consisted of facades and partials that leaned up against a steel-mesh fence that enclosed the entire property. The western town, like the moonwalk, had lost the battle with the foliage with only a few dumpsters offering any resistance.

But for no reason he was drawn to the livery stable. He told himself he was only killing some more time and would give this backdrop only a quick once-over.

Lifting the heavy metal bar up and over, he pressed the warped flanking doors open a smidge and squeezed in. Again for no apparent reason, he checked out the dusty buckboard, harnesses, bridles and other gear hanging from the supporting posts, and the rickety wooden ladder propped up against a landing about thirty feet away.

Ambling around, he noticed the huge oil drum sitting in a far corner under a hay loft filled with greasy rags redolent of motor oil and rancid gasoline. Dangling from a chain directly above the oil drum was a rusty motor, probably taken from the Model T sitting way over in the far corner.

Moving left, he came upon a pit, partially obscured by the buckboard and filled with a pile of burlap grain sacks.

Edging back, just out of curiosity, he climbed up the ladder and eyed the hay loft and a flimsy wooden door close by. He lifted the latch, entered a cramped piney room and took in the sagging cot and a wash stand serviced by a hand pump. After a half dozen tries, the crank only produced a trickle of rusty water. The only ventilation came from a slot in the wooden screens next to the cot. Twisting around, staring down from the landing onto the plank flooring, he spotted a half-dozen bales of hay wedged next to the grain pit.

Climbing down the ladder, Ben muttered, "Grist for the mill, Benjamin. You never know." But, then again, why had he studied all this so carefully? The cop world sound stage made some kind of sense but what did this livery stable have to do with *something streetwise with backup while shaking off the denizens of the underworld*—the kicker he'd tossed out to appease Angelique? What did the livery stable have to do with anything?

Coming to his senses, he got out of there, closed the barn doors and clamped the metal bar in place. He had to quash these nagging, incessant omens if it killed him.

Chapter Fourteen

A few moments later, heading back to the writer's bungalow, he spotted Leo clambering out of a golf cart that had stalled by the café. By the time Ben reached him, he'd turned the ignition key a dozen times and assaulted the dead battery with some flavorful Russian invectives. Sporting the same California-black outfit he'd worn last night at the Polo Lounge, and with his bald pate shimmering in the sunlight, Leo curled his thick lips upward into a lopsided grin.

"No worries, dude. All things not gold yet, is true, but my hand to God, becoming silver as we speak."

Before Ben had a chance to ask for a definition of "silver," Leo spun him around, escorted him across the way to the writer's bungalow and stopped short at the entrance.

"To you, bungalow is neutral zone between outer space and old west, plus cop city and haunted house up tech alley."

Again, trying to get a word in edgewise, especially about the dubious use of the extra set pieces, got Ben nowhere. Pointing to the scrawny orange trees nearby, Leo said, "Like oasis beckoning to you, and what could be better? Nothing. I am right or I am right?"

Leo carried on about how he had laid the groundwork, provided Ben with an easel in anticipation of his storyboard sketches leading to "what I am hawking to finance boys as tax shelter. Which Gillian is then right away pitching to production company right after you are providing the goods. I'm telling you, out of old ashes is rising ... Is rising what?"

"The phoenix."

"Exactly. Beautiful, beautiful, is old name of studio in days of glory. Perfect. Whole package is gathering steam and before you can say long Slavic prayer, out of ashes is rising the Phoenix."

Finally cutting in, Ben pointed out the limited access to facilities and reduction of staff to a skeleton crew comprised of one clueless guy named Lester; a person whose dim   prospects of getting paid would make anyone leery. On the face of it, it was hard to believe this Phoenix would see the light of day, never mind get off the ground.

At this point, Leo totally lost it. Plucking handfuls of oranges the size of miniature billiard balls, Leo began hurling them at unseen enemies: through the wide-leafed banana plants, past the rubbery thickets and beyond to the ruptured space pods.

"Oh, so now I must talk business with rinky-dink scraping-bottom-of-barrel writer? How money flows and is changing shapes is for his brain also? Funding, accounts in Budapest where bank lends you, no questions where collateral is from, also his business? Proceeds, wired clear of taxes, baking like bread in Bank of America too is for his brain? And no names behind numbers for preliminary expenses is also deadbeat scribbler's business?"

"Look," said Ben, not understanding a word of it, "you tell me not to worry. You tell me it's none of my business. You pepper me with financial double-talk. And all I ask is for some plain old reassurance."

Recovering, Leo quit hurling the oranges and shambled back to the golf cart. He fiddled with the key as if a couple more clicks would somehow revive the dead battery. Talking to himself and then to Ben, he finally said, "Is what I get for wheeling-dealing so everyone can enjoy the fruits? Is what I deserve?"

A few deep sighs and Leo was back to being Leo again. He yanked out his cell phone, punched in a number and mumbled something incoherent that ended with, "One o'clock for sure. Yes, I am going. Yes, is okay, is all okay."

Leo smoothed the black strands of hair by his temples and returned to Ben's side by the stunted orange trees.

"Benjamin, for last time, who says hack must know how project is bankrolled? From where you get this idea, please?"

Ben shrugged.

"Answer please? Who is last to know, if ever?"

"Yours truly, the hungry hack."

"Positively. When opportunity is knocking, who is answering and not looking gift horse in the mouth?"

"A grateful, opportunistic hungry hack."

"Absolutely, positively. Make or break we are talking here. Make or break." Pulling out a wad of bills, Leo shoved some money in Ben's dress-shirt pocket. "So, to mover-and-shaker I am going now and you are minding your business for sure. With sealed lips, otherwise word gets out, everybody races, everybody loses. Is name of game in town, yes?"

Though dying to ask, Word gets out about what? Ben let it go.

Leo scribbled down his cell phone number and added it to Ben's bulging shirt pocket. "At quarter-of-six you are calling. I will have answer and, hoping on lucky stars, drill for getting you this positively crackerjack job. Okeydoke?"

Tired of fighting it, Ben gave him an, "Okay."

With nothing else to be said, for a time both of them fell silent. As if to make up for yesterday's agitated Santa Ana, the air remained dry and still, the sky the clearest blue. As a bonus, the incessant traffic noises stayed far off in the distance, except for a lazy drone like a homing device seeking the two of them out.

At the same time, Ben realized his post-Labor-Day resolve had slipped another notch. If everything would only keep still for a minute, he could conceivably pull this off.

Just then, Gillian appeared astride a second golf cart like a model on a parade float. Today's outfit was a lavender satiny-pants-suit, fitted to her slender form; the top lacey and open at the neck. The chestnut do was, as ever, lacquered down framing her oval face. The translucent nail polish and lip gloss shimmered; the three-inch heels on her side-less, backless, slippers a perfect match. She was so poised, there was no indication that here was an employee from Paramount/Viacom about to rush back from her break.

Her cart glided to a halt close to Leo's by the café veranda. Leo hurried over to her and said something typically incomprehensible. Apparently satisfied with Gillian's response, Leo turned his head in Ben's direction. "So, Gillian is giving you kicker and project is off and running in your brain and sealed lips and wishing on a star."

Like a man under the gun, Leo scurried away, leaving his defective cart behind.

With no sign that Gillian would deign to give up her perch, Ben walked over to her side. "Well there then now, can it be?"

"Can we dispense with the patter, Benjy?"

"Funny, that's what I was going to say. Great. So let's have it."

"Are you alert? Are you intrigued?"

"Lady, you better believe it."

"All right then. Do you recall the video game you bungled at the house party in Malibu?"

If he was reading her right, the game she was referring to was *Crossfire*. And if memory served, you the player (as ex cop Bruce) learn at the outset that your wife and baby were murdered by druggies. You're out for vengeance the second you come home and discover their bodies. Thus, if Ben hadn't chosen to enter the house, the game would've ended. But even on *easy mode*, Ben lost track of the druggies hiding upstairs. Prompted by a voice-over to shift to the next scene, Ben had Bruce cut down a dark alleyway rimmed by fire escapes. Within seconds he was met with a barrage of crossfire and was instantly gunned down. It was silly, but after three attempts, Bruce still got three in the chest. At that juncture, Ben swore off video games forever.

"Well?" said Gillian, tapping her false fingernails on the cart's steering wheel.

"Okay, okay. I blew it and gave way to a pair of jaded starlets who did a lot better."

"Not only that. But what did they keep bitching about?"

"After blowing away an army of toothless thugs, they'd had it. Claimed the macho stuff was as lame as the lady-countess tomb-raider crap. Kept eyeing me as if it was my fault."

"And? What did they say?"

"I don't know. 'Show us something, man. Bring it on.'"

"So?"

"What do you mean 'so'? They are the focus group! That was the test marketing! They were clamoring for an iPod with touch-screen joystick controls. And open-ended hard core scenarios."

"Uh-huh."

"Come on, come on," said Gillian. "Don't pretend you don't gobble up the buzz, don't hear what's trending. That you laid it on thick with Angelique totally out of the blue."

With his mind clicking away, it dawned on him that she was currently in a relationship with some gaming media designer in the Valley—another part of the industry Ben knew zip about.

"Gotcha," said Ben, as though he was on point all along.

"Well I should hope so," said Gillian, constantly checking her flimsy designer watch. "Are we or are we not in an upgraded world?"

"We are indeed," said Ben, recalling the Amazon on the treadmill egging on the jabbing night nurse as if she wanted a lot more.

"Ergo, Angelique needs a sure-fire vehicle with intense visual exposure and saturation. One her old form can be jigsawed in with real, not CGI, backgrounds."

As if Leo's sputterings about financing weren't enough, Gillian rattled off so much shop talk, all Ben could catch were snippets like "... emotional impact ... *Angie's Run*— perfect ... game to film adaptation ... potential of 124-million units worldwide ... first sequence grabber leading you on like a killer elevator pitch ... "

Breaking in before he went into brain-lock, Ben said, "Okay, okay. But what does that have to do with conning me to check out actual crime scenes? And the hype about Pepe at the writers' workshop? What does it have to do with this wreck of a studio? What is the simpleminded upshot?"

"The upshot is an annual growth rate of 20-percent and an untapped market topping it by another ten."

"That's not what I asked."

Gillian, however, was on a roll. She was standing now, so psyched she'd flung her slipper off her right foot and hadn't even noticed.

"Ask any girl under thirty," Gillian went on. "Would you rather spend your time watching a screen, waiting for the story to happen? Or would you rather take charge? 'Retro but new'—you nailed it. A real-time experience. Mission after mission no matter how dicey and to hell with the consequences."

Still at a loss, Ben came back with, "Then let me just ask you this. My job is to--"

"Good God, isn't it obvious? Come up with a hook, backed up with whatever smarts Pepe can provide. To put in my hot little hands a thumbnail sketch complete with captions I can pitch to bozo execs who can't read and have the attention span of a toddler."

"Okay, I hear you, I hear you," said Ben, recalling the videos and the soap as Gillian plopped down on the go-cart bench to catch her breath. Just as suddenly, she demurely wedged her toes back into her slipper, pulled out a compact from her clutch bag and re-perfected her façade.

"Otherwise," Ben added, "you keep leasing ancient reruns for Viacom and the proverbial handwriting is on the wall."

'Oh, puh-lease," said Gillian, applying a dab of lip gloss. "Just shut up and, while you're at it, work in a double."

"A double?"

"You heard me. A double, a stand-in. My Lord, what does it take? See you in a bit."

Left in the lurch, Ben noticed neither Gillian's fading form as she headed back toward the front gate, nor the dissolving drone of her go-cart. Having no idea how he was going to come up with a cheap thrill for girl gamers, let alone shoehorn an Angelique stand-in, he shuffled back through the stunted orange trees, absentmindedly turned the knob and entered the bungalow.

He passed through the alcove, found a switch for the three overhead fans and stood there glancing at the action-flick posters lining the walls. He told himself to quit slip-sliding and just buy in. The last time he worked, he'd been summoned to storyboard a pilot featuring a potty-mouthed hotel heiress on the loose. It seems the producers were getting cold feet over logistics. Ben had no sooner begun thumbnail sketches of the resort hopping itinerary when he got word the project had been scrapped in favor of two underemployed potty-mouthed waitresses on the prowl on Melrose. In turn, hapless agent Oliver threw up his hands in favor of tending to his orchids.

So, at this juncture, Ben should bloody well do what he was told. For the first time in living memory he was there at the inception and given carte blanche.

This firm conviction held steady for all of two minutes. Then it was, But still and all, why the rush? Why was there no time for development? It took months before a project-- any project—started to see the light of day. Take the potty-mouth fiasco. Take anything Ben had had a hand in. With this scheme it was as if *Starshine* had to be repackaged quickly. And just as quickly work in a double.

Not to look Leo and Gillian's gift horse in the mouth. And yet ...

Then he noticed it. A rumpled sleeping bag lay in the corner highlighted by glints of dappled sunlight. Strewn about were a couple of Styrofoam cups and wads of Krispy Kreme doughnut wrappers.

Walking over and hunkering down, he fixed his gaze on an Avalon Studios card, the one with Angelique's signature pink curlicues. He also noted one of the cups was embossed with a trace of lipstick.

"Right," said Ben. "Just what I need."

Chapter Fifteen

With this next glitch, Ben's juggling act became more problematic. The itinerant maiden in the bib overalls obviously crashed last night at the bungalow. The bungalow was his slotted work space. Getting her squared away, along with the other two immediate concerns, would allow him to concentrate solely on his job.

Heading east on Beverly toward Beechwood, Ben decided to kill two birds with one stone. There was a good chance Mrs. Melnick, Oliver's landlady, would reassure him that Oliver wouldn't be back for a few more days to reclaim the Prelude. That would give Ben enough time to have the car fixed and slip the girl temporarily into Oliver's pad. The maiden would surely agree that a secluded hideaway was worth the slight inconvenience of a bent grill on an obsolete pickup and a helluva lot better than trying to hole up on a studio lot about to swing into gear.

There was, of course, Aunt June's as an alternative. But Ben had promised to keep it off limits. Aunt June's cactus fortress was out and Oliver's rented hacienda was the best bet.

Suddenly finding himself famished, he swung into the upscale shopping area on Larchmont, popped into a pricey bistro and wolfed down a Hawaiian tortilla wrap stuffed with rock lobster, pineapple, mango and swabs of wasabi mayonnaise. This he washed down with another iced Kenya AA.

Soon after, he took a couple of side streets and tooled down Beechwood. But when he pulled up in front of Mrs. Melnick's duplex and spotted her in all her glory, he realized he'd be lucky just to get her ear. There she was at the edge of her rock garden, her squat body gyrating, her scrunched-up face animated, carrying on with a gaggle of stoop-shouldered neighbors. She obviously had news as her honking bark kept underscoring the name "Howie." Which, for Ben, meant yet another stumbling block.

As it happened, Howie and Ben had attended public school together. The major difference, aside from the fact that Howie had a mother and father, was the fact that Ben had gone on, whereas Howie never worked a day in his life. As soon as he became of age, he declared his independence, occupied the other half of the duplex, ate all his meals with his parents, and dutifully collected his allowance. He also continued his lifelong pursuit: gathering trivia relating to the entertainment business, attending live TV broadcasts, and attempting to get on game shows. While his introverted father collected rent from Oliver and tenants in his dilapidated apartment buildings south of Pico and Robertson, Mrs. Melnick became Howie's personal manager. Lately, she'd sworn as soon as Howie's star began to rise, she would help Ben with his flagging career; an offer Ben took with the largest grain of salt on the planet.

Flustered, Ben waited till Mrs. Melnick's crowing abated and, at last, her audience straggled off. He eased out of the car, but before he had a chance to reach the swale, Mrs. Melnick waddled over and blocked his path. In the near distance, Howie stuck his mop of hair out of the front door of his side of the duplex and waved. Shielding his eyes from the glare bouncing off the glossy-white façade, Ben waved back, holding Howie at bay with, "Be with you in a sec."

"Well well," said Mrs. Melnick, flaunting her orange muumuu and unfortunate permanent, piled so high she looked like a victim of incipient brain fever. "You heard, right? From Iris I bet. You were eating your heart out. But, mild-mannered class act that you are, you had to come over and offer congratulations. Plus maybe cash-in, huh?"

Shaking his head, he considered blurting out his simple question about Oliver's travel plans and quickly taking off. But, knowing Howie's doting cheerleader of a mother, he would have to ward off an additional dose of crowing.

"I see you're dying, Benjamin, so as a special favor, I'll let you in."

Ben glanced at his watch. It was almost three. The traffic would step up and congeal any minute. The last item on his agenda was connecting with Chula and passing on his concerns about his accident if only he could zip past this Melnick hurdle.

"To make a long story short," Mrs. Melnick went on, "it dawned on me that whatever Howie was doing wasn't working. All these years I've had to listen to 'my son this, my daughter that.' So I asked myself, What angle can we play? What's Howie got nobody else has got?"

Deftly moving to Mrs. Melnick's side, his back to Howie and the glittering duplex, Ben said, "And what's the answer?"

Ignoring Ben's prod, Mrs. Melnick related how she dragooned Oliver's significant other, an assistant producer on *The Tonight Show,* into coming over. The pretext was that she had checked in on Oliver's orchids and thought they might be dying.

"So naturally," Mrs. Melnick said, "I got hold of Budd, you know he spells it with two Ds. And we talked about the hothouse system breaking down. What do I know, right? But anyways, I said the one with the ivory petals and hot pink lips looks peaked. Not to mention the ones that look like explosions in a paint factory. Not to mention the ones that look like butterflies, lady's braids and little birds. And the one that smells like chocolate and the other one that smells like angel food cake."

"Excuse me. I'm in a rush and I only wanted to know—"

"A rush? And you're driving Oliver's car? Is this wise? Are you taking care of it? If I were you—"

Practically screaming, Ben said, "Can we please have the kicker?"

"You got it, you got it. I said to Budd maybe Oliver should forget the orchid show in Lauderdale."

"You didn't."

"I did. Because Budd misses Oliver something terrible. Crafty me, I comforted Budd, said, No worries I'd ring Oliver, crying his plants are sick with loneliness too. Then I wangled my way round to the subject of Howie and you'll never guess. Budd was so grateful about the wilting orchids and getting Oliver back, plus he loved my idea about Howie."

"So Oliver's ... ?"

"Flying back. You know, I wouldn't be surprised if I wasn't right about those cockamamie plants."

"And he'll be here when?"

"Who knows? Soon. Maybe tonight, maybe tomorrow."

"That's just great," said Ben, twisting away from her.

"Hold it," said Mrs. Melnick, tugging on his sleeve. "You're missing the angle, the pot of gold, you gotta hear this. They're billing Howie as the world's youngest oldest virgin! Fresh, undamaged goods. He's booked for a quickie Monday. If there's a call-in from sexually active ladies —his doctor tells me at his age it's not good for his bodily functions and you know how a mother worries. Anyhow, if it flies, and there's a follow-up after the first date and maybe some preliminary hanky panky—"

"Please, I've got to run before I'm caught in the slipstream. Tell Howie I'll catch him later."

As he broke for the car, he suggested she consider the aftershock to Howie's system.

Her jowl dropped a few inches, her beady eyes locked. Recovering, she hollered back, "Such dry humor. You *are* eating your heart out. And who could blame you?"

At times like this, Ben wanted to chuck anything remotely connected to the entertainment industry.

It was only five miles from the Melnick duplex to Chula and the Farmer's Daughter Motel. But with the escalating traffic, it took Ben a good thirty minutes to find a way past clogged Fairfax, around and down until he finally veered into one of the coveted parking spaces across from CBS.

The motel was another of those two-story L-shaped slabs divided into cubicles with one queen-sized bed, spongy mattress and a boxy frig on the floor permanently set to cool-but-never-cold. All that mattered to those who'd just checked in was getting a jump on the free tickets to the daytime shows across the street.

Ben hopped out of the car, skirted by the dank oblong pool and rushed into the lobby, hoping that Chula was more amenable than the surly albino he ran into this morning.

This time he got a break. There behind the cramped front desk, murmuring short answers over the phone in Spanish, stood a young woman with features as soft as her voice. Her hair was jet black, long and braided. Completing the image, she wore a muted blouse over a supple beige skirt, no makeup save for a little blush over her cheeks and no accessories except for a delicate gold bracelet.

As soon as she replaced the receiver, Ben greeted her with a polite," Que pasa?"

There was no reply. Just a sweet smile.

Trying once more, Ben said, "Que tranza?" but the smile only widened.

Ben tried another tack. "This town is amazing. I just ate at a Hawaiian Mexican bistro. Had a Polynesian tortilla wrap. To date, I've sampled every Angelino dish except the real thing, like Pescado a la Veracruz, Sopecitos de Camaron or mole rosa de taxco. I mention these only because Carlos Jose, better known to we lucky few as C.J. —Pepe to the uninitiated--lists them among his favorites."

The wide smile lingered a while longer. Finally, she patted Ben's hand as if he were a lost child with a separation complex and said, "It's okay. You must be Ben."

"How did you guess?"

"All those words."

"Sorry, just a little anxious. I will do my best to pull back a tad."

Doing so, he soon learned that she was a Montessori teacher. At the moment she was spelling her cousins Josie and Liliana so they could visit boyfriends and relatives in Mexico City. All in all, she seemed to have what one of Aunt June's housekeepers called a venga lo que venga, a come-what-may attitude toward everything. Ben couldn't help being jealous.

The phone rang again. Chula handled it quietly and quickly, and jotted something down amid the stacks of glossy tourist leaflets. Hanging up, she smiled that smile of hers and said, "I heard about that little boxing match yesterday."

"Oh well. You never know what gets into C.J."

"Nevertheless, you should never question his mom's virtue, especially in front of his boys from the barrio. They're so susceptible and you know how Mexican men feel about their mothers."

"Look, the truth is I only want to pass on a few concerns to C.J. Okay? Do you mind?"

He had tried pulling back. He had tried on a come-what-may. Now he was getting testy. He never got testy. Maybe it was all this talk about mothers and families. Maybe it was the unfinished business with the maiden. Maybe it was all the pressures that were getting to him. At any rate, he politely gave her a capsule version of the accident and asked if there were any criminal ramifications or whether it was strictly civil. She jotted the question down.

"Okay, but here's the tricky part." He told her about C.J.'s call last night concerning some nutty accountant which had to be a practical joke and had nothing to do with him. He also mentioned what little he could make of Leo's money-finagling practices. He hadn't planned to do any of this. With all the running around, it just came out.

Chula put down her pen and sat on the padded stool behind the counter gazing at him in wonder.

"Right," said Ben, grabbing a sample menu from a tourist trap and scribbling on the back. "Just in passing—you see, C.J. ran into Leo at the gym. I mean, just for fun, I'll list a couple of kinda iffy details."

The phone rang again, Chula spoke in Spanish, picking up where she left off. With her dulcet tones in the background, Ben jotted cursory references to cash flow from Budapest to the Bank of America and money changing shape with no names behind numbers. Knowing that Leo had asked, Was this any of Ben's business now that he had his foot in the door? Knowing better than to overload the circuit, Ben did it anyway.

He folded the back of the menu neatly and handed it to Chula who, in turn, remained glued to the phone. As he waved goodbye and turned to go, she cupped her hand over the receiver and said, "When do you need an answer?"

"No big hurry. No problem. When you hear from him."

"And where can I reach you?"

Good question. He still had no cell phone. And even if the project was promptly green-lighted, the writer's bungalow had no phone either. What would be the point?

"I'll call you," Ben said. .

Just as he pressed on the glass door, she called out again. "And what about your birthday?"

"What about it?"

"C.J. says we should get you something for consolation."

"Cute, that's real cute. Tell him it's any time after the day after tomorrow. Tell him also that I've got irons in the fire and there is much more to me than meets the eye."

He left the motel muttering, "Great exit line you gave yourself, kid. Here's hoping you didn't come across as a total jerk."

After some impossible stop and go, finally reaching the dealership a few miles south on La Brea, he let the car off for repairs and grabbed the customer service phone just in time to check back with Leo.

"Dude, good good," yelled Leo on the other end as if Ben was hard of hearing. "Listen, I am to ask question before you get absolute answer. What is it you do with business cards?"

"Beg your pardon?"

"For business, from Angelique with pink curlicues?" yelled Leo even louder.

"Is this a trick question?"

"Could be. You still got them?"

Ben thought for a second. He wasn't about to tell Leo he'd handed one of the calling cards to the maiden after crashing into her pickup; ostensibly the same card he'd recovered lying on the floor of the bungalow. For want of a better answer he said, "They're all accounted for."

At first, Leo seemed stuck. Then he said, "Meaning you have still got them?" When Ben said they were still in his possession, Leo countered with, "You are staying put, I will call right back."

Ben did what he was told. In less than two minutes, Leo was back in touch. "Good news, is all okeydoke."

"You're saying there are no more contingencies. We're on."

"Yes, go, move to studio. All work tonight you are handing over while going is good. Using back lot and studio for locations. Like whatever Gillian is telling you."

"Hold on. In Gillian's parlance, you're saying you want me at the writer's bungalow forthwith?"

"With--certainly, of course *with*. What you think, *without*? You bring what you use for storyboard, what is asked for, everything."

Ben glanced through the plate glass window at the trunk of the Prelude. The other day he'd failed to return a shopping basket from Ralph's Market. All he had to do was toss in some remnants of Aunt June's cleaning frenzy and wing it.

"Okay," Ben said without thinking twice, "I've got stuff that'll probably do. But I was hoping to get in a little practice first."

"No practice. You are whipping up sure-fire hook and getting off the phone. Gillian is expecting handoff like in football."

Leo garbled out the schedule and hung up. Ben gave himself a quick coffee break in the customer lounge and took stock. If he was reading this right, off the top of his head he had to come up with a thumbnail scenario that gave the gamer no easy way out. Once she entered the setting—that is, the studio—and began to play, the game took off to the point of no return. To make it work, the proxy on the screen needed some resemblance to Angelique. But, of course, with a lot more going for her like youth, stamina and physical prowess.

All well and good. But this time would everything actually hold still while he worked? As he, someone who'd never been the sole creator, let alone related to this kind of character, let alone had any acquaintance with real trouble —could he sketch away la-di-da while night fell on this shabby playground? If so, granted he could somehow call on C.J. for tips, it was possible.

Moving right along, as a favor the Honda service manager dropped him off at the studio gate. Ben tossed in what he needed from the keepsake carton, plus the binoculars for no particular reason, plus the Dr. Seuss book to con himself as a reminder he was on the verge.

Clutching the shopping basket, ambling past Lester's quizzical gaze, he pressed on hopeful as can be.

Make that hopeful but unconsciously looking over his shoulder just in case.

Chapter Sixteen

Two days before on that same Sunday, Deke reckoned it was close to fifteen miles to Castroville and he was in no mood to walk, given the condition of his back and his tight schedule.

He'd taken a break, reached into his overnight bag and snatched out Elton Frick's smartphone to see if there were any voice-mails for the nerdy accountant. That way he could tell if anyone was on the lookout for Frick or he was, just as he'd seemed, a little guy with no friends, family, partners or anyone giving a damn. A nobody who was either lying low, out of the picture or both. Nothing Deke need concern himself with in his hunt for the missing goods.

But it had turned out that wasn't exactly the case. There'd been somebody who'd called earlier from the S.E.C. and there was another message from the D.E.A. No telling what either of them wanted. Deke did recall that Frick cautioned him about the S.E.C. But all Deke knew about the agency was they investigated accounting frauds which was Walt and the Outfit's lookout. Up till now anyways. As for the D.E.A., Deke had no idea how in hell drug enforcement figured in.

Putting that all on the backburner for now, he told himself if he could track down the goods here in Castroville, get a bead on what they were and a way to parlay them into some kind of cash flow, he'd be home free. Far from where the Feds, Walt and the Outfit and any other goddamn thing could reach him. End of story.

He walked on.

In short order somebody finally drove by, braked and picked him up. His benefactors were a neatly dressed elderly couple who were Jehovah Witnesses from Watsonville. It seemed they spent every Sunday at this time looking for some good deed to perform. Or finding a person who needed to be saved, which was all the better. As usual, Deke sat in the back seat and let them carry on.

Fifteen minutes later, they hit Castroville with the couple still unsure how to proceed. As they approached the first traffic light, they began arguing over whether or not a righteous-looking man thumbing a ride on Blackie Road was not a prime target but only in need of a lift. Especially when you consider the fact he wouldn't tell them how he happened to be on Blackie Road without any means of transportation. Especially when you consider the fact he wouldn't tell them anything.

Deke slipped out at the flapping Castroville sign that hung over Merritt Street like a signal flag for a railroad crossing. The man and wife drove off, continuing to snap at one another as if Deke's departure was beside the point. .

Getting his bearings, he took in the ubiquitous green-and-yellow signs and awnings. There was even a giant plaster artichoke looming by a sugar-cube of a restaurant. Deke went in, had a weird dish of artichoke hearts, Canadian bacon, asparagus, eggs and Hollandaise sauce which he washed down with an artichoke-colored, lemony iced tea. In the course of his meal, focusing on his only lead, he learned from the blowsy waitress that the packing plant had closed down two weeks ago. When he asked about the company car, she sidestepped the issue and whispered that she'd be available to provide answers to any of his questions in forty-five minutes at the shift change.

Back outside, he meandered by the file of storefronts dotted with more standard green-and-yellow logos such as "Pezzinni Farms, chock full of artichokes and artichoke items." There were a few neat little churches, a drug store and a supermarket but they were all closed.

Many of the signs and placards were in Spanish, a language he should have learned down in Florida but had baulked at the idea. He didn't trust the people. Something odd about the way they seemed to be saying one thing and spoke to each other in their own tongue as if they had something else in mind. Deke recalled that right from the start his ol' man felt the same way and hired Walt to keep a sharp eye peeled.

More meandering around by old Spanish-mission buildings sporting bright banners, some billboards advertising the annual artichoke festival back in May, come-ons from garlic promoters from Gilroy, and broccoli farmers touting their nearby outdoor marketplaces.

Getting nowhere, what with the heat, his back acting up again and the loss of more precious time, he returned to the blowsy waitress. In between jangling her silver-and-turquoise bracelets and lowering her turquoise-smeared eyelids every time she brushed by him, she let on that she'd be glad to drop him by the trailer he was looking for. When he asked, What trailer? she winked some more and said, "I thought you were interested in the company car?"

There was more jangling and winking until she finally admitted she'd known the woman forever. She also told him that Madge was much much older and there was no love lost between them. Taking him aside, she said it was less than five miles to Madge's broken-down place and her Town and Country wagon which was just as broken down. She also hinted that while she waited for him to conduct his business, it was only another mile or so to the ocean and a nice Quality Inn. Not that she was a tramp, just friendly and curious. Mostly interested in getting the lowdown on "queen Madge" and having a good time. Besides, Deke would have to admit it was more than a fair bargain.

"You a repo man?" she asked, her voice getting more husky, her tone a bit more bitchy. "Figure to drive off with that woody of hers 'cause she can't make the final payments? Now she's lost her job at the plant, I mean. That I'd like to see. Hey, it's perfect. You can hop in Madge's wagon, leave her stranded and follow me for some down time. I love it."

Deke did his customary nod, figuring the wagon must be a classic in great shape to warrant having to pay it off. .

"And, hey," she added, "I hear she's raising pigeons. Calls them her little doves. And some of them have already flown the coop. Lost her job, pigeons, and now about to lose her snazzy ride. It's gonna be a red letter day."

Deke could never get over how talkers would rather make up stories than take the time to listen. Rather let some information slip than stand a little dead air. Or even wonder what the person who was barely putting up with them was really after.

"You sure you don't want a sip of this?" said Madge, sitting back under a raggedy awning by the trailer door. "It's a genuine Sonoma Red Sampler."

With a carefree glint in her eyes, she raised her glass and took a few languid sips. To Deke's mind, she may have been ten years older than the trampy waitress, but was a helluva lot better looking.

"Hey, tell you what," she said, pursing her cupid-bow lips and patting a fancy carton by her side. "I've got half a case left and I might be willing to share."

With her eyes beaming, she plucked up a few bottles. "Lookee here. This one's deep ruby with a spicy, dark cherry taste, fruity and silky. The Merlot's got black current and plums and a toasty, oaky smell. Then there's this one spiked with raspberries, black pepper and cinnamon. As long as you've dropped by, I mean. Just a taste. Just for fun."

"About the station wagon," said Deke for the tenth time.

"Oh, right," she said, replacing the bottles. "No fun, just all business."

Deke peered around while she poured herself another drink from the ruby-colored bottle, swished some of the wine in her cheeks and swallowed slowly. Dead ahead, he noted the irrigated fields of little bushy-green artichokes spread in all directions. Off in the distance, a parched brownish-gray outline of low-lying range cut off his view. Behind him, well out of sight down the dirt lane, the waitress was sitting tight in her yellow convertible with the top down.

It was now well after five. The shiny mint station wagon with the artichoke logo—the one the two jerk-offs from Starshine were tailing--sat a few yards off to the side in front of a dumpster and a pile of old tires. Despite locating Madge and the car, all Deke had accomplished was to gain her confidence by mentioning such things as harvesting, the use of canastas, sorting by size, conveyor belts and the like. As far as he could tell, she'd mistaken him for some corporate type connected with the defunct packing plant but possibly friendly.

Carelessly dangling her wine glass, Madge cast her woozy gaze in his direction and smiled. "Hey, true or false? Do I or do I not look like Marilyn if she made it to my age?"

Deke didn't know how to answer. "Marilyn?"

"Monroe. Don't tell me. How can you be in this business and not know back in the day she was crowned the first artichoke queen? 'Course I'm not tellin' when I was crowned. But then, you know, she was known as Norma Jean. 'Course I didn't change my name. And it was only luck I wasn't discovered too ... and got stuck here. String of bad luck with men who wouldn't do right ... Tell me it was the bad hand I was dealt or you are dismissed."

Drifting into a sad funk, Madge started humming to herself, mouthing the lyrics of an old Emmy Lou Harris tune:

"I'm the queen of the silver dollar
I rule a smoky kingdom
My wine glass is a scepter
And a bar stool is my throne ..."

Putting up with her a little while longer, Deke noticed her high cheekbones, tousled graying hair and her blue eyes that would've been sparkling if she wasn't so sloshed. That and a mischievous smile and the curvy way she filled out her blouse and faded jeans. All together he did have to admit she reminded him of somebody who'd been in movies a long while back. Someone who played some lonesome gal watching the trains go by.

Not knowing much of anything about Marilyn Monroe but trying to get something out of her, Deke said, "You're right. Now that I think of it, I do see a bit of Marilyn in you. Now about that wagon of yours... "

Madge wiggled herself upright and did a little curtsy. "And you can not believe I am in my fifties and have a granddaughter just turned twenty-two."

The car horn down the lane and around the bend beeped twice.

"What was that?"

"Nothing."

"Oh." Her eyes half-closed, Madge's gaze drifted off. "Hey, you see those coops back there ... behind the shed? You know what? Those birds mate for life. They do, yes, ma'am, yes, sir. I'll take my little doves over men any day. Present company included."

Running out of patience, not about to let her go on about the mating habits of pigeons she couldn't keep track of, Deke strode over to the dumpster and examined the tires. They were bald Fisks, double bias and full of dry rot, the kind they hadn't made since way back in the last century. In his mind's eye he pictured those same old wrecks he'd messed with back in Cut Bank: Packards, Studebakers, Hudsons, Desotos and General Motors models they no longer made.

Then he checked out the dumpster. Sorting through the junk food wrappers, he came across some crumpled *Los Angeles* and rock magazines and a sticky program from a Monterey pop concert. As he flipped through the soiled pages he paused at an ad for The Prado Hotel. The big print claimed it was a luxury watering hole for the entertainment industry. The small print read, "For those whose star is on the rise." The page was circled in red with a big question mark scrawled on the side.

The car horn beeped again, only much louder.

"Hey," said Madge, standing behind him, swaying ever so slightly. "What is this? Oh, I get, I get it. Spotted the wagon up in Monterey, did you? Thought it was me on a toot after you guys closed us down. After telling me it's back to picking, pension or pack it in. Well I got news. I am still my own woman and taking my sweet ol' time."

Still wobbling, she followed him around as he hunkered down and studied the tread marks on sections of the dirt lane that were still a bit damp. As far as he could tell, the vehicle veered into a couple of wooded stakes, spun its wheels and headed out. While Madge was muttering over his shoulder about how even at the packing plant she was always known as Miss Artichoke, Deke examined the broken wooden stakes. There was a faint streak of paint on one of the posts about waist high.

Hunkering down again, he figured the size of the tires to be 215 x 75 x 15 or thereabouts. Radials. To replace the originals you'd have to pay ten times that much, wait a month and, even then, would only get a few thousand miles out of them. Which was no problem if all you wanted was to ditch the Town and Country, switch to something less obvious, hightail it to L.A., hawk your stolen wares, and then hole up at the Prado.

The horn beeped a few more times, longer and louder than ever.

"Wait a minute," said Madge, appearing to sober up a bit.

Disregarding her, Deke went back to the dumpster, ripped off the Prado ad and stuck it in the inside pocket of his suit jacket. As he got set to go, Madge circled around and stood in his way.

"That magazine junk is there 'cause I cleaned it out, not 'cause I put it there. I've made my mistakes sure, but nothing like what she could be up to."

"Go on."

"With what?"

"About her. Name or license plate will do fine."

Suddenly wide-eyed, Madge said, "You go to hell. You go straight to hell."

"Only asking."

But Madge had turned on him and he knew he would get no more out of her. "Suit yourself," he said. .

He left her, made his way down the dirt strip and rounded the bend onto the dusty road. He could sense her traipsing behind him, but at this point it didn't matter. Neither did the sight of the trampy shape dead ahead, hands on her wide hips, wagging a finger.

"Hey," Madge hollered out behind his back, "don't tell me it's you and the sleazebucket? What is this, payback time? Some kinda trick?"

Deke kept walking. The wine glass spun over his shoulder and shattered against a rock. It didn't matter. Nothing in these parts mattered anymore. All that was left was ditching the "sleazebucket."

He climbed into the convertible. The waitress slid behind the wheel and beeped the horn in a rat-a-tat rhythm as her bitchy farewell and took off. She asked him how it went. He said it went fine. She asked about the repossession. He told her to quit yakking, he had to think.

He pictured himself at the Prado in Beverly Hills, stringing along the Outfit's point man and moving in and out real quick. As long as he could find the connection between what was missing, the Prado, and an old green '52 pickup.

Chapter Seventeen

The very next day, caught in a hodgepodge of straggly hills, switchbacks and hideaways, Deke pulled over and left the rental car. No way he was going to chance running into something on this winding drive so he decided to walk up.

As he approached the top of the incline, he heard a hollow smash of pottery and a high-pitched scream. Trudging up closer, which sure as hell was doing his back no good, he heard another crash, another scream and a slap. Two more screams and he caught a glimpse of a gal holding the side of her face and making obscene gestures at the sky. As he fixed his gaze on the fake frosty highlights in her hair and her tight-looking bod, he knew it had to be this Angelique character and he'd found the right place.

He moved back down a-ways, snatched his cell phone out of his suit jacket pocket and hit the redial.

"Yeah," said Walt, his gravelly voice echoing in the sudden stillness, "what now?"

"I'm here. But I'm not about to step into some domestic dispute."

"Look, I don't want to hear it. I don't want to hear nothin'."

"You called it."

"Wrong. The goddamn point man sent for you. Likes your style, remember? But in case you're losin' your hearing, I don't like your style, never did. And I sure don't like what you pulled outside of Salinas. Hell, you want to work alone, Deacon? Cut your own throat? Go right ahead."

There was a long slurping sound, as if Walt was punctuating this last remark with a deep pull from a frosty ale and a wipe across his walrus mustache.

"So," said Walt, back on the line, "in case you're losin' your memory too, I have had it with bunglers, shifty financing--the whole kit and caboodle. For my money you and the goddamn point man deserve each other."

"Okay, Walt, forget it."

"Damn straight. The very second you clean up this mess--and let's not forget the freakin' accountant the Outfit is still on my ass about. They don't buy 'no news is good news.' They want some closure. Is he alive? is he dead? is he on ice or what?"

Deke broke off the connection, pocketed his cell and slipped past the Jaguar through the open gate. Ignoring Angelique, who was slumped down on a chaise lounge next to the pool checking out her left cheek, he headed straight for the sun porch. He noted that the shape of the house, like the serpentine drive, was made up of high, concrete curves, as if designed by some pastry chef with a thing for pink swirls.

"I wouldn't go in there just yet," Angelique whimpered behind his back like a sulking teenager. "He's still picking up the pieces and isn't fit for human company. That is so-o Ray, taking it out on a girl or anything handy."

The name Ray struck a chord but no image came to mind.

Deke scuffed back a few feet till he was by her side. He tried to avoid looking down. Not because she was wearing a bathing suit of yellow ruffles and shreds that covered practically nothing. But because the glare from the sun was bouncing off the pool water, pink tiles, her outfit and bleached hair. Along with everything else, it was giving him eye strain and a headache. The everything-else included the bimbo waitress from Castroville who gave him no rest till he finally ditched her; plus the drive from the airport yesterday afternoon, getting lost on the freeways and to hell and gone; and, to top it off, the skinny gals and punk rockers jumping each other last night in the suite next to his at the Prado.

"So you're the tracking service," said Angelique, abandoning her simpering, whining act.

"The what?"

"The detective, whatever."

"Could be." Continuing to avoid the looks she was giving him, he rubbed his watery eyes.

"Hard night?" said Angelique, making things worse by pulling out a hand mirror.

"In a way."

"Come on, lighten up, talk to me. What are the chicks wearing?"

"Chicks?"

"Girly girls, starlets at the Prado. Come on, I know you're staying there. What have they got on?"

"Slips and slippers, I guess."

"Oh, that is so-o Joline. Came out with that lingerie look a week ago. Purple rules the red carpet now. Lavender, color of royalty, Hollywood's hottest hue, right?"

"I wouldn't know."

"But you must have noticed. Violet silk camisoles, lilac, dark-purple tank tops. What's the scene around the pool? With the open cabanas and chicks slinking around the lacey bamboo, floating on the water like goddesses, right? 'Angelique,' this hottie said to me the other day, 'how do you keep looking like some Venus?' No bull, really, I swear. But still, in this town, you gotta keep up."

"Sorry, can't help you." Hearing no more noises, Deke set out again for the sun porch.

"Wait," said Angelique, trying out a purring sound. He glanced back as she reached under the chaise lounge, fumbled around and pulled out a bent cigarette from a crumpled pack. Pouting, giving him another come-on, she held the cigarette by her glossy lips and let it dangle there.

Deke reached in the suit jacket pocket, struck one of the little wooden matches against the side of the box, gave her a light and flipped the match into a hibiscus bush. Then, just to make sure, he said, "About this Ray. Does he have a nose like a beak?"

"That's the one. Ray the hawk. Hawk anything. Keep handing you a line and slap you around as long as you put up with it."

Deke nodded. Now he knew exactly who he was dealing with.

"Hey, nice suit. Pin stripe, huh? Helmut Lang, elastic wool, tuxedo shirt. Cool."

Wasting no more time, he walked clear away from her.
"Hey, what is it, my cheek? Think it'll show? Like that's
the last thing I need, huh?"

The lull ended the moment Deke set foot onto the
porch. The screeching electric wail came from somewhere
past the curtained glass door.

"That is so-o-o Ray!" Angelique hollered. "Can't play a
lick but sure can fake it."

Deke stepped inside and slid the glass door shut
behind him. If the pool area was an eyesore, this playroom
did it one better. The overhead lights flashed off Ray's
chrome-plated guitar and speakers in the far corner; the
walls covered top to bottom with metal-mesh curtains; the
surveillance cameras and the vents blowing frigid air from
all directions. Even the floor and ceiling had a polished
sheen, and so did the broken shards of glazed pottery lying
by Deke's feet. The only soft spot was a gaming table in the
center, with a plush-green felt top, standard Vegas
markings, inlaid wooden chip trays and padded sides.

Ray himself was wearing a silver T-shirt, a white linen
jacket with the sleeves rolled up and white satiny pants. He
also had on the same blue reflecting goggles he wore in
Vegas when Deke last saw him. As far as Deke knew, Ray
had his finger in everything but nothing in particular.
Always mouthing off like a Sin City tout. But who knew
what was under the bullshit?

As wiry as ever, with that pointy chin and nose too big
for his face, he shifted his bony fingers up and down the
frets still wailing away. The slap and broken jug a minute
or so ago plus the twitch in his cheeks was all the more
proof Ray was losing it.

Spotting an ice bucket and bottles of mineral water on
a cart in the near corner, Deke ambled over and poured
himself a drink. Just as he was about to swallow a pain
pill, Ray pulled the plug and the screeching came to a halt.

"That's what it's like, man," Ray said in that nasal
twang of his. "When somebody guts you, there's a short
circuit. No chords, no vibes, no nothin'. It's shot."

Dropping the guitar and letting it rattle around for
emphasis, Ray waited for a response.

Deke swallowed the pill and washed it down.

"You follow?" said Ray.

"Uh-huh."

"'Uh-huh' is your answer?"

Deke nodded.

"Listen, you need to appreciate something and that something is this. You have value because no one sees you coming: not the CPA who tried to screw me over with some frickin' audit, not my own two dicksters you gave the slip to, and certainly nobody here where you could pass for anybody."

Ray scuffed over to the gaming table, ripped the cellophane off a new deck of cards, split it, riffled the cards, fanned them out and slid them from side to side. "Now as anybody knows, everybody wants in on the hustle. In Vegas, if you're a floater, it's hit the tables, luck out, crash and burn, and you're out of it. But when you're a player, when everything's riding on it, like a shark, you got no rest."

Deke poured himself another glass of water. All Ray was telling him was that he was at the end of his rope.

"Give me something here," said Ray.

Deke raised his glass.

"Okay," said Ray, "I'll take that as a 'yes'. You see, what we got here is the world's most number of wannabes who'll do anything. Even if instead of the spotlight, they're askin' for it. Headin' straight for the La Brea Tar Pits."

For emphasis, Ray pointed to the overhead cameras and lights and flipped a few cards at the chip trays. Two landed in the slots, the rest fluttered to the floor.

Deke stood pat in the corner.

"What am I sayin'?"

"You thought you had it covered but you got stiffed."

Ray reached around, came up with a wide blue rubber band and began stretching it and twirling it around his fingers as if trying to decipher exactly what it was that he was saying. Finally he said, "So let's hear it. Am I right or am I right? What's the skinny? What's the score?"

Deke told him that the rockers, starlets and hangers-on didn't gather at the Prado till around six-thirty. At that point, they squeezed into the banquettes that lined the pool, lit the candles and waved as he drifted by.

"Beautiful beautiful. Yes! You could be a new studio exec. The latest face in the revolving door. So? So?"

Using the lingo he picked up, Deke went on. "No setup. Right off, a surgeon's implanted a bomb in somebody's wife and she's missing."

"Movies. You're talking movies, right? Must be. Good, it's only flicks. Keep going." Ray began circling the pool table, twirling the rubber band a little faster.

Deke recounted more trade talk, continuing to play the cool cowboy Ray expected.

"Which means," said Ray, groping for a leg-up, "our problem is an inside job and the Prado lead was a decoy. Which leaves this Pepe."

Not sure where he was going with this, Deke let it ride.

"Who is he? Where did he come from? Is he on to us, trying to horn in? What is the word on this guy?" Ray snapped the rubber band hard against the padding as if this Pepe character was already on his hit list.

"Listen," Ray went on, more antsy than ever, "I caught this message on the machine, 'Just to let you know, Angelique, Pepe's in on it.' I'm talkin' a cool woman's voice. Is she from the Feds? The Outfit? What? Then I spot her— this is a different her, I'm talkin'-- sneaking up the drive; then down at the bottom with this guy, then gunning it the hell out of here."

"Who?"

"Who what?"

"The one you spotted?"

"Never mind. Who's calling the shots here? So then what? Back to your end. You ran it down, right?"

"What?"

"The real deal, the Pepe lead. What am I talkin', Greek?"

Going along for now, Deke told him the Mexican parking attendants at the Prado said they'd also heard that a Pepe was in on everything but they weren't sure what. Then they got suspicious and blew him off. Said if he wanted more information, he'd have to go to the barrio where Pepe was from. The way they said it, Deke wasn't sure they weren't leading him into a trap.

What he didn't tell Ray was, with his bad back, he was not going to wander through any ghetto in East L.A., dealing with people he didn't trust and didn't trust him, dressed-up in this pin-striped monkey suit just asking for it. Which was why he'd located a Levi jacket at a costume shop on Hollywood and Vine and braced himself for the worst.

Deke did let on that a gang, some Los Cobras clique, swore at him. They banged on the hood of his rental car, rocked it and tried to tip it over. What he didn't tell Ray was that he had to gun the motor to get the hell out of there. One of the kids bounced off the windshield, two off the hood and one took a whack in the thigh as he swerved hard and sped off. He did, however, admit that a bony kid warned him not to mess with Pepe whose identity was secret, whose reach was everywhere and Deke had better say his prayers.

Ray gave the padding of the gaming table a few more welts. "You know what the problem is? Generosity. I give Angelique her head, let her hire whoever she wants. I mean, hey, all I need is a new front. But somehow ... somehow ..."

Ray switched from the rubber band to snapping his fingers and spun over to a meshed-covered door leading deeper into the house. "I will tell you something and that something is this. It is coming to a head with this Pepe. I can feel it, I can taste it. How he got in on it, I don't know but you will need some insurance."

Ray's cheek went into another set of involuntary twitches as he brushed by Deke and disappeared. In turn, Deke stretched his back as the pain pill started to kick in and offered him some relief.

Over the swish of the air-conditioning he heard Ray making a call, shouting at somebody and then giving in.

A minute later, Ray was back clutching a sleek stainless steel briefcase. "Okay, okay, okay," said Ray handing it over. "A little insurance like I said, plus index cards, legal pads, whatever, as you keep playing the part."

Ray went over to the gaming table, pushed a button, reached into a drawer, snatched out a business card, scribbled something on the back and shoved it in Deke's jacket pocket. "At first I thought Angelique's ditsy cards tipped our hand. But I just heard it's only the two and they're accounted for. I got all the rest here she had printed. Nothing on the street, so what am I missing here?"

As his mirror-blue goggles faced Deke dead on, Deke wanted to ask, What am *I* missing here, you mean? But he knew better. Ray would get even more frazzled and start running off at the mouth again.

"So listen up," Ray went on. "You are getting on your horse back to the Prado, get the jacket pressed and ditch the tux shirt. I got word a silky purple T-shirt is the next thing. 'Cause if the tux shirt is in yesterday, as any dummy knows, it's on it's way out today. There's a shop around the corner, next to the Vegan boutique, open till seven. They'll fix you up."

Deke was about to tell Ray where he could shove his purple T-shirt, but let it pass.

"Anyways, when you're set, look in on this." Ray patted Deke's pocket. "Since timing and looks is all, this'll lead you to the hole which you will frickin' plug!"

Deke realized that in the warped movie in Ray's mind, Deke was once again some kind of janitor. No matter how many bonehead moves he'd made, Ray figured he could always hang back, let Deke mop it up so Ray could wipe the slate clean. That's how far gone he was.

"Keep in touch," said Ray, patting him on the shoulder. "Nine gets you ten the Mexicans will bunch up. They got to move, can't just let her keep it. I tell you, it is goin' down."

Deke was dying to know, Let who keep what? But before he could figure how to say it without tipping his hand, Ray was putting the finishing touches on his daydream.

"Now when you check in with me," Ray said, "no longer than sixty seconds. After that call to Angelique which I deleted, you never know what bugs the Feds are using nowadays. I am talkin' tonight, no later, you read me? I am talkin' everything and everybody back where they belong. I am talkin' frickin' *pronto*."

Ray returned to the gaming table, banked some dice against the side walls and watched them bounce. He threw the dice harder and started mumbling to himself. "Can you beat it? You slip outta Sin City, play it close to the vest and for no reason it unravels on you. Twice. And now what? I got accounts frozen ... dicksters horning-in ... just 'cause I got vision. Where's the justice?"

"Why tonight ?" said Deke.

"Read the message on the card and do what I say. She's got to unload, I tell you. If it don't move, it dies."

Again it was a *she*. Deke eased out into the glare of the sun porch, his exit punctuated by another screech on the electric guitar. .

Angelique was in the pool now, tossing her head back, trying for another sexy pose. As he strolled by, she splashed his trouser legs. "What's the verdict? Good to go?"

"Just about."

"And what about my business cards?"

"No problem."

"Awesome."

Deke kept walking toward the gate.

"Aren't you even gonna offer me a fresh cigarette?"

"Don't smoke," said Deke flipping the latch.

"Then what's with the little wooden matches?"

"You never know." Before Deke closed the gate behind him, he asked who she'd given the cards to and why? Her only answer was that she wanted this writer, this Ben guy to be impressed and start letting the word out that Angelique was back on top.

Deke left her and walked past the gate.

"And what's with the slick briefcase?" Angelique called after him. "You get a present and I get knocked around? Terrific!"

She jumped out of the pool, trailed after him and pulled him back. She claimed she was the brains behind this new venture and insisted on his cell phone number. With nothing to lose, Deke gave her the number and resumed his retreat down the winding drive. Scanning the possibilities, and as near as he could figure, the deal came down to what Walt called "financial resources hittin' a snag."

Appreciating the long cool shadows toning everything down, Deke knew there was only one thing for it: getting there first, laying his hands on those resources. And leave them all to yak themselves to death.

He slid behind the wheel of the beige Ford rental, made sure there was nobody coming by, and unlatched the case. Predictably, the "insurance" courtesy of Ray was in a leather pouch. He slid out the silvery Walther PPK/S: light, slim, the best palm pistol bar none. He checked the safeties, injected one of the three 8-shot clips and tossed the piece from hand to hand. It had been a long while.

Flipping through the notepads, pens and all, he unzipped one of the hidden binders and spotted the belt slide. In this one particular instance, Ray had thought of everything.

Just before heading back to the Prado, Deke pulled out the pink calling card from his jacket pocket. Unlike Ray's usual bullshit, the scrawled message on the back was clear: "Check out this address. Find Angelique's double."

Chapter Eighteen

At a loss, Ben stepped back from the easel. As a rule, when people would ask him what he did for a living, he would say he was, more or less, a screenwriter: an idea man, if you will; a fix-it guy, a quick sketch artist. When that didn't do the trick, he would simply add that he was a team player, on call, ready to help out for the next project-- TV show, commercial or whatever.

But here he was as late afternoon wore down, on his own, staring at the first page of a set of formatted panels. Each panel poised over an empty slot for captions. Nine blank panels over nine blank slots per page, waiting to be sketched, noted and clipped together like an oversized comic book for Gillian's perusal. Only Ben didn't have a clue how to begin.

Ordinarily, by this time it would look like a rough set of camera shots. Still images that suggested moving images: an establishing long shot, say, then a close-up of a girl; then a montage leading the eye on and on as other figures came into the background; the expression on the girl's face changing; a medium shot of the girl running past, entering a barn, disappearing into the shadows until, following the brief captions, you just had to turn the page. And so it goes, hopefully, through the whole sequence.

But ordinarily this would only come about after a bunch of sessions with other writers, producers, production company spies, and some showrunner (if it was TV) put his or her two-cents in. Ben would then add his ideas to whoever came up with this project in the first place. And he was *then* told: "Hey, Ben, crank out a thumbnail sketch of what we got so far and let's see if it flies."

In short, Ben had never been in this position before. In short, everything about it was strange.

Frustrated beyond belief, Ben grabbed a soft-lead pencil and kneaded eraser and sketched in the back of a female figure in overalls ascending a steep, curving drive. A stick figure of a male holding up a calling card came into view above her, along with the hood of a Jaguar in the background. Panel three found the girl clutching the card and backing away. In the next panel, through an opening in a gate a near-naked figure lay a short distance away by a pool. Panel five: a close-up of a ratty-looking male wearing goggles. Another close-up accenting the girl in bib overall's wide eyes and cupid-bow lips. Then aerial views in panels seven and eight as she turns and runs down the drive, ending with a medium shot of the back of a pickup driving away.

It wasn't great, it wasn't that promising but at least it was a start.

At another impasse, realizing he had to come up with a grabber before Gillian popped in, he snatched the binoculars out of the grocery basket, walked out of the writer's bungalow and looked around. He took in the long shadows glancing off the ficus trees and the café veranda and, turning around, eyed the hitching posts all the way down to the pitch of the livery stable roof. The temperature was cooling down, twilight coming on, and he was in that pressure zone where anything was grist for the mill.

He thought again of the maiden. True, her sleeping bag was gone, along with the food wrappers and Styrofoam cups. But he could swear he heard the drone of the old truck motor and the grinding of gears. Which could mean she'd circled past Lester's gate looking for a back entrance. Or already knew there was one and was just making sure. Possibly come to settle accounts with Ben, that is, if you took to heart her message on Iris' machine. Or came to hole up again tonight, or to keep hiding from Ray or someone.

"Simmer down," Ben said to himself as he wheeled around and strolled over to the side of the café. "You are reaching, spinning your wheels."

With nothing better to do, no further imagery coming to mind, he passed the café and worked his way up, through the moonwalk and the wide-leafed banana plants.

Climbing atop the rickety remnants of a space pod, he balanced himself, adjusted the focus on the binoculars and peered all around. No back gate, no opening that he could see.

He kept going till he came upon the secluded Swiss chalet cottages, with their fairytale balconies fabricated for Douglas Fairbanks and Mary Pickford. Or was it Nelson Eddy and Jeanette MacDonald? He couldn't remember. Besides, it was locked-up tight like most everything else and he was still stuck with nine frames of a storyboard going nowhere with no reason to turn the page.

Returning to the bungalow, he switched off the overhead fans, cranked open the windows as wide as they would go and looked about.

Then he started berating himself. Nobody worked like this, hoping someone would show up and fuel his tale. As any of his cronies would tell you, when in doubt, do the tried and true: do a spin on a spin. Or appropriate anything he'd gleaned this morning from MTV or the stupid soap. Why fight it? In a pinch, who needs originality?

But the only lasting impression from that cursory stint at the gym was how much the maiden resembled the young Angelique. A factor Angelique had vaguely hinted at; a factor Gillian wanted shoehorned into the mix. Besides, why would a young woman who looked like Angelique be so drawn to this studio if there was no connection? Was it only to confront Ben directly and demand payback?

Though keenly aware he was mixing fact with fiction, and for want of a better option, Ben stuck with the maiden's possible storyboard plight.

Which still got him nowhere without a link to this back lot.

But if he had one last ditch ploy it was always, *In a pinch, there's got to be something close at hand—open your eyes, use it.*

Scanning the bungalow's interior, all there was were a few potted palms spent and drooping. The scarred Formica-top desk in the far corner was equally forlorn. The rattan couch occupying the center with its flowery seat cushions and the throw pillow on the coffee table only reminded him of the maiden and her need for some place to crash.

At the same time, the cover of Dr. Seuss's *Oh, the Places You'll Go* sticking up from the shopping basket seemed to be baiting him. Telling him to get off it and keep moving. As in, "See the rainbow paths leading to the top? Pick one, you simp, any one and get on with it."

So it was back to the easel, another sheet, page two and he was at it again.

Second scene: the maiden sneaking into the studio ... into the bungalow ... past the alcove; a jog forward and a shift into the kitchenette ... returning, checking out the fans overhead ... the crank-out windows and jalousies facing the stunted orange trees.

Next sequence: locking herself in ... wolfing down doughnuts and coffee ... curling up at the foot of the couch ... then sneaking out again and taking off ...

But where? And why? Playing hide-and-go-seek for what reason? What's really at stake here?

Ben drew another blank.

He left the bungalow, turning the other way this time, past the hitching posts, raised planked sidewalks and the facades of a saloon, boarding house and general store. He hesitated by the barn doors of the livery stable, cut back around through the coarse chaparral and made his way behind the building. He reached up and yanked on a rope attached to a pulley overhead in an attempt to scale a dumpster to gain a better vantage point. But he no sooner started to clamber and hoist himself up when the rope snapped, the huge shutters overhead smashed against the screened windows, sealing them shut.

Picking himself up and brushing himself off, he realized that if she truly was skulking about, if this boneheaded move didn't spook her, nothing would.

Minutes passed. But just when he'd given up on movement for movement's sake, he heard the deep drone of an old engine, a shift of gears accompanied by a grating sound like something rolling over sandpaper. Then quiet, save for a clank and a rustling not more than a hundred yards away.

He reminded himself that Gillian could be by any minute and he'd have to wing it once again. But this time he'd have to produce. The storyboard so far was worth zilch without a juicy springboard.

At the moment there was only the faint whoosh of traffic up on Melrose and the occasional sound of cars zipping by Lester's stand on Van Ness. Dying to know where she was and what she was up to, he circled around the dumpster beyond the back of the stable.

Here in the waning light the foliage was tinder dry. He worked through the manzanita sagebrush, thickets of chaparral shrub and craggy scrub oak and clumps of deer grass till he came upon a wall of eucalyptus. Poking around, he discovered the eucalyptus served to mask the steel mesh enclosure that rimmed the property. He slipped through a narrow break and a tangle of vinca vines till he reached a metal gate.

He disengaged the slide bolt and stepped out into an alleyway. As near as he could make out, he'd come upon a revamped low-rise apartment complex. There were shiny window fittings, the smell of wet concrete and stucco, and crushed shards of aluminum at his feet. Contractor's vans had apparently squeezed by earlier, making their way to the rear. He followed the crunched trail, turned the corner and there it was.

The truck bed was empty except for the ropes that held the tattered tarp. The cab was vacant. Below the California license plate was a yellow and green bumper sticker advertising last year's artichoke festival.

He hurried back, re-bolted the gate and, avoiding all the prickly scrub, circled the other way round past the empty corral, cut over and hesitated at the barn doors. Someone had eased them open a crack.

One glance, he told himself. Peek in and hightail it back to work.

Peering hard into the darkening recess thanks to his dumb move with the rope and shutters, he spotted the wooden ladder. This time it was propped up against the landing by the hay loft. He could barely make out her form without widening the opening but he could hear her tugging and dragging things. Possibly some sacks, it was hard to tell. Letting out a weary sigh, she seemed to have slumped down somewhere up on the loft. No longer a maiden in Ben's overblown imagination, but a willowy girl definitely up to God-knows-what.

In that same moment, the put-put of a go-cart announced that Ben's spying stint had abruptly come to an end. For now, his only hope was to placate Gillian and get rid of her while the girl rested. And then deal with the girl and finally come to terms with this fantasy/reality riff.

By the time he made it back to the work room, Gillian was already eyeing the storyboard sheets. She shifted position as Ben caught his breath. Her after-hours outfit consisted of mauve lounging pajamas; the lacquer in her chestnut-brown do had given way somewhat as had the cosmetics daubing her face. She wore sandals this time, lowering her height, forcing her to raise her head a bit to maintain a condescending pose of authority.

"All right, Benjy," said Gillian, settling her gaze on the first sequence and tossing the others onto the couch, "I think I see where you're going with this. By the way, where were you just now? Never mind, don't tell me."

"You were saying?"

"You've got two identical looking figures, one about to enter the other's lair plus a lurid figure in the background."

"And the other guy?"

"What other guy?"

"Never mind." It was amazing that even when he put himself into a frame he was indistinguishable.

"Thus," Gillian said, "we quickly establish the seamy world the player is entering. By the way, where is this? Any problem getting footage?"

It never occurred to Ben that Gillian had never driven up the serpentine drive. But what difference did it make?

"No worries," said Ben. "Getting that opening footage is a given."

"Excellent. We can also intercut those crime-scene shots as a teaser. Good move on my part, as it turns out."

"On your part? You mean it was your idea to send me out on those alleged photo ops?"

"What did you think, it was Leo's? Oh puh-lease. He packages, he finagles, but creatively? Don't be ridiculous."

"Ah yes. The first test to see, if push came to shove, it would be worth scraping the bottom of the barrel with me."

Ignoring him, she moved behind the couch and continued to mull things over. "And we can toss in more serviceable visuals to jazz up the backdrop."

As Gillian continued to pace, intermittently running her fingers through her hair, loosening the lacquer binding, Ben moved over to the windows and peered through the slats in the jalousies. There was no reason why the girl would come by, what with the go-cart parked outside and Gillian carrying on, but he looked out anyway.

"Okay," said Gillian, moving on. "No dialogue, got her off and running. Of course, you've got to pencil in a few captions to satisfy the mentally challenged execs I'll be dealing with. Let's just say at this juncture—"

"I've made a start," said Ben, still amazed she'd injected a "seamy world" into his doodling around.

"Then why have you stopped? Why are you flitting about?"

"Flitting happens to be a well known creative device."

"Don't hand me that. Stick with me, Benjamin."

But Ben didn't want to stick with her. All he wanted was to get back to the stable. But Gillian wouldn't let up. She loosened her hair some more until a strip of it fell over her ear. She clip-clopped away and tapped her fingertips together. It finally dawned on him that Gillian was the one at the party on Malibu who kept pushing it, saying, "You'd love it, wouldn't you? All you girls would love your very own escapades. Love to get your hands on it soon as possible." Gillian was the one clamoring for an outlet, some way to escape from the mindless hours leasing TV relics. Some quick leap to V.P. of a cutting edge entertainment. And what could be quicker or better than a hot video game? It wasn't just Starshine that needed an instant jumpstart. It was darn near everybody.

Widening the gap in the jalousie slats, Ben said, "I read you, Gillian. I'm on it. One nasty joy ride coming up."

"Speaking of which," said Gillian, poking at the opening panels with a glossy fingernail, "where is Pepe's imprint? Where are the hard-core portents I asked you to serve up?"

"Only a phone call away when needed, remember?"

"Cut the tap dance, Benjy. When was the last time you conferred with your pal? "

"A little while ago, if you must know." It wasn't a total lie. He'd asked Chula to ask C.J. to look into certain matters. Plus he really was making progress. To keep the ball rolling, he had to brush Gillian off, but she wouldn't budge.

"So tell me, Mr. Prine," said Gillian, as though seeing right through him, "how did you contact him? There's no phone here and you let your cell phone service expire over a week ago. So I assume, since my check at the conference took care of your car repairs, you are flush with the coin Leo slipped you under the table. So humor me and display the el-cheapo cell you must have picked up under a cheapo pay-as-you-go plan."

Realizing she had him there and he couldn't very tell her about the stupid accident, all he could say was, "Something came up and, given this first work day after the long weekend, plus the tasks and short notice you guys gave me, I simply ran out of time."

"Brilliant. So how were you planning on feeding this thing? How, may I ask, are you going to stay in touch with your go-between?"

"Well, missy, there's Lester's phone. And before I can re-confer, I had to wait for your feedback. Not to mention this is the locale of the primary set pieces. And there is no way I can continue to check them out and utilize them *before* I check back in with my interlocutor. Comprende? I am thinking, thinking, and you are wasting precious time."

After another quizzical look from Gillian, Ben added, "Give me a break, will you? It's only seven-fifteen."

The quizzical look lingered.

"Fine. Take me to the gate. Just know that our Pepe is not simply on call. Not with all the vice and nefarious goings-on that can't be spoken of lest we spook the tourists."

Ben had no idea what he was talking about. All he'd gleaned about C.J.'s undercover work were inklings here and there. At the moment all he wanted was to dispatch Gillian and get back to the girl, provided, after all this chit-chat, she hadn't bolted again.

He gave Gillian a nudge but she stood her ground.

"Look, lady, you liked my opening. Hard-core options you want, hard-core options you shall have."

"The truth, Benjamin. Why do I suddenly get the impression you've got two things going here?"

"Who knows? Who cares? I am on it. It is percolating. Truly, honestly, deeply."

Gillian snatched the opening thumbnail sketches. "Nevertheless, I'm keeping these as collateral."

What that meant was anybody's guess. But Ben was in no mood to go around another circle.

She retrieved her shoulder bag, gave her do a quick once-over with a comb and scented spray and escorted him out of the bungalow. One more quizzical look as he took his seat next to her and she put-putted the pair of them up the tech alley.

Pulling in next to Lester's glass-enclosed station, Gillian glared at him. "You've been invited to the dance, buster. Don't make me sorry I extended the invitation."

Ben had nothing more to offer.

"I will give you till ten. If you come up empty, if this thing tanks, if I have to go back to the drawing board, you, my little friend, are dead in the water."

Apparently it didn't occur to her that the steel-meshed barricade was wide open and Lester was nowhere in sight. She slid behind the wheel of her BMW convertible, backed out and sped off into the darkening afterglow. Heading up Van Ness. Doubtless over to her office to scour her computer files in case she might very well have to cut her losses.

Chapter Nineteen

In limbo, Ben stood there motionless. Gillian may have had her suspicions, but he was still in the game. Nonetheless, he couldn't help thinking about normal people. They would never find themselves in this loopy predicament, constantly trying to keep more and more balls in the air. He wondered what they were doing at this moment. Washing the dishes perhaps, talking about the lighthearted events of the day with the kids, feeding the dog, getting ready to settle down and watch a warmhearted family show.

Snapping out of it, he went inside Lester's station, swept aside the empty Pepsi cans, bags of chips and peanut butter and jelly crackers that littered the counter. As long as he was here, Ben decided to accomplish something. Besides, there was no way he could race back to the stable in time and he knew diddly about operating the go-cart which he had no business touching in the first place. So he punched in an outside line and dialed Chula.

After four rings, Chula picked up. In that soft, reassuring tone of hers, she informed him that tapping the grill of the girl's pickup was an insurance matter, gracioso and a waste of C.J.'s time.

"Not a police matter?"

"Correct. But this thing with this Leo Orlov ..." Her voice trailed off.

"Yes? Go on."

"They've had their eye on him. But C.J. is so upset about this vaquero maldito who ran over his kids, it was hard to follow what he was saying."

"A cowboy? Are you serious?"

"A cowboy type ... I don't know. You know how C.J. gets. Anyway, some of the kids are okay, bruised and banged up and shouldn't have been playing hooky on the first day of school. But a few others are ... "

"Are what?"

"In the hospital. So, C.J. is wondering who put this vaquero on to him. Was it this Leo, the one you said from the gym?"

"Leo again."

"Yes. Like I am telling you, I couldn't quite follow, couldn't take it all in. At the same time, they got another crank call at his station, in Vegas and San Francisco."

"Oh no. Not the crippled accountant in the Rockies?"

"I suppose. 'Coming from the mountains ... has a cowboy drawl'. Who can follow it?"

"Follow what?"

"Some connection too, C.J. is saying. When he calms down, maybe it'll seem different to him. But right now, I must tell you, his brain is racing."

Since Ben had no idea what any of this was all about, all he could tell Chula was he doubted there was any connection between Leo, some cowboy and what befell C.J.'s kids in the barrio. Let alone some ranting accountant if that's what he really was. All the while Ben felt more time passing, everything getting more and more jumbled, including the abiding image of the girl stashing something by the hayloft and scurrying off into the night.

"Anyway," Chula said, "I guess you'd better keep your ears open and let him know."

"Let him know what?"

"Anything you might get wind of."

"Oh sure, you bet."

Chula noted Lester's number and rang off with a reassuring, "Okay, take care."

Turning back, Ben spotted Lester dead ahead in the deepening shadows, sneaking around past the cylindrical media center. He seemed to be holding his air rifle low, bending his knees, like a kid playing Indian scout.

Ben shook his head, passing beyond Lester's playtime, hurrying by the stretch of soundstages. He could just hear what his cronies' at the Farmers Market would say chortling over morning coffee and croissants:

This is the part when you should've finally wised up.

Used your brain.

Seen it coming.

For crissake, Ben, how whacked out can it get?

Picking up his pace, Ben cut over and headed down the tech alley, barely noticing that the door to Studio Three was slightly ajar.

What brought him out of it was a sudden tug on his shirtsleeve and a blur of tousled honey-blond hair and dusty bib overalls.

Chapter Twenty

"I'm saying I could use a hand," said the girl.

"A hand?"

"Look, in case you didn't get my phone message, in case you clean forgot--you owe me."

"Now where have I heard that before?" Completely taken aback, Ben knew that with all that was going on, he had to at least take half of it with a grain of salt to keep from going into brain-lock.

"Look," said Ben," as it happens, I am on deadline. I have already looked into your lodgings problem. However, if you let me know what you've been up to, I'll give you a hand later. Okay?"

At this stage of their little tiff, they were milling around under the high arching grids of the soundstage, close to the holding cells, interrogation cubicles, briefing room and the like.

Exasperated with Ben's response, she clamped both hands on the metal railing leading up to the motel facades and haunted attic on the second tier. As she confronted him again, the dim overhead work lights made the circles under her eyes even more pronounced. Jamming her hands into the side pockets of her overalls, she blurted, "How can you act this way? How can you turn a blind eye when there's a redheaded nut case stalking around?"

"Lester. So that's it. You're talking about Lester."

"Whatever. He's got an air rifle. He could climb up any second."

"Climb up where?"

"On this roof."

"So what? Apparently deserted studios make him restless, especially when he hasn't been paid."

"All the more reason. You got to stop him before he shoots."

141

"Shoots what?"

"The pigeons, the pigeons!"

In the ensuing dead silence, Ben wasn't at all certain he'd heard her correctly. "Hold it, are you telling me this is all about an off chance Lester is gunning for some stupid pigeons?"

"They're not stupid. And if I weren't so out of it—listen, if anything happens to those pigeons, if even one feather's been harmed, you are really gonna get it, buddy."

"Brilliant. To humor you, I'll steal his BB gun and race around while you and your idiot pigeons beat it. As a result, I will have lost precious time coming up with a hook for my scenario. Meaning, and I quote, as far as any future is concerned, 'I am dead in the water.'"

Arms crossed, eyes downcast, she went straight for the door.

"Don't do that," Ben said, despite himself. "Don't pout, don't go."

As she hesitated, he said, "I'm sorry. Truce? Okay, one last chance?"

Why he said these words he would never know. What he should have said was, "In point of fact, my debt to you extends no further than a slightly bent front grill on a truck not long for this world. What this all comes down to is some kind of quid pro quo. Shall we be reasonable or not?"

Responding, however, to what he actually said, she dawdled some more, her hand working the metal bar back and forth, and finally said, "I pulled you in here 'cause this is what I figured. What with the card you gave me with Angelique's pink curlicues and all, and you seeming more or less harmless ... What I mean is, still no Angelique coming by, and now with the pigeons up there and this Lester stalking around ..."

"Never mind. I am going to regret this, I know. But since there's an obvious tie-in between you and Angelique, I will check and see if there really are some endangered pigeons and take it from there. Who knows? In some discombobulated way, this may all work out."

As he moved by her, he noted that even up close she was an enigma: partially hardbitten, partially vulnerable.

She could be taken as a wholesome farm girl or someone doing a number. There was no way yet of nailing down her character in his storyline.

"Come on, buddy," she said wearily. "You gonna move it or what?"

"Ben. My name is Ben. And yours? Can I at least have that?"

She did another of her ceiling scans.

"Look," said Ben, "if you can't even tell me your name, what's the point?"

"Molly," she said, staring right at him this time. "Just make it Molly."

"All right, Molly. I'll see what I can do."

He left her, pressed the door shut, circled around and clambered partway up the steel ladder till he heard the cooing sounds. Somewhere on the roof of this airplane-hanger-like structure was a cage harboring no more than a few birds. He climbed down, returned to the tech alley and headed back toward the front gate. His mind reached for something sensible to tell Lester but nothing registered.

Lester's beanpole form suddenly appeared out of the glare of the spotlights about twenty yards ahead. His long, bony fingers tightened around his air rifle as he squared off to block Ben's way. "Where you been and what the hell's goin' on?"

"Ah yes, that same old question."

Ben quickly joined him, the mesh barricade serving as a backdrop in the near distance along with the occasional blur and whoosh of a car traveling up Van Ness.

"First off," said Lester, "this Gillian rings me on her cell from the bungalow wanting to know where you're at. Now I don't mind that, of course. Only good thing that's happened, gettin' to play Lester the protector for the ladies. Especially when they're in them skin tight pajamas and—"

"Can we drop this? I only came by to ask you to stay put."

"Do what? Forget about the noise sounding like a shot or a backfire from somewheres in the back lot? Forget this Iris character who made me cart her to the bungalow with a sack of tins?"

"Iris? You're kidding?"

143

"Don't I wish. Then, when you ain't there, she goes nuts."

Lester plucked out his mobile phone from its sheath and held it up for emphasis. "And she's called every ten minutes since. And all this after over eight hours I've been at it and not seen so much as a dime from that bald headed Russian. Wouldn't surprise me if this whole thing was a total screw. Like as not, betcha some far east telecommunications consortium steps in after this Russian bails out, I get replaced and have to call my union and sue."

Unable to put up with the contortions of Lester's sliver of a face as he punctuated everything with the barrel of his air rifle—unable to put up with any more static whatsover--Ben pulled out a few bills Leo had plied him with and said, "Here, on account."

"What for?"

"To hold still and man your post. Stick to the gate for a while. Can you do that at least? Can you?"

"Why? What's it to you if I scout around, seein' there's nothing else to do?"

As fast and best he could, Ben told him he desperately needed everything to completely stop. He had to lock something in before Gillian returned. The way things were going, what with Iris now tossed into the stew, if everything didn't simmer down, he didn't stand a chance in hell.

Lester handed Ben the air rifle, riffled through the bills a few times as if to make sure they were genuine, and said, "And after you get your story thing squared away, we both settle up with Leo."

Ben nodded and started to leave, but Lester was still not satisfied. "And what about the weird noises and stuff?"

"I'll get back to you, I swear."

As if on cue, Lester's own mobile phone began to buzz. "Yup, here we go again." Lester pressed a key, said, "Yes, ma'am, you're in luck, he's standin' right here," and slapped the padded receiver in Ben's hand.

"Finally," Iris hollered in his ear as Lester retrieved his rifle. "I'd like an explanation, please?"

"Priorities. No time, Iris."

"Leo is your priority, buster."

144

"Please, I'm begging you before I crack up."

"Just as I thought. It's stress. No worries, I took care of it, left you a tote bag full of—"

"Tins and tubs of the usual.Goodbye."

Cutting off the signal, he handed the mobile straight back to Lester and told him if Iris calls again, he is incommunicado. Salvaging what he can for everybody's sake.

As he started to make his way back to the tech alley, Lester shouted out, "Yo, there was another call. From that old pop singer on MTV. It was right after that hot pants Gillian rolled in."

"Enough, okay? Enough!"

Lester yelled out other things, including the fact it really rankled him when people told him to cool his heels.

Ben let Lester's complaints fade off as he picked up his pace. By now the stars were out and the moonglow bounced off the metallic facades, stripping him of the last of his illusions. As his old college professor would put it, once external fluctuations got really going, things are bound to flare up. In short, only if Ben's luck held out a tad longer could spontaneous combustion be averted.

Returning, he pressed the door handle of Studio Three and slipped inside. A quick scan brought him nothing. She was nowhere in sight.

"Molly? Molly? It's me. No problem, your pigeons are safe."

He glanced up at the spiral staircase and spider encrusted attic and moved in and around the makeshift dungeons, wrought-iron gates and open graves on the ground floor. He looked inside the police station and scurried over to the ramp leading to the motel façade. Perhaps she didn't trust him. Perhaps she brought the cage down from the roof and split.

Casting his gaze up to the grid, attempting a calm, reassuring tone, he said, "It's all right. Lester's been paid off. He's sitting tight. Tit for tat, now you can humor *me*."

A door to one of the motel rooms swung open. In the pitch dark of the upper recesses, she seemed even more exhausted, her windblown hair hanging loose, her shoulders sagging.

"You scared me," said Molly, in a voice as tired as she looked.

"Sorry. What were you doing?"

"Dropped something. And it's none of your business. I thought you had to get back to work?"

"Oh, that's cute. Before you threw me off course, you mean. That's the whole point."

Scuffing partway down the ramp, Molly said, "You really pay this Lester guy off?"

"I did."

"Well, if you think that makes us even, you're wrong." As if dismissing any further need for his services, she went back to rummaging around and retracing her steps and then faltered. Turning back she looked a bit dazed.

"Listen," said Ben, "if you want to freshen up or you could use a little energy boost, my sort-of cousin left some stuff in the bungalow. Then we can get on with it. What do you say?"

He babbled on about tins of protein mixes infused with Siberian ginseng, royal jelly, spirulina and what-have-you. The usual revitalization kit for flagging slackers like himself.

"No thanks," said Molly, her disembodied voice shuttling somewhere above between the back of a motel door and the spidery lair.

"Better still, I spotted some tea and stuff somebody left behind." Grasping for any way to use her, he added, "As a respite, I mean, in a nice, quiet, familiar atmosphere."

"I hear you. Maybe. Now go."

"Absolutely. Got to go now. You bet."

He eased out the door as gingerly as he'd slipped in. This last exchange made him feel like a despairing teen inviting the head cheerleader to the prom.

He hurried back to the bungalow and willy-nilly pressed on. Clipping another set of formatted sheets to the easel, he sketched in a blurry suggestion of a cowboy ramming into C.J.'s delinquents. Another set of panels followed with shots of Molly rummaging around Studio Three and a close-up of a pigeon cage atop the studio roof. As a storyline, this also came to zilch and wound up tossed on the floor.

At another impasse, he wandered into the kitchenette and put some water on to boil, hoping for a gentle knock as Molly came for tea. For better or worse, he needed her to propel the story to a point of no return. But he wasn't able to admit to himself that he was the one who needed a respite, longing for her company and a way to block out whatever gonzo forces may be closing in.

Chapter Twenty-one

Wearing his Levi jacket over the silky mauve T-shirt he was dying to ditch, Deke slid into a vacant booth at Islands Polynesian Delight, placed his cell phone on the inlaid tile tabletop and waited for Angelique to call back.

By now he'd driven around a bunch of times and saw no sign of an old green pickup. In the twilight afterglow, with the hunger getting to him, he reminded himself not to confuse motion with action.

The second rule, which went with the first, was not to move at all till he had something to go on a damn sight better than this. And getting definite information out of Ray, who believed the Feds could tap him if he stayed on any device more than sixty seconds, was harder than getting Angelique to use what little brains she had. But at least Angelique had snuck out, rang Deke's cell and offered to call the guy manning the studio gate. She did it, so she said, because she had to hook up with some dead ringer or at least get in touch with this Ben character. Failing that, she would get hold of her fitness trainer who put her on to Ben's situation. Bottom line: Angelique was in need of Deke's tracking service as much as Ray but for a different reason. And Deke was in need of some clear cut beeline to the payoff.

It was now ten after eight. He had a few minutes to wolf something down and take it all in till Angelique touched base. Which, come to think of it, wasn't such a bad idea. This Ben character might be some kind of link. Any kind of link would be better than hanging everything on Ray's hunch about Angelique's handoff of a calling card. And his hunch this Mexican was about to horn in. Banking on both hunches leading straight to the missing stash was way too scattershot.

And so was checking on that wimp Elton Frick's voice mail again. And finding out both Fed agencies figured Frick was spooked by organized crime. That's why Frick wasn't calling back. And that's why they were looking into it.

Too much static all around. He needed something he could get a bead on here and now.

As Deke did his best to hang tight waiting for Angelique's call, a young punk dressed in a matching flower-print shirt and pants, brushed by and took his order. The only thing recognizable on the menu was an Island burger with chili and pineapple chunks. The chili was made of soy and tofu, but the beef was supposedly from a steer. Plus they couldn't have messed with a cold bottle of Coors.

The punk thanked him as he scooped up the menu and stopped in mid-motion. "Nice T-shirt. Say, you wouldn't happen to be a talent scout or something?"

Deke gave him a blank stare.

"Just asking. Our acting coach at the Strasberg Instiute says you never know. That's the same Strasberg--long departed, of course--who made Marilyn Monroe a star."

Deke cast his eyes away from the punk and onto the tiled tabletop. Marilyn Monroe again. First Castroville and now here. Even more static.

"Okay, just tossing it out there," said the pushy punk. "But like coach says, in this business you play the moment. You see an opportunity, you grab it."

Deke tapped on the tiles. The punk finally caught on, excused himself and flitted off into the blare of the *Beach Boys Live* and the obstacle course of grass huts and tropical birds. The glazed macaws were perched overhead painted in turquoise, lime, orange and flamingo red.

Deke snatched the crinkled L.A. map from the top pocket of his jacket, slapped it on the table and scanned the West Hollywood streets. Last time he was here, the chase also took him every which way. This particular watering hole was set back on a boulevard that wasn't a boulevard. There was a chunky gold building down the street like a fake eastern temple, shoddy store fronts, radio towers that looked like mangled oil derricks, a weird

Chinese-looking theater, then a cluster of chrome bimbos that looked like a hood ornament for a 1950s Caddy.

Everything was so flung around, you were never *there*. To find Paramount or this Avalon Studios, you had to scout around up La Brea or Fairfax, cut across Melrose and turn down. And all the while cars zipped by on either side and tried to cut you off. Either that or everything slowed to a crawl. But if you tried some side street, you'd like as not wind up on the Santa Monica Boulevard and to hell and gone.

To Deke's mind, at least in Vegas, all of it was piled up on the Strip. You couldn't miss it if you were blind drunk and had amnesia. There it was till they tore it down and stuck an even bigger load of crap in its place: shooting fountains, an Eiffel tower, the statue of liberty plunked in a fake ocean, and a screaming roller coaster. Inside, you got an old lion stuck in his cage, topless girls, every kind of blown up show, crowds streaming in and out of the casinos and banks of slot machines. From there you had your high-rollers betting $5,000 a hand, the buzz at the roulette tables, baccarat, blackjack dealers with their dead eyes peeling cards from a shoe. You want it, it's in your face and you were smack-dab sons-of-bitches *there*.

What it had come down to was that Deke had goddamn had it. Sick of being bottled up and jerked around. Sick of the spasms in his back. Sick of the jokers to the right of him, clowns to the left. Sick of what was up with the Feds, the Mexican, Walt and the Outfit. He was a footloose tracker and, one way or another, he was going to by-God stay footloose.

The punk came back with Deke's order and made no more play for Deke's attention. But still no call from Angelique. He set his cell phone aside and wolfed down the meat and mealy-sauce-and-fruit combo. By this point, it had gotten so bad he almost missed Sin City. Missed getting a thick steak and all the trimmings any time of night and day. Missed being called in 'cause some bozo had signed markers, comped a huge credit line, or some bag man was skimming off the top. No problem. You smoked him hightailing it to the desert or Red Rock

Canyon. Then you were out of it, back to the shack up in Cold Creek. Over and done.

Draining the Coors and asking for another, Deke took out the little notepad and nailed down his plan. Intercept those "financial resources" and get the hell out. Over to Vegas for a juicy tradeoff with the Outfit. Then cool it down overlooking the Sierra Range: wild brownish red in the morning, a coat of fresh snow atop Mount Charleston in winter. The desert road to the Valley of Fire ... dancing sunsets on Red Rock Canyon walls ... swinging over to Sunrise Mountain, Lake Mead, up and over to wherever the hell he goddamn pleased.

About twenty minutes later, he paid his tab and scooted out. Over to the beige rental car a few blocks away; his sightlines cut off by a humongous billboard display: some grinning nutcase, half of him dressed in a wedding gown, the other half in a tux, fat pink and blue letters spelling out *Split Decision*. Seemed everywhere he looked, something about this town kept twanging his back.

Finally, his cell phone did its jingle. He gave Angelique only a few seconds for her song and dance about how hard it was to keep sneaking away from Ray to make a private call.

"Talk to me," Deke said, "or forget it."

"That is like so rude. Like I deserve this?"

"Then forget it."

"All right. Damn, this was supposed to be so-o fun."

"The girl. You said she was coming down to do double duty. What was she driving? An old pickup maybe?"

"Who knows, who cares? The point is, Lester was doing his rounds last night and came across the card Ben must've slipped her. The point is, she didn't show up at my place and there's still no sign of her yet, besides the card and some doughnut wrappers and all. But if she's looking for me ..."

Angelique lost her train of thought before she came back with, "The story is, only Studio Three and the bungalow are open and there must be some kind of misunderstanding."

"And this writer, this Ben character?"

"That's the worry part. He's playing hide-and-seek."

"Who told you this?"

"Iris, my trainer, who else? She was just there, called back a bunch of times and finally caught him by the gate. Sounds like he's got something else going."

"Like what?"

"I don't know. Look, I need a project real bad. Gotta make sure this comes to something. Gotta get back on the power list before I fade and die."

Breaking in on Angelique's meltdown, he learned that Iris was at her fitness center this minute waiting to fill Deke in.

Deke made some more notes. A glance at the map gave him a two-step trajectory. He was on it now and all he had to do was follow the trail.

Deke drove a few blocks west and got a break headed down Fairfax hitting only light traffic. Parking behind the gym in a no-parking spot, he unbuttoned the suit jacket swearing he would never again wear anything that made him feel like a male whore. Then snatched the stainless steel attaché case out of the trunk for added effect. Afterwards, when he swung back up Melrose and over to the studio, he'd put on the Levi jacket and play it his own way.

Before locking the car, he checked under the front seat making sure the slim-line Walther and belt slide were carefully tucked out of sight.

As he drifted through the glass doors of the gym, he got sidetracked by a bunch of gals in the room to his right. The space was lined with mirrors rimming a shiny wooden floor and they were all wearing bright halters and shorts with their hair done up in a ponytail. In the few seconds it took him to realize the instructor was much too young to be Iris, he nodded as heads turned to check him out. It seemed they were in the middle of a routine, reaching like they lost something way up high, crossing their arms in front, swinging them all the way around and obviously in no position to help him out. He pivoted to avoid the instructor's eyes but turned too fast and felt a twinge down low in that same spot in the small of his back.

Ignoring the spasm, he scanned the layout. The space beyond the front counter was much larger and held the treadmills and flickering TV monitors. Down a flight of stairs was a lineup of all kinds of machines, weights, bench press equipment and such much further back. And that's where he spied her, way over in the corner, well past the tall brunette and little blonde going neck and neck, stride by stride on parallel cross trainers. The only trouble was the pounding speakers overhead wailing and thumping about 'good lovin' that hurt his ears. Adding to the racket, the giant fans were grinding and blowing the night air in a cross current. Having to raise his voice to get something out of this Iris character was dumb. But she looked too busy to move her outside and he didn't have time to ask her to step into an office.

Just then, a body-builder type bulging out of his V-neck tank top lumbered out of the shower rooms behind the counter. Deke asked if he would mind turning the sound down. Snapping open the attaché case and pulling out the notepad and silver ball point seemed to get a rise out of him. But mostly it was Deke's mauve T-shirt that the body-builder called "very dishy" that did the trick. The bodybuilder asked if Deke was from out of town on business. When Deke said he had an appointment with Iris, the guy switched stations to Broadway show tunes and kept it on a low decibel level. He also said not to worry about interrupting her. Iris was only disinfecting the machines for their nightly dust-up. He added that he was free at ten and would be more than glad to show Deke around.

After giving him a thanks-but-no-thanks, Deke headed down the stairs, straight between the dueling cross trainers and the water fountain and across to the far end. Iris still had her back to him as she sprayed the handles of something that looked like a huge snowmobile that had hit an embankment and spun on its tail. Her knees were on the seat of the contraption as she squirted away at the chrome handlebars with a plastic bottle filled to the brim with soapy foam. A paper towel rolled onto the floor. Deke picked it up and handed it to her.

"Thanks," said Iris. "Angelique send you?"

"Uh-huh. Can we get right down to it?"

"You said it. Hey, wait a second, what happened to the beat?"

"I asked the guy at the desk to turn it down."

"Oh, yeah? He didn't just tweak it. He switched to slurpy shlock. You can't pump iron to slurp. I'm telling you, everything right now is totally out of whack."

Before pressing on, Deke gave her a once-over. She was built like a squat lady wrestler but wore a silky yellow windbreaker with the sleeves rolled up, yellow shorts, socks and matching tennis shoes. Her thick grey hair looked like she'd clipped it with sheep shears. No makeup, deep tan. The lines in her face told him she was well over fifty. Her beady eyes and low, rusty voice told him she shot from the hip and he could cut to the chase.

"Get it?" said Iris, wiping down the handles again to make doubly sure. "What I'm saying is, think about it. Ben's all over the place. You got one dorky guy manning the gate who knows from nothing. Leo asks if the Mexican who works out with the heavy bag is Ben's secret friend. This is just the other day, mind you. Tonight, Leo calls and asks again, wants to make sure."

"Of what?"

"That it's going down, what else?"

"With Ben?" said Deke. "The writer guy?"

"Who else?"

"And Leo is … ?"

"Never mind. The point is, Ben has to be leaned on, pinned down before the whole thing tanks. You read me?"

"Yup," Deke said, as she hopped off the Chin-up/dip. She moved over to the Pec Fly. "By the way, this one isolates the pectoralis major. But judging from the stiff way you handle yourself, you'll need more flexion and less muscle work. Keep that in mind once we get through this rough patch. But enough. Are we through?"

"Just about." Pulling out the notepad from the attaché case, jotting down a few more pointers, Deke said, "Now about this Pepe fella."

"Ah, you know him?" said Iris, going over to the Preacher Curl. "Interesting. Seems he may be the problem instead of the solution. Calls Ben up in the middle of the night. Oh, yeah, I heard, I caught it. Got my finger on everything. I have to, as you can plainly see. You getting the picture now?"

"Uh-huh," said Deke, making a checkmark.

"Good," said Iris, spraying in two directions and alternately wiping down the dual Hip Abductors. "Off the record, I am pushing this for Leo."

Deke circled Leo's name having no idea who he was or how he fit in.

"Still and all," Iris went on, "since Ben needs this so bad and, underneath, may have the goods plus the means —but enough said. Isn't it time you got on your horse?"

"The means? Something going on the side, is that it?"

Iris attacked the Lat Pull-down with a double spray. "What am I, talking too fast for you?"

"No, you're doing just fine. And what about the girl?"

"What girl?"

"A ringer, a look-alike."

"Oh, you mean the sketches. The ones Gillian just grabbed."

"So this Ben character was with her."

"Using her, you mean. Or maybe she's using him or both. Who knows? Isn't this complicated enough for you? So, like I said, pin him down."

With her tone getting more and more testy, she added, "Pin him down so Leo can have his shot."

"Leo wants his shot," Deke said, making a final note.

"Out, out of here," said Iris, rising from the padded rollers of the Leg Curl and the Leg Extension. "What is it with you? Too uptight to move?"

Before he had a chance to duck, she whacked him across the back. Not hard, but hard enough.

Deke covered up this next spasm by moving away and looking around. He settled his gaze on the tall brunette and the little blonde who had just ended their contest on the cross trainers. He grimaced and watched as they caught their breath and mopped each other's faces with big white towels. When he turned back around, he found Iris glaring at him.

"One last thing," Deke said, still waiting for the spasms to subside. "This Pepe, what does he look like?"

"Did you see Mr. Muscles at the counter? If Pepe is who I think he is, add long, jet-black hair, the face of Zorro and a crazy look in the eyes."

Deke gave Iris a final nod and walked over to the water fountain just as the tall Brunette and little blonde sashayed by and headed up the stairs for the lockers arm in arm. He snuck a pain pill in his mouth, filled the paper cup and guzzled the ice cold water down.

Back in the car--the Walther tucked in the belt slide just behind his right hip--he held his cell phone close to his mouth and let Ray have it.

"Give it to me, Ray, before I move in."

"Hey, what did I tell you? We gotta make it short. You never know what bugging devices they got now."

"I don't care if it's one word. What is it? What's worth all this pain?"

"Look—"

"Tell me or get yourself another flunky."

"I'll tell you and that something I'll tell you is this. You will tell *me* and I will tell you nothing."

"Okay then."

"Wait. What do you know?"

"I know you're so strapped, you can only lease one building, a bungalow and a joker at the gate. Which tells me there's no way you can front Angelique's operation without collateral. Without those missing resources, you can't launder squat."

"Are you talking to me? Are you talking to Ray like this? I am calling Walt. I am nailing his ass and telling him--"

"You do that. He'll remind you, what with the accountant scamming you over the lame books plus this latest screw-up, the Outfit's already got you by the short hairs. So, assuming some combo of Ben, the girl and Pepe haven't already divvied things up and I can cut it off ... But hell, waste some more time. Please yourself."

Ray was so unhinged at this point, all he could say was, "Jeez, hold it, hey ..."

Deke gave him two minutes to call back and give him the kicker. In the meantime, surprised at himself for coming on strong like that, he shrugged it off, ditched the pansy top and put the dress shirt back on. At least it was broken in and something a man could wear. He probably should've also put the suit jacket back on to keep up appearances but what for? Once he spooked the lone clown manning the gate, how much of an appearance would he have to keep up? So he yanked his Levi jacket out of his overnight bag.

Then, just for the hell of it, he riffled through his notes. The riffling reminded him of time limits, high stakes, all the chips and the two hole cards down. If he was reading things right, it looked like Ray wasn't that far off. Of course, Deke wouldn't know Pepe's hole cards and Pepe wouldn't know his. But if it came to that, Deke would need an edge.

He eyed the Walther and patted the belt slide by his hip. He tried to recall the last time he fired a hand gun. Did he wing the guy or just shake him up? He couldn't remember. At any rate, he'd need the insurance no matter what Pepe was packing. Especially if he brought along some of his Chicano hoods out for revenge.

Or, in any case, if this Ben and the girl gave him a hard time.

Chapter Twenty-two

Ben's last-resort ploy didn't exactly pay off. Instead of going along with him, Molly shuffled into the bungalow in a daze.

From his vantage point in the kitchenette doorway, Ben watched her meander over to the desk where Iris had plunked down the tote bag full of health food paraphernalia as heavy as curb stones. She peeked in, yawned, shook her head and just stood there.

Not about to say or do anything to spook her, it dawned on him if he could keep her awake, she might give him a clue about her predicament. That clue, in turn, could take his storyboard to the clincher. And that was why he snatched an Earl Grey tea bag and dangled it as a lure, indicating something hot laced with caffeine might just do the trick.

She looked up, nodded and shuffled toward him.

As she approached, he poured generously from the pot he'd been brewing into an oversized ceramic mug, added a spoon full of honey and spun out of the kitchenette. She accepted the offer without a word and floated back to the rattan couch. With her legs crossed and tucked beneath her, she took slow measured sips.

In the span of these few moments, Ben noticed she moved like a dancer, not like a farm girl at all. More like one of the nymphs at a recent U.C.L.A. dance concert, lost in a futuristic time warp.

Unobtrusively as possible, he ambled down and sidled over next to his drawing board opposite her. Perhaps they could engage in a little small talk, the way average people did who weren't coming undone. Then, once he'd put her at her ease, she'd open up and, before you knew it, he'd be off and running again.

Careful as can be, he plucked up the discarded panels. If he could cut from the shadowy form of a ramrodding cowboy, to Molly hiding out and rummaging around the cop-and-Halloween set, plus the pigeon cage on the roof, and then cut back to the cowboy—one of those classic *meanwhile-back-at-the-ranch* edits--maybe Gillian would buy it. And Ben would have time to pick up the rest of the pieces. As long as he could shoehorn what was up with Molly stashing those sacks in the livery stable. Come up with something along those lines. Otherwise it was still a bunch of thumbnail sketches leading nowhere.

After a few more beats of suspended silence, Ben said, "Nice ribbon."

"Mmm," Molly murmured, looking childlike with the new addition of a pink hair band.

"Was that what you were looking for? Back there in the haunted attic?"

"Never you mind."

"Just wondering."

"Well stop wondering."

"Well if it's not the ribbon, maybe I could help you find whatever it is. Later."

"Drop it, okay, buddy?"

"Ben. I told you my name is Ben."

"Okay, Ben," said Molly, back to her old standoffish tone but too weary to put any energy behind it. "In case it isn't obvious by now, I have hardly slept. The stuff I lost was over the counter, No-Doz, nothing to get worked up over, and this tea isn't doing a bit of good."

"I see, I get it," Ben said, keeping as offhand as possible. "What with no legitimate place to sleep ... hauling pigeons up on the roof. Plus chugging up and down the canyons with an old clunker of a truck. Make anybody exhausted. But I do have the answer if you'll bear with me."

"Look, I'm only sitting here to get my second wind. Then finish what I was doing ... I guess." Here was that look again, peering out at nowhere, sorting through some hazy options.

"Unfinished business, right?"

"Mmm."

"With those sacks."

She responded with a nod, then a shake of the head.

He keyed on her eyes again, consistently her most expressive feature. They fluttered, opened wide, drooped and opened again. Obviously at a point where she'd love to give in, curl up and drift off.

Shaking herself out of it, she uncrossed her legs. Humming some obscure country western tune, she rubbed her chin on her chest and swung her head back and around and let it drop. After a few more of these, she stood, stretched, eased around the back of the couch and did a straggly figure-eight around the desiccated palms in the far corner.

Returning to the back of the couch, she said, "Okay okay. The real reason I came in here. About the movie."

"Sorry?"

"Don't give me that. Angelique has to show some time. You handed me the card, remember? No sign of her this morning ... and her dumb phone is unlisted. But here you are with your easel and your writing gig or whatever. So it figures."

Checking her watch, she shook her hands and arms like some kind of wake-up call. "I'm saying, I can not believe people have been by for no reason. It's getting late but you're still here. So you must be expecting someone. When, for heaven sake? When?"

"Okay," said Ben, realizing the gentle offhand approach was out. "Assuming Gillian is still giving me the benefit of the doubt—"

"Who?"

"The one shepherding the project. If she is, there's still a little time. A very little time."

"I knew it, I knew it. Then I can talk to this Gillian who'll get back to Angelique and work something out."

Somewhat satisfied, but then squinting at him, she said, "Hey, why aren't you doing your thing? What's with the tea and the small talk? I thought you were on deadline."

"I *am* on deadline. I am groping—the tea and the small talk were part of a quiet yet desperate grope. In a word, I am stuck."

"Oh, get off it. What do you need?" Scuffing over to him, bending over the shopping basket, she gazed bleary-eyed at the Dr. Seuss book sticking straight up like a tab. "What's this?"

"Nothing."

"Come on, come on, let's have it."

"A birthday reminder, if you must know. All part and parcel of the ticking clock."

"You're kidding," said Molly, pointing to the candy cane swirls under the title *Oh, The Places You'll Go.* "I mean, how old are you anyways? And what are you trying to pull?"

"Nothing," said Ben. "You wouldn't understand."

"Talk to me," Molly said, leafing through the pages. "Tell me please, I'm begging you, this is not some kinda kiddie thing."

On his feet, about to lose it, Ben spelled it out for her. "You see those rainbow paths of yellow, green, purple, blue and orange? You see where they lead, you see the kid all the way up on top? That's where I'm supposed to be. That's where I've *been* supposed to be. Look on page twelve: *You'll join the high fliers who soar to high heights.* Well, sister, time is running out. The last-chance birthday is upon me, you're not coming through, and I am this far from oblivion."

"This far from what?"

"Oblivion, erasure, eradication after letting Aunt June and just about anybody and everybody on this planet down."

In the state she was in, it took Molly a few moments to even try to take this in. "I'm sorry, my brain is so fuzzy I don't get what you're saying."

Leafing through the pages again, talking more to herself than Ben, she said, "Wait a minute. What's this? The one with the big circle around it? 'You're too smart to go down any not-so-good street ... in that case you'll head straight out of town.'"

"Ah," said Ben, "there you have it. The enigma, the great dilemma. Maybe the road less traveled is for later, much much later, after you've made it. Then you can light out, sit around the ol' campfire and say, 'Here I am. Finally, at long last. This is my story, this is my song.'"

There was no response. Nothing.

Dejected, Ben flopped back down in his chair.

With her eyes drooping, Molly tossed the Dr. Seuss book aside and returned to the couch. "Right, never mind, forget I asked. So, back to business, about this gig. Twin sister or doubles act? We're talking my age, correct? I mean, if I play it right. Yes? Isn't that so?"

She slumped back on the couch and stuck her feet on the coffee table, barely missing the mug.

Ben gave her a halfhearted nod.

"Okay, that's better. All right. I'll help you out if you drop the not-so-good-street stuff. I mean, we're both trying to make it, right?"

"Bingo."

"Awesome. So what do you need?" Fluffing up a throw pillow, leaning back against it, she let her head to loll to the side.

Hoping against hope he could make up for the time wasted, Ben gave it another try, grabbed a hunk of charcoal and waited for something to click.

But instead, after a few yawns she went off on another tangent. "Oh, wow, just to be part of it all. I passed by the Prado and saw some real celebs. "

Eyes still drooping and with her voice getting more and more slurry, she paid no mind to Ben's frustration. "I pulled over on Rodeo Drive too, spotted a couple of girls, my age, through the tinted window. Highlights, foil strips, some guy pouring on the gold so their hair looked sun-bleached. Leaving the roots so they looked hot ... no worries, no regrets."

Ben had no comeback, except to say it was cute, like the pigeons. He kept staring at the blank panels, the piece of charcoal clutched in his fingers.

"Cute, huh? Pretty easy for you, bud. Are you in over your head? Is your mom tramping around Sausalito? Is your granny a wino?"

"Come on, Molly, give me something."

"You bet." She let out a sleepy moan followed by an almost inaudible, "Oh, man, I am so out of it." Fluffing up the throw pillow, she finally let something slip. "But I got stuff I gotta do first ... hide something a whole lot better."

"Uh-huh," Ben said, trying to fake that offhand tone. "Sounds like a plan."

"Mmm," said Molly, her eyes comfortably closed "In a minute, in a sec."

"But why bother? Thought you wanted to meet Gillian?"

"Mmm."

"Hey, tell you what. Maybe I can help. Work it in."

But she drifted off again, slid over on her side hugging the pillow.

Turning back to the easel, Ben sketched-in a suggestion of the pickup truck, tailgate down ... a cage full of pigeons resting inside the truck bed, a few sacks hovering behind them ... tying it in to Molly scurrying around the back lot in the shadows.

Molly tossed and turned and let out a few more incomprehensible murmurs.

"Hid it in the barn, did you?"

No answer.

"Of course, somewhere near the loft."

Another affirmative "Mmm."

"Couldn't hide it well 'cause Lester spooked you. Had to move the pigeons as well. And, judging from your license plates, you've been running yourself ragged."

Yet another "Mmm."

"So, much better to stay put, wait for Gillian, while I make sure the secret's good and tucked away."

When she snuggled up a bit more, he went over to her and whispered, "No problem, Molly, you got it. No trouble. No trouble at all."

There was no murmur this time, no sound at all. Only the deep breathing of an exhausted young woman fast asleep.

It was all so simple. He was looking for trouble. He was this close. If he could parlay the hidden stash into a juicy point of no return, it would be a win-win. A hook to feed Gillian so they'd green-light it in a flash. *Hey, chicks, what are you waiting for? Check it out. Be the girl, play the game, it gets worse and worse. Do anything, babe, and take it all back.*

He flipped the light switches and set the three overhead fans in motion. Even though it had cooled off, the air inside was getting stuffy and it would mask his exit.

As he passed through the alcove and squeezed the front door shut, it crossed his mind that the contents of her sacks were suspect to say the least. Which was promising but a bit worrisome to boot.

He scurried past the shabby facades of the Western town keeping only Gillian's directive in mind: come up with something seamy, off the mean streets and totally now. With or without C.J.'s help, what did it matter? The second Gillian, aided and abetted by Leo, confronted him at the bungalow, he would deliver.

The bags were only a springboard, he kept telling himself. A device to jolt his imagination while doing Molly a favor.

If he wasn't in such a rush, he might have also pondered over what Gillian and Leo would make of it if they came across Molly lying dead asleep on the couch. But it had all come down to stowing away some sacks, hyping their contents, racing back to his easel and winging it in record time.

The second he reached the stable, he lifted the rusted iron bar. The overhead rollers resisted, forcing him to shove even harder till the doors gave way enough so that he could barely squeeze through.

Once inside, he saw that, with the heavy window shutters closed tight thanks to his clumsiness, it was almost pitch dark. He immediately banged into a wooden post. The rancid odors of axle grease, motor oil and stale gasoline from the oil drum and hanging Model T motor were overpowering. With Lester tramping around with his squirrel rifle, it was patently obvious why she only made a cursory attempt to hide her wares, latched the barn doors shut and, with Iris headed for the bungalow, took off for Studio Three lugging her bird cage.

He banged into another post before he got his bearings. Threading his way past the musty harnesses, he located the wooden ladder and clambered up to the hay loft. The rest was easy. It didn't take long to locate the tarp from her truck bed and uncover the sacks. Although his eyes were getting accustomed to the dim shapes and shadows, he had no idea what kind of sacks they were. They seemed like the same plastic and burlap ones they use in the post office for hauling packages.

No matter. He only needed to find a better hiding place so he could beat it back to the bungalow while reaching for the most illicit thing these light-and-chock-full sacks could hold. A cheap thrill enterprise, a no-no the girl gamers would love to take on and beg for more.

His first notion was to slip the latch and dump the sacks in the makeshift bunk. Another possibility was to hide them under the moldy sacks of grain in the pit behind the buckboard. He opted for the latter, pitched all half dozen over the side along with the tarp.

Scrambling down the ladder, he jammed the lot of it under the rotting lumps of grain, made for the entrance, bumped into another post, squeezed through the opening, shoved the heavy double doors back in place and secured the iron bar.

A quick survey revealed no sound or movement approaching down from the tech alley. A glance at his watch under the filmy glints of moonlight told him he had, at the outset, less than twenty minutes to fill in the blanks. Which, given the fact that nothing dicey enough came to mind, left only the prospect of cajoling Molly, telling her he'll never reveal the whereabouts of her plunder if she let on what it was or even could be that would be worth all this grief.

Rushing back, slipping on the scattering of oranges by the walkway, he noticed the door was slightly ajar. Which was odd because he could swear he'd shut it tight. And the blinds were closed. He'd left them partially open to let in the night air.

Perhaps Molly had split? But that was unlikely considering how fast asleep she was and the fact she needed him as a go-between. Anxious to meet Gillian. And then there would be Leo who held the purse strings.

Scanning the area, there were absolutely no signs of activity. No golf-cart parked under the shadows of the ficus trees fronting the sealed café. No indication of anyone's early arrival.

He eased through the alcove and peered inside. The fans were whirring just as he'd left them. And Molly hadn't stirred. The big difference was the sight of a rangy figure wearing a faded Levi jacket. What was even more troublesome was the nod of recognition despite the fact that he and Ben had never met.

Chapter Twenty-three

As the guy chain-locked the front door and steered him into the kitchenette, Ben froze. Even the intermittent sounds Molly made tossing and turning on the couch in the next room didn't snap him out of it.

With the rangy figure blocking the way, he was trapped inside the narrow rectangle of space. He had no idea what he was dealing with, what with the guy's wind-burned leathery face, dry twang, dress shirt and slacks and that open Levi jacket. And Ben had no idea when and if he would start to function and raise at least a single protest..

"Maybe you'd like to make a call," said the guy, reaching in the top pocket of his jacket and flipping open his cell. "Seeing how you don't have a phone on hand."

Averting the guy's squinty eyes, Ben turned to the sink and toyed with the drain stopper. At least his hands were moving. Maybe his ability to speak would follow suit.

"How about the police? Maybe I could call for you?"

Ben took this as a joke. As though the guy knew full well Ben was high up on the L.A.P.D nuisance list and had sworn to keep a low profile lest he be brought up on charges.

"Right. Wouldn't want to let them in and spoil your game."

When Molly's restless murmurs rose above the sounds of the whirring fans, the guy said, "What is it? Want me to toss something your way before bringing the girl into it?"

Another joke. Weren't those the same words that started this whole fiasco--Gillian's offer to toss Ben a bone? From now on he would regard this phrase as a red flag.

"Well? What's it gonna be?"

"Look," said Ben, surprising himself, "I don't get it? What do you mean, 'bringing the girl into it'? You act like I know what you're talking about. Like I'm some kind of accomplice or something."

Ben went back to the drain stopper, images of Gillian and Leo's impending entrance flitting across his mind. "This is ridiculous. Who put you up to this, Lester?"

Ben was so rattled, though he'd started groping for answers, he didn't know what else to say. He'd paid Lester off to sit tight and man the front gate. So Lester would've never let this guy in unless there was some kind of security issue. Which, given Lester's skulking around after Molly, must be the case.

"Is that it?" said Ben. "What do I have to do, guess?"

Cutting off Ben's sputtering, the guy said, "Now what in hell does that have to do with it?"

"I don't know. I'm thinking, I'm thinking."

"Well you'd best quit thinking and lay it on the line."

Wincing, the guy braced his lower back with his knuckles and sucked in some air; a routine, along with everything else, Ben had no way of deciphering. At the same time, Molly's murmuring was growing a bit louder.

Then, as if the atmosphere in the kitchenette wasn't stifling enough, the guy backed Ben up against the sink. "Look, friend, the girl's coming to. Everybody, including Angelique and your feisty cousin are getting antsy."

"Iris, you've talked to Iris?"

Shaking his head, the guy turned on his heels and went back to check on Molly. The overhead fans in the work room whirred on.

Ben edged over, saw that he was only looking at her, not shaking or touching her in any way. Back to the sink counter Ben went, fussing with the box of cone-shaped coffee filters. He flipped them right-side up, placed them neatly back in the box and wondered when, if ever, his brain would start to kick in.

The second the guy returned, Ben said, "Okay. Not to appear dense, but why are you working on me? What is it you think I've done?"

All Ben got in return was that same squinty stare.

"What is it? My sneaking around? Is that why they called you in?"

Molly's yawning prodded Ben that much more.

"Okay, I get it now. You see, as a hack, when nothing comes to me, I get ideas from whatever's around. Then I jump back in, sketch, babble, whatever it takes to keep the ball rolling."

Moving right up to him, Ben said, "Look, I know you think you're doing your job. But I am under the gun. I suggest you consult with whoever put you up to this and let me get on with the finishing touches."

"Right. Look the other way while Pepe steps in. How dumb is that?"

It wasn't much, just a palm pressing against Ben's chest, but it was enough. With the little shove and the words "Pepe" came the realization this was no security man. In turn, Chula's report about a cowboy stalking Pepe in the barrio and running over C.J.'s kids struck brain. This was the very guy.

"Listen," said Ben, "You have got this all wrong."

"Tell me about it," said the cowboy. "He calls you late at night and is hooked up with Chicano hoods. Iris says you got something going on the side. You draw a sketch of wiped-out sleeping beauty here, her old truck and the sacks in the truck bed. And then you take off again."

"Ben?" said Molly, yawning and calling out. "What's going on?"

The cowboy jabbed a forefinger right at Ben's face. "See what you done? Now I got to get it all from her."

That said, the cowboy stepped into the work room.

Ben sidled down, hopelessly trying to wave him off.

Woozy as can be, Molly pushed off from the rattan arm of the couch, knocked the mug off the coffee table and peered up at Ben. "Don't tell me. You stalling again?"

Molly ran her fingers through her tousled hair and looked over. When she saw the cowboy leaning against one of the tacky posters on the far wall studying her, she flopped back down, grabbed the throw pillow and buried her face.

Fighting off a growing sense of panic and a metallic taste in his mouth, Ben said, "Okay, here's the deal. As it happens, Molly here is only resting up for her appointment with a producer and a project developer. Which, of course, is why I am here, providing the material for the initial pitch. Hence the storyboard. You see? But if you don't believe me, if you'd like to see for yourself, stick around. They'll—"

"Be right over," said the cowboy. Lester got the call. So we'll have to bring Miss Molly around while you ditch them. And while Pepe waits for a signal that never comes."

"What do you mean, bring her around?"

"Toss some coffee down her gullet and bring her to. I could've been in and out with no one the wiser. But you had to stall like she said. Endanger others. Worry my aching back."

"Wait a minute," said Molly, mumbling into the pillow. "Who is this guy?"

The cowboy moved stiffly to the edge of the couch. His tone was growly and deliberate, like he'd been saving this up but wasn't used to having to explain himself. "I am not gonna put up with any more bullshit. I want a bead on the switcheroo, the setup and the timetable. Then the goods. So I know what I've got going for me clear of any Mexican cartels. Ben here is gonna ditch the jerkoffs. You both'll come up empty but no worse for wear."

In response, Molly could do no more than peer up again from her pillow.

"So, missy," said the cowboy, "you are gonna move your little butt into the little kitchen. 'Cause you don't want me to drag you there. 'Cause you want to get outta sight and get your head straight, quick as can be."

"But ... ?"

"Now."

As easily intimidated as Ben, Molly raised herself up and got off the couch. Still groggy as can be, she looked back and gave Ben a puzzled, anxious look. All Ben could manage was a feeble gesture as she straggled off through the portal and out of sight.

"Open the blinds some," said the cowboy, "so it looks normal and I can catch what's happening."

"What if they barge in?"

"You're gonna see to it they don't. The second you spot them, you're gonna blow 'em off."

No jabbing forefinger this time. No need. The cowboy was standing watch by the portal and Ben was back in brain-lock.

Absentmindedly, Ben straightened up the couch pillows, picked the tea mug off the floor and put it away inside a desk drawer. While opening the Venetian blinds partway, his listened for any sounds of distress coming from Molly. Hearing nothing but puttering sounds coming from the kitchenette, he wandered into the alcove, unlocked the front door, stepped out and waited.

Presently, he heard the gurgle of the coffee maker back in the kitchen; then, a few minutes later, the put-put of the go-cart. He moved forward as soon as Leo hopped off. Gillian shut the motor and hung back. As Leo's bulk shambled toward him, Ben met him halfway.

As always, in preparation Leo smoothed the remaining strands of hair by his temples. His thick lips, however, were pursed in attack mode and his broad, Slavic brow was crinkled. Nearing the shadows of the scraggly orange trees, wearing the same California-black outfit, he resembled a henchman in an old B movie.

Gillian clopped forward on her sandals and then abruptly halted. Her rumpled silk lounging pajamas and mussed-up do, plus the way she was giving Ben a slow burn, signaled it was over before it started.

The part of his brain that was working told him the best recourse would be to pass them a note, have them call the police and then take off and run. But Molly was back there with the cowboy. He couldn't leave her in the lurch again. And, in some weird way, he was still as eager as the cowboy to find out what she was up to.

Faking a grin, Ben stepped closer to the miffed duo.

"Is amusing?" said Leo. "Is high-concept hook you got for us? Is rest of storyboard pages which I am not yet seeing? Is reason you are smiling so up the toilet we are not going down?"

"Well," said Ben, "that's what I came out here to talk about."

"I told you, Leo," said Gillian. "What's the point?"

"Hold please," said Leo, advancing right up in Ben's face. "Angelique pick you because you will make her into action figure and not sex kitten. Plus you have the jump on everyone with Pepe supplying hard-core grit. Yes?"

"Yes. And, happily, I'm on to that hard-core grit as we speak."

"That is so pathetic," said Gillian, the slow burn permanently stuck on her face.

"Enough," said Leo. "Is high time, is past high time. You will hand material over now."

"Love to. But you see—"

"You playing with me?" said Leo, clapping one of his meaty hands on Ben's shoulder. "Because I am bark worse than the bite? You stiff me? You stiff your cousin Iris? We have no contract, idiot. I have no contract. I need position! Without position I go down shit's creek without paddles!"

"Forget it," said Gillian, yanking Leo away. "We'll go with my step outline."

"Your step outline is from hunger. Is rehash with no hook. Is old hat with no hat and pictures for dummy yes men who say no."

Removing his hand from Ben's shoulder and retreating a few steps, Leo switched gears. "Benjamin, you give Gillian good start. I am loving the double in old truck, dead ringer driving, hiding and seeking in back lot like runaway gypsy. But now, my hand to God, we need big danger."

"I'm in on it, believe me. Later, okay?"

Gillian tugged on Leo's arm, Leo pushed her away. "Okey-doke. Tell it to me, Benjamin. Before deportation back to Odessa. What is bad business that is going down you are in on? What, who?"

It was the hard squeeze of his arm and the sense of what might be happening in the bungalow that did it. "You, Leo."

Releasing Ben's arm, Leo said, "Say again please?"

"Producer by day, at the cleaners by night."

"Cleaners?"

"Laundering, Leo. Did you ever hear of it? Isn't that really what it comes down to?"

"You are telling me ... ?"

"I'm telling you somebody's going to get hurt and I can't fake it anymore."

"Where you getting this?"

"Where do you think? You picked him. You wanted a close eye to boost the sleaze quotient."

"So?"

"So, among other things, Pepe's close eye is eyeballing you."

Instantly, all the animation drained out of Leo's face. He stood motionless, then turned and shambled back to the cart. From the little Ben knew of Leo's brand of Russian, he was telling himself his shady dodge had sprung a leak and he was about to go under.

Gillian lingered for a moment. After studying Ben as though her contacts had fogged up on her, she said, "You know something. I was so pissed when I got back to my cubby hole at Paramount, I took a chilled Pinot Grigio from the frig and got sloshed. I knew it, knew you were out of your element and would somehow fuck it up. Never again, Benjy, I swear. In Leo's immortal words, 'My hand to God.'"

With this tag line still reverberating, Gillian clip-clopped over to the go-cart, switched on the puttering motor and sent them both on their way.

Ben shifted over to the edge of the tech alley, not in pursuit, but simply to watch the last vestige of his so-called career dissolve. Just before he turned back, he noticed the shiny car parked nearby, blocking the doorway to Studio Three. He half wondered why neither Gillian or Leo mentioned it. But, then again, they had other things on their mind.

Ben hurried back to the bungalow, cut through the alcove and reentered the work room. There he found Molly wide-eyed standing by the portal to the kitchenette watching the cowboy closing the blinds. Molly appeared to be frazzled but unharmed; the cowboy champing at the bit as he returned to her side.

Without a word, Ben ripped his excuse of a storyboard off the easel, wadded it up, tossed it as far as he could and plopped onto the chair behind the desk.

"Okay," said the cowboy, calling over to Ben, "you juggled that pretty good."

"Right," said Ben, elbows on the desk top, head in his hands. "That's what I do. That's what I'm good at."

"Which just leaves Molly here to provide the finishing touches. End of story."

Chapter Twenty-four

At first the cowboy let Molly carry on. He braced his lower back and leaned against the tacky movie posters while she stayed opposite, prattling away and nervously straightening the leaves of the dusty potted palm.

The good thing was that her eyes were alert and searching, like the first time Ben spotted her on the running board of her truck. And, yet again, nothing like that first time. Here, she was blurting out bits of useless information, like the fact her mom kept hooking up with a series of promoters, sending Molly off to dance classes while she shacked up. And then dumped her on Granny the wino, to labor in the fields when mom was between gigs. Getting the word out that she, like Molly's Granny, had a kid by accident when she was only a teen. Which made good ol' mom a prize for anyone looking for a footloose showgirl in her prime.

When the cowboy asked what the hell she was yakking about, Molly said it was one of her mom's rejects who pawned her off on Angelique as a backup dancer. Also, she'd been playing errand girl between bookings to keep in line for her big break. Not like her Miss Artichoke Granny who wasted away in a packing plant. Except that lately, when Angelique's star plummeted, Molly panicked and announced she was willing to do anything to help out. "Whatever you guys need. Long as I'm still on board."

Still plunked down at the desk by the front windows, Ben strained to get the gist of Molly's story under the whir of the overhead fans. He was at once curious, dejected and climbing out of his skin. Along with the abiding metallic taste in his mouth, there was a weird chill running down his thighs to the tops of his feet. All this, coupled with Molly's imploring glances some thirty feet away, drove Ben to fiddle with the contents of Iris' survival kit. He reached in, took out the clunky tins of protein mixture one by one. It was senseless, as useful as emptying out the coffee filters in the kitchenette. But he had no more words to offer, no more plans, no way out.

After another hitch in Molly's ramblings and yet another imploring glance, like a neurotic stock-boy, Ben had all eight cans stacked up neatly.

Molly rubbed more dust off the palm fronds and stopped gyrating and glancing at Ben. "So that's it," Molly said. "That's the deal about me and Angelique."

"What deal?" said the cowboy, his voice straining this time. "Start with dumping the station wagon. The setup from there to here hooking up with Pepe. "

"Pepe?"

"The setup, the spillage and the timeframe."

Molly shook her head and walked around in circles. She muttered something about delivering diet supplements ... making stops in Santa Cruz, Monterey and Morro Bay. And then finding the game plan had changed.

"Right," said the cowboy inching closer to her. "You jumped at the new goods, switched sides and took the truck route instead."

"No," said Molly, moving away from him. "I just guessed something was up, something risky, something illegal."

The cowboy's cell phone jingled. He plucked it out of his Levi jacket, listened for a second and said, "Later, Ray. No, no sign yet of Mexicans. Now get off my back."

A poke and a flip of the cowboy's wrist and the cell phone came winging in Ben's direction and landed on the couch; the lit blue screen indicating there would be no more interruptions.

"So, missy," the cowboy said, speaking slowly as if Molly was hard of hearing, "we got you taking the back road. Then, all of a sudden, Ben wants in. You're caught between. You got Ben and Pepe's crew. You got Ray. And you got Angelique's double cross of Ray with your wannabe actress gig as the brass ring."

"That's crazy. That's all mixed up."

"Like hell. No goddamn wonder you're so fagged out."

"Say something, Ben. Help me out here."

But at the moment, whatever thoughts Ben could muster were centered on linking Ray, the scrawny guy with the beak by Angelique's pool, Molly running off at the sight of him, and what the cowboy was after.

"Spit it out," the cowboy said. "What's the new product? How many drops you get to make if you go with Angelique? Or Pepe? Or if you stick with Ray and save your skin?"

"Quit it," said Molly twisting back and forth. "You are seeing this all wrong."

"I am seeing it from here to Burbank," said the cowboy, directly behind her now, barking out his guesses as Molly cupped her hands over her ears. "Malibu. Pasadena. Culver City, Universal City, every goddamn city. Westwood, Brentwood, Inglewood, every kinda wood."

"No!"

"Hey look," said Ben, speaking out at last. "Since there's obviously some big misunderstanding here, I say we at least give Molly the benefit of the doubt."

The cowboy strode over to Ben and swept the cans off the desk so hard they flew over the shopping basket, smashed into the coffee table and rattled onto the floor.

Shaken, Ben hunkered down and retrieved the cans. They were something to hold onto: large, smooth and cylindrical. But most of all, crawling around was a way to block out the craziness he couldn't erase or smudge over with charcoal.

As he scoured around, he eyed the cell phone still resting on the cushion above him. He thought of pressing the power button to keep the charge from running out. But he abandoned the idea out of fear of what the cowboy might do.

In the time it took Ben to retrieve the cans and put them all back, Molly had retreated into the kitchenette, gulped down some more coffee, yelled out, "Why won't you listen to me?," slammed a couple of cabinet doors and returned.

With his feeble clean-up chore finished, Ben stood motionless, the bulging tote bag nestled against his side.

Off on another tack, Molly explained how she'd gotten into a fight with her Granny over the station wagon as Granny got more and more suspicious. Then gassed up the old truck and bought a set of worn tires from Dell's Junks and Wrecks out on Molera Road. Next, she'd glommed a few of Granny's homing pigeons in the hope she could foist them on Angelique and still be in the movie or whatever it was. Demonstrate how to attach vials to the pigeons' feet. Let Angelique come up with the drops, move the new risky stuff, whatever it was. Create a flyway from her roof. Or have somebody else do it. She'd done her bit as delivery girl and darned well deserved a break.

Catching the exasperated look on the cowboy's face as he rubbed his lower back, she pointed at Ben. "But when he bumped into me, and when I saw creepy Ray by the pool, I took off. Thought maybe I'd catch Angelique here alone. And since Ben owes me, handed me Angelique's card, plus this shack was unoccupied ... and the movie people were due, had to be. Hey, you saw them, you made Ben screw it all up."

"To hell with it," the cowboy said. "To hell with all bullshit. Just ... gimme ... the stash."

With Molly's gaze fixated well past the front windows, Ben said, "She can't. She doesn't know."

Out of nowhere came a hand gun, small and silvery. Then, like a drill instructor, the cowboy pulled the magazine out of the bottom of the grip. "See the red dot? You slap in the clip, flip off the safety and you're set."

He cocked the hammer.

"What is this?" said Ben.

"Watch. With the hammer back, you get a lighter trigger pull. If the first shot don't do it, you're in automatic and the bullets fly."

He pulled the magazine out of the bottom of the grip and waved it in front of Molly's face. "Ready?"

"Wait," said Ben, "I'm trying to tell you something."

Still speechless, Molly transferred all her energy to her shifting feet.

"Too late," said the Cowboy.

"Stop," said Ben. "What are you, out of your mind?"

The cowboy smacked the clip in place.

Before Ben had a chance to say, "I'll tell you, I'll show you," Molly broke for the front door.

The cowboy lunged and caught the back of her hair, spun her around and sent her crashing against the coffee table. Reflexively, Ben raised the tote bag as the cowboy leaned over, grabbed her arm and twisted it. As she screamed, Ben smacked the cans across the side of the cowboy's head. Ben's curses now as hysterical as Molly's cries and the cowboy's furtive ducking until one of Ben's blows struck him in the back. The cowboy moaned and released Molly's arm as Ben struck again and again. The cowboy lurched forward, banged against the upended coffee table, shoved it aside and began clutching his lower spine. Groping wildly, Ben stripped the gun from the cowboy's fingers and jabbed the muzzle in the exact same spot.

"Out, out, out of here!" Ben yelled, jabbing him again. "Safety's off. Next I pull the hammer back, right?"

The cowboy weaved forward, threw open the front door, stepped out into the night air and straggled past the shadows of the ficus trees as Ben stayed close behind.

"In the car," Ben said. "And you better make it fast before I let you have it."

It was all a bluff, tossing out a line from an old Warner Brothers flick. Ben had no intention of pulling the trigger, even firing a warning shot. Only hoping the cowboy would think Ben had completely gone berserk and truly was in cahoots with Pepe the bandit. Praying the cowboy would crawl into the car and take off before realizing Ben had no idea what he was doing.

And somehow it actually happened. The cowboy slid behind the wheel, gunned the motor and backed up, tires squealing and screeching. More squealing and screeching as the car jockeyed around, sped up the tech alley, careened right and kept going. Perhaps seeking immediate relief for his aching back, perhaps contemplating his next move, perhaps just about anything. Ben had no thoughts about Lester and the front barricade, not even the possibility that the cowboy might run Lester over like he'd done with the Chicano kids. Ben had only thoughts for Molly.

Flipping the safety on, Ben raced back to the bungalow, latched the front door, jerked the Venetian blinds shut, clicked off the lights and knelt by Molly's side.

Bleary-eyed, she gazed up at him and feebly began pounding on his arm. "Where did he come from? Tell me, tell me."

"I don't know. I'm sorry. Sorry as hell."

Fending Molly off, Ben placed the hand gun on the floor and slid it away; within grabbing distance if it came to that but with the muzzle pointed the other way.

Clutching the front of Ben's shirt, Molly said, "I have to know. Why me? How did this happen?"

She asked a dozen more questions Ben had no answers for. Then, hanging onto him, she muttered, "Granny got to the Greyhound station and had cold feet, did you know that? Sleazo mom never made it past the airline reservation counter. But I got here. This was my time, man. This was my time!"

She let go of him, wept quietly and snuggled against his shoulder. He put his arm around her but all he could muster was, "I know, I know."

When her sobs diminished into whimpers, he squinted into the darkness, looking for the blue light of the cowboy's cell phone. Knowing he should call Lester, or Chula to get C.J. down here, or the station--even if the dispatcher scoffed at a nuisance call from an abandoned old Hollywood studio.

He finally spotted the faint glow of the cell by the broken leg of the coffee table. But he couldn't move, couldn't disturb Molly, leastways not now. He hoped the charge would hold out a little while longer. He hoped the cowboy wouldn't recover and come storming back.

At any rate, here they were, in the dark beneath some cheesy movie posters, fans whirring, hand gun close by.

After a time, Molly began to sing, like an inconsolable little girl trying to lull herself to sleep:

I'm the queen of the Silver Dollar ... I rule a smoky kingdom ... a wine glass is my scepter ... and a barstool is my throne ...

The lyrics didn't make much sense. Ben said, "I know," again. Then, "It's okay." As the song faded, he hung on to her tight to keep himself from shaking to pieces.

Chapter Twenty-five

"Okay, Ben," said Molly, edging over toward him, "who did you just call?"

"Chula, his girlfriend. She'll get hold of him."

"And who's he again?"

"A friend, an undercover cop."

"Oh sure, I'll bet."

"It's true."

It was now after eleven. They were in the dark by the fake tombstones on the ground floor of Studio Three, well back of the entrance. The one thing they'd agreed on was the need to vacate the bungalow. Remaining there like sitting ducks was just asking for it. Especially if the cowboy didn't hightail it to the emergency room. Or collapse onto a motel bed with a bag of ice on his frazzled back.

"And who's this Pepe," Molly went on, "and his crew we're supposed to be in cahoots with? Where does he come in?"

"He doesn't."

"How do you know?"

"How do you know anything in this town?"

"Exactly. How do we know this Chula isn't really mixed up with--?"

"Look, what do you want? Lester didn't answer and we've got to get you out of here. Come on, Molly. What's it going to be?"

Stalling again, Molly ran her fingers across the spiky wrought iron fence that rimmed the graveyard till she located the rusty gate. And there she lingered. "But what about the sacks? What about the pigeons?"

"I told you. You take off and lay low. I sit tight till C.J. gets here. I hand the stuff over and fill him in. Tell him you didn't realize what you were doing, words like that."

"How do I know? How do I know what you'll do?"

"Great," said Ben, traipsing over to her. "I'll show you where I hid the sacks and we'll load them in your truck. We'll even load the pigeons."

"But--?"

"Exactly. What's C.J. going to think if he spots us? And what'll the cowboy do if he gets here first?"

Getting more and more frustrated with her, Ben began tossing out anything that came to him.

"Okay then, when C.J. gets here, I'll tell him nothing happened, I made it all up. In the meantime--if you can still keep your eyes open, that is--you'll have already zipped back to Laurel Canyon. Sure, great idea, take the cell phone. It's probably good for at least one more call. At this hour, it's only polite to give Ray and Angelique some advance notice. And then all three of you can come to grips with who has been double-crossing whom."

Ben brushed by her, passed the police station interior, reached inside and found the desk sergeant's counter. He retrieved the cell phone, hand gun and the binoculars he'd snatched from the shopping basket. Slipping the strap around his neck, he stumbled around and returned to her side. She shook her head as he switched on the cell and held up the glowing monitor.

"Here," Ben said, "see, it still works. You're all set. Take the gun too, take everything. Hurry, before you start listening to reason."

"What is this?" said Molly.

"Nothing much, just tearing my hair out."

"Listen, you, just 'cause you saved my life maybe, and I let you hold me and all, doesn't mean you're calling the shots. So back off, will you? I can't hear myself think."

Telling her he'd just about had it with this squabbling, he almost dropped the gun as he moved over to the ramp opposite the entrance and shoved the cell phone in his back pocket.

Fine," he said, placing the gun gingerly by the metal railing. "And if the cowboy does get here first and I can't hold him off, be sure to share your thoughts."

183

After another one of her blank stares at the ceiling, she shuffled over to him and pressed her forehead against his shoulder. "God, I am so beat."

"Obviously."

Stifling a yawn, she took a few steps up the ramp.

"What are you doing?"

"Looking for the No-Doz I dropped up there. I am so wasted and so hyper. I mean, if I don't take something or find some place to crash ..."

"I don't believe this. What does it take to strike brain?"

"Thanks," Molly said, tramping back down and away from him. "All right, anything, anything."

"Meaning?"

"Meaning, I give. Anything to get away from you."

"Great," said Ben, moving toward the entrance. "Then we play it my way."

"Not so fast. You're saying Aunt June's place is vacant and safe."

"How many times, Molly? How many times?"

"And this C.J. can be counted on?"

"Yes!"

A little more stalling before Molly finally went along.

Giving her no time to backtrack, Ben grabbed the gun, pressed the metal bar and opened one of the double doors. There was no sign of any activity whatsoever.

"Right," Ben said, reaching in his shirt pocket. "Can you follow these directions?"

"I am not that far gone. Where are the keys again?"

"Under an adobe brick in a crayon box behind the Madagascars. The two gold ones will get you through the front; the remote under the second brick will open the garage and close it. Be careful skirting the cactus."

"Aunt June is away till Saturday and the neighbors won't spot me?"

"Yes, yes, yes. The house is sideways and the neighbors are in hiding. You will sleep undisturbed around the clock."

"And you?"

"Never mind. I am armed and considered dangerous."

"What about your cousin's place?"

"After this? Are you kidding? Now will you please move those feet?"

"All right, I'm going."

Ben held the hand gun low by his side, just like in the movies, just like he'd done as a little kid. They went over the drill, which was also pure Hollywood but, in the state they were in, it didn't matter. Ben would slip out into the night, scan the immediate area, wave and cover as Molly darted to each checkpoint. If the coast was clear, Ben would scurry across and join her. If not, she would split and Ben would hang back to delay any intruder till C.J. arrived.

On Ben's signal, as if they were two playmates, the maneuvers began. Rushing across the tech alley; then down to the ficus trees fronting the locked café, the far edge of the bungalow next to the fringe of the Western town; then to a spot behind the saloon dance hall and dumpsters and the back of the livery stable. Next, it was in and around the tangle of vinca and manzanita, clumps of sagebrush and thickets of chaparral and scrub oak.

The only drawback was the darkness. Gone was the bright moonlight which had given way to a gauzy overcast. Though the cloud cover made their darting figures harder to spot, once they hit the tinder-dry foliage and long shadows made by the blocky wooden structures, it was even harder to spot each other.

Disregarding Ben as if she were home free, Molly cut through the narrow break in the chaparral, reached the stands of eucalyptus that masked the back fence, worked the slide bolt and was gone down the strip of gravel on the other side.

After losing his way in a thatch of chest-high deer grass, by the time Ben followed suit, the pitiful whine of the pickup's reverse gear was almost upon him.

Raising his hands, he rushed onto the gravel strip. Molly hit the breaks as he spun around and checked out the side street. A quick glance revealed only the file of low-lying apartment buildings in the throes of renovation.

Ben ran back to Molly's side and found her slumped over the wheel, the motor still chugging. "Hey!"

"What?"

"Are you going to make it?"

Molly shook herself erect. "Sure thing. Just resting my eyes."

"I don't know. If you fall asleep at the wheel—"

"I won't. Will you kindly get off my back?"

After checking out the side street again, he reminded her to use the couch. And leave no sign that anything remotely female had infiltrated the premises.

In turn, Molly stretched, widened her eyes and gripped the steering wheel hard. "Don't hold me to anything I said or did. We'll settle up first thing."

"Nice. Okay, just head west, hang a left at the first intersection and keep going till Olympic. Then hang a right and you're golden."

There was no kiss, no pat on the arm, not even a thank you. Ben checked out the street one last time, gave Molly a high sign and the next thing he knew she was gone.

He traipsed back to the rear gate, aware of the smell of damp concrete and eucalyptus, the sound of aluminum shards and loose gravel underfoot, and a faint trace of moonlight glinting off the muzzle of the gun. In all the rush, he'd almost forgotten he was carrying a loaded weapon.

He released the slide bolt, made his way through the break and paused by a stand of scrub oaks. What now? Hopefully intercepting C.J. and handing over the stuff. Afterwards, finding a place to spend the night. Perhaps the motel where Chula ran the desk.

Some wistful part of him cut in and pictured dull quiet things, like the Farmers Daughter activity across from the motel: the fabricated waterfall, the trolley car and little shops at the Grove ... sipping Kenya AA in the Coffee Bean and Tea Leaf hangout. The images dovetailed into more wishful thinking, like telling his cronies he might have some irons in the fire. And they, as usual, informing him whether any of these projects might fly.

The illusions were immediately replaced by the certainty Gillian would have him on top of everybody's persona non grata list. Gone was the clarion call *You're on your way up, soaring to great heights.* Gone was the daydream of a gathering around the campfire at trails end.

Even in her daze, Molly had noted the words *You're too smart to go down any not-so-good street. In that case you'll head straight out of town.* Advice he'd given to the conference wannabes at the outset. But too-smart Ben was so desperate to hang on, he never knew when to get off.

With the realities staring him in the face, he reckoned Molly was probably safe for now. Of more immediate concern was a fluttering sound. Perhaps coming from the nearby street, as though someone had shut off their motor and was coasting in neutral.

Tensing up, he tried to reassure himself that the attempt to reach C.J. was not in vain. If Chula had taken him seriously, she must have relayed the message and C.J. would be on his way. All that was left was a hop, skip and a jump. Then a short wait in the shadows by Soundstage One within shouting distance of the front gate.

Then it dawned on him. It was too easy. As if he and Molly *were* a couple of kids playing hide-and-seek. Why hadn't he wondered why the cowboy gave in so easily? Was this guy really afraid Ben would fire the gun? And if the cowboy's back was really shot, how had he managed to maneuver his car so deftly and, again, why? Was it because he was lying in wait to see who came and left? Probably. Moreover, a receding empty truck bed meant the goods were still here. And Ben was still here—the one who, under duress, revealed that Molly didn't know where the sacks were. The very same Ben Prine who'd left Molly unguarded while he scurried away and only a few minutes later returned. Therefore, as any fool could see, this Ben character had hidden the trove close by and was simply waiting for "Pepe" to make the handoff. Which, any way you looked at it, was absolutely true.

A crunching sound coming from the gravel strip cut through the silence. Stopped. Grew louder. Stopped again and was supplanted by a clink of the slide bolt.

Ben shifted to his right, crouched low and scurried through the patch of deer grass to the edge of the corral.

Then, for a time, nothing stirred. Apart from the faint traffic noise north at Melrose and an occasional whoosh closer by to the east on Van Ness, his was the only movement. As far as he could tell, that is.

He was about to circle around and drift forward toward his rendezvous with C.J., when he heard a clang. It came from the vicinity of the dilapidated dance hall behind the saloon up ahead.

Then a second clang. If it was who he thought it was, the cowboy was back in action rummaging through the dumpsters, searching every conceivable hiding-place. If so, a retreat to the back gate would prove fruitless. The cowboy could simply beat him to it and cut him off. If Ben continued to circle around the corral, past the livery stable and take off once he hit the bungalow, the cowboy was in position to shoot up and intercept him at the café.

Another clang. A glint of moonlight held for a second and gave way again to the thickening cloud cover.

Ben reached into his shirt pocket for the cell phone but then thought better of it. No matter how low he pitched his voice, it was so quiet he was bound to be heard. Besides, the longer he kept hanging out in the open like this, the more vulnerable he became.

He opted for the little room in the recesses of the hay loft. If the cowboy squeezed the barn doors open and looked inside, what would he see? The closed back shutters blocked off any hope of moon-glow, and there was no electricity, no switches, no other source of light. All the cowboy could make out was the dim outline of the posts and hanging tack in the foreground. And maybe the oil drum, hanging motor and shell of the Model T in the far right corner. And maybe even the buckboard deep in the opposite corner. But sacks of rotting grain were lodged in a covered pit behind the buckboard and Molly's sacks were below that. The little room was way too far back, up and over and, ostensibly, non-existent. Judging from the hell-bent way the cowboy was scouring the back lot, he was not about to linger over anything.

Wary of the gun in his hand, constantly making sure the safety was on, Ben eased around the corall to the stable, lifted the wooden bar over the iron brackets and pulled the doors open just wide enough to slip through. As quietly as he could, he squeezed the doors shut, working against the squeaking rollers.

He found the air inside heavy and steamy with the
shutters closed; the smell of old motor oil, gas, hay, rotting
grain and leather even more insufferable. He wanted to
chuck the whole idea. Then again, if he found it so
unbearable, how would an exasperated guy with a bad
back take it?

Using the acrid smells as a guide, along with his
outstretched hand to keep from smacking into the posts,
Ben inched toward the propped-up ladder. Halfway there,
he tripped over an old saddle blanket and realized he'd
gone too far to the right. Making an adjustment, he sidled
over and bumped into the open oil drum. A slight jog to the
left and he located the wooden rungs. He straightened and
steadied the ladder and clambered up, keeping the hand
gun away from his body, the muzzle pointing down.

Once safely up on the loft, he put the gun down, faced
in the direction of the barn doors and worked the ladder to
his left, past the stacks of hay, all the way to the wall so it
would appear the loft was suspended in the air. And this
pungent, claustrophobic, old-timey livery stable was,
doubtless, unoccupied.

Back to the center of the loft. He retrieved the gun,
edged his way over, groped around and found the loop of
rope that served as a door handle. He tugged on the rope,
stepped inside and secured the latch. With the shutters
pressing against the window screens behind him, the room
was pitch dark, the air close and stifling. Hopefully there
would soon be a door slide and squeak from down below, a
quick count, and the cowboy would be gone.

He sat on the cot. The springs creaked, the ticking tore
exposing the rotting mattress.

He began to sweat. He ripped off a length of ticking,
went over to the washbasin, cranked the hand pump a few
times until trickles of rusty water doused the rag. He
patted his brow and the back of his neck. Then squatted
down and searched for a crack by the flimsy door so he
could have some idea what was going on.

For a moment he felt like a sniper as he peered out.
Make that a sniper and a mark both with the jackpot
hidden about twenty-five feet below him.

Back to the hand pump. After a few more cranks and another mop of his brow, he thought he heard the scrape of the overhead rollers as though someone was testing the barn doors. Just to make sure, he crouched back down in time to see the huge doors split apart. Backlit by a smidge of moonlight, the cowboy's shadowy figure appeared.

This was the moment for the quick count, a cursory look-see and perhaps a reluctant sigh as the barn doors slid back where they belonged. But it wasn't to be.

Chapter Twenty-six

The cowboy reached inside his Levi jacket and struck a match. It was a tiny flame but enough to illuminate the posts closest to the entry. He walked forward, his back ramrod stiff, his boots scuffing the rough planks. He kept it up, took in his immediate surroundings, struck another match and progressed further.

When he reached a point between the saddle blanket and the hay loft, Ben knelt down, unable to squat a moment longer. Flipping off the safety, Ben thought of a series of commands, but they all seemed as ridiculous as the one he used on him before: "Hold it right there ... hands up ... reach ... freeze ..."

Another tiny flame, this one highlighting the motor hanging over the oil drum followed by another scratch on the matchbox. This time the ladder was lit up in the far corner. The cowboy grabbed it, moved it over, steadied it against the edge of the loft and mounted it one rung at a time.

Unable to see from this vantage point, all Ben could do was listen to the scuffing footsteps, on their way toward him from the stacks of hay to the center of the landing. Ben raised himself up, grabbed his right wrist and held his shaking forefinger close to the trigger.

Yet another scratch of the matchbox. A tug at the door's rope handle. A long hesitation. Then the footsteps trailing away.

Hunkering down, peering again through a crack in the slats, Ben was barely able to make out the cowboy's descent from the ladder. More scuffing against the rough-planked flooring and the cowboy's shadowy form reappeared behind the oil drum.

"Seems everybody's folded," the cowboy said, "except you and me. And you've boxed yourself in. So, looks like you got only one card to play."

When no answer came, the cowboy said, "Eight shots in the clip, by the way. Then again, it could be seven."

Ben had no idea what to do. It could be a hunch on the cowboy's part that Ben was hiding behind the door. It was warped and stuck for all the cowboy knew. It wasn't necessarily latched from the inside.

Then it hit him. The cowboy had heard the squeaking overhead rollers when Ben entered.

"Okay," the cowboy said. He shoved the ladder over until the top was almost directly opposite Ben's sightline. Perspiring like crazy, Ben gripped his wrist tighter and thought of pulling the hammer back. Instead he took slow deep breaths and wiped the sweat out of his eyes.

"There now," the cowboy said, moving back to his position behind the oil drum. "As near as I can figure, these oily rags will just smoke. But there could be flames. At any rate, that'll leave you at most two minutes. Any longer and your lungs'll be shot with CO and deadly fumes. If it weren't for the closed shutters you could last a bit longer."

The cowboy tilted the drum and rolled it till it sat directly under the hay loft.

"But if these rags should catch, the dry hay'll take off and the fire'll ventilate itself. Collapsing the roof probably. But that's even worse. Especially after I bolt the barn doors from the outside."

It wasn't so much the words, it was that dry, raspy tone again. In the bungalow, it was bullets and semi-automatics. This time it was fumes and flame.

"Another thing," the cowboy went on. "Old weathered lumber chars at a fast rate. And if you stay put and shoot holes in the shutters, the fire'll travel even faster to get to the oxygen. You'll be done in by flashover."

After the next dead silence, the cowboy rapped his knuckles against the metal drum. "Hey, you getting this?"

Still not at all bothered by the lack of response, the cowboy continued in the same offhand way. As though he was really in his element.

"Anyway you look at it, you're gonna have to drop the hand gun. 'Cause you won't be able to see diddly, leastwise shoot the damn thing. Meaning, you're gonna have to scramble down the ladder, knock on the barn doors and beg to hand over the stash."

Unable to still his racing mind, Ben cranked the pump and drenched the shredded rag till it dripped all over the floor.

The second Ben unlatched the flimsy door, the cowboy struck another match, held it high for Ben's benefit and called out. "Time's up," he said, as he dropped the match in the oil drum and strode away.

As soon as the smoke began to billow, the barn doors shut with a resounding clunk. Ben fell to his knees and snatched the cell phone out of his pocket. He hit a wrong button that flashed a 503 area code. On his second try, he managed to hit 911 just before the smoke darkened and thickened. The second someone picked up, Ben hollered, "Fire ... back lot ... Avalon Studios!" rang off, retrieved the hand gun and crawled to the ladder.

His eyes were stinging and running, and even with the wet rag over his mouth he wasn't getting enough air. If the cowboy was right, he had only about ninety seconds left.

Slipping on the safety, he tossed the gun over the side, grabbed the top of the ladder with one hand, held the rag over his mouth with the other, and swung his legs over. The ladder swerved, Ben dropped the rag and grabbed the ledge, let go, hit a couple of rungs, twisted around and jumped. He skinned his knee as he crumpled to the floor and writhed around. Disregarding the wrenching pain, keeping his face close to the floor boards and cleaner air, he drew quick, shallow breaths, using up more seconds till he found the rag and the gun a few feet away.

Gagging into the rag, he released the safety, pulled the hammer back, got to his feet and shot, aiming at what he took to be the top of the barn doors. He kept it up, the shots going wild, maybe letting in more air, maybe attracting attention, maybe making things a helluva lot worse.

With the smoke swirling up to the rafters, he stumbled back to the oil drum and tossed in the gun, reckoning that at least the weapon would be inoperative.

Gagging uncontrollably now, unable to see much of anything through his streaming eyes, he rushed toward the doors, whacked into post after post till he pounded his fists right and left, screaming, "Okay, okay, you got it!"

The doors slid open somewhere to his right. A hand shot out, yanked him into the night and threw him on the ground, exacerbating the pain in his right knee.

Retching and spitting up globs of crud, Ben muttered, "Behind the buckboard ... under the trap door ... under the rotten sacks of grain."

"You think I'm gonna go back in there, is that what you think? You're gonna go back in there."

But try as he might, the cowboy was unable to lift Ben off the ground. He clutched his back, cursed and snatched the rusty rag Ben was hanging onto for dear life.

Perhaps deciding to cover the smoking oil drum with the saddle blanket, snatch up the trove and make off free and clear. At any rate, all Ben could think of was to get to some clean water and relieve his scorched throat.

Half-stumbling, half-scrambling, Ben went across the planks that fronted the old Western town, past the hitching posts and into the bungalow. Rushing into the dark workroom, a lurching swerve took him through the portal into the kitchenette. Sticking his head under the sink, he turned on the faucet full tilt, gurgling, gulping and spewing the cold water out of his mouth.

This went on till he could swear he heard the beep of a horn. Shutting off the faucet, he heard it again.

Totally drenched but thinking *Maybe, just maybe*, Ben doused a dish towel. He dabbed the flayed skin above the tear in his ripped trousers and cried out. He was not only bleeding, he was riddled with splinters. Still gagging and spitting, he hobbled back outside, alternating between holding the towel over his mouth and gulping in the fresh night air.

His leg throbbed, his throat burned, his watery eyes kept streaming, clouding his vision. He turned left in the direction of the tech alley and found nothing, no vehicle, no more beeping. A turn to the right in the direction of the pungent smoke sent him dragging himself forward, blinking and straining his eyes.

Just then, a shrouded form seemed to slip through the billows. Covered by a saddle blanket perhaps, it was hard to tell. Three sacks dropped to the ground one by one, maybe more. There was some faint coughing but nothing compared with Ben's spasms. Ben pulled the dish towel away from his mouth and sprawled onto the hardpan soil in front of the ficus trees. He fumbled in his shirt pocket for the cell phone. The blue monitor flashed but his eyes were too watery, his vision too blurry to make out the numbers. Working by touch, he tried to locate 911 again, realizing he may not have gotten through before.

Hitting the speed-dial by mistake, he muttered, "No, not Portland Information. Good God, will you just get me 911?"

He repeated his fire-alarm message when, out of nowhere, the cowboy reappeared closer by as if just remembering something.

Ben rang off and tried to fathom what the cowboy could possibly want. Why was he walking toward him? He had his loot. It had to be the cell phone—the speed dial. Here in LaLaLand he had no name, no identity. He and the snatched bounty couldn't be traced. But the stored numbers could. Someone picking up at an Oregon exchange might be more than happy to tell all about this character. And so, when it came to it, would good ol' beak-nose Ray.

If Ben had had any energy left, he might have attempted another retreat. But it was all he could do to keep from passing out. So he just sat there on the rough ground watching the cowboy drift closer. Maybe he could roll over on his stomach clutching the cell phone, give him a hard time. But even that seemed unlikely.

More gagging and retching. As though making fun of him, the cowboy paused on his stiff-legged way and hacked into the back of his hand. When he was only a few yards away, he stopped again. This hesitation came on the heels of the blare of a horn. The same horn Ben swore he heard off in the distance while gulping and spewing the cold tap water.

No horn this time. Instead, a slam of a car door. At the same time, before Ben knew it, the cowboy was on top of him trying to tear the cell phone out of his hands.

Ben struggled for a moment and was about to give it up. But somehow through his bleary eyes he caught a glimpse of the wild shoulder length hair and brawny form that belonged to C.J.

A backhanded slap sent C.J. out of view. The frame froze with C.J. to Ben's left, the cowboy opposite. The space in-between was occupied by the outline of the burlap sacks in the near background, a smoky haze in the distance.

Ben sat up, C.J. turned toward him. Ben waved him off as the cowboy said, "Now what?"

Ben went into a rocking motion trying to ward off more gagging and spitting. In the interim, the cowboy muttered, "Oh hell," and sent a roundhouse right that just missed the side of C.J.'s head.

Without uttering a word, C.J. immediately went into his shadow boxing routine, bobbing, weaving and back-peddling. Dipping his shoulder, he rehearsed a few combinations: left jabs, crosses and uppercuts. Feigning a left hook to the cowboy's head, C.J. moved in and began stalking, this time letting out a few choice invectives. Whether he understood Spanish or not, there was no doubt the cowboy knew that C.J. relished the opportunity to get back at him for what he did to his boys.

The cowboy shuffled around and then stood his ground. Another roundhouse right misfired and glanced off C.J.'s shoulder. Through toying with him, C.J. countered with a left hook into the cowboy's ribs. A right cross clipped the cowboy's chin and a flurry of left jabs landed somewhere in the cowboy's midsection. With his arms flailing every which way, punching wildly, only a few of the cowboy's blows managed to hit the mark. Then, catching the cowboy flatfooted, C.J. feinted throwing another jab to the stomach and landed a hard high cross smack in the cowboy's face that snapped his head back.

But nearby shouts accompanied by a pulsing red light broke things up. Camera flashes added to the melee along with squawking intercoms and ear piercing sirens. All of it ruining what promised to be a perfectly good fight.

Chapter Twenty-seven

Ben protested but to no avail. He tried to convince the EMTs and the paramedics that he'd escaped from the barn before conditions worsened and it all caught fire. They didn't listen. No one listened to him. But how could they in all the noise and confusion? And with him gagging and sputtering while straining to get a glimpse of the aftermath of the C.J./ cowboy bout? After being summarily hauled into the ambulance, a tube was shoved down his throat and an oxygen mask was clamped over his face while IV fluids dripped into his veins.

And this was just for openers. Once inside the calamitous ER, blood was drawn along with a lot of talk about blood gasses, oxygen saturation, noxious fumes and levels of CO_2. A saline solution was employed to mop up the blood and gunk around his knee. Then a surgeon went to town with a sharp forceps on the clusters of splinters. The area was sterilized, dressed and bandaged, and a toxoid tetanus shot added for good measure. Not to mention a series of antibiotic injections.

As if this weren't enough, he was carted off for a chest x-ray in a mausoleum-like chamber where he was outfitted with a lead vest and sandwiched between rectangular plates. While all this was going on, some disembodied voice ordered him to hold his breath as she toyed with her buzzers.

Eventually, he found himself inside a cramped cubicle rimmed by daiquiri-colored cinder blocks and a metal closet crammed in the corner. The open closet door afforded him a peek at his dank, sooty dress shirt and shredded khakis with its long, bloody rent where his right knee and thigh should be. There was no sign of his socks and tattered moccasins.

How and when they got him into the matching daiquiri-colored hospital gown, was anyone's guess. But here he was, in the middle of the night, lying on an elevated hospital bed adjacent to the occasional din of a bustling corridor. At the moment, there was an oxygen clip affixed to his nose and a lozenge for his parched throat that tasted as bad as the rest of him felt, which included his throbbing right leg and aching sore eyes. These sensations and the now-familiar drip of the IV combined to convince him all this was actually happening. He was grateful that the probes had ceased but unable to shake off the notion that his abused body had been dumped and abandoned.

His reeling mind began to blame it all on the carousel's painted pony and the faux Santa Ana that had blown Ray, Angelique and the cowboy into town. It was also the fault of the ramshackle back lot that, as a last hurrah, had drawn everyone in. Like mad, gun-toting Norma Desmond in *Sunset Boulevard:* hell-bent for a revival of her heyday no matter what the cost.

He also tried to lay blame on Dr. Seuss' book, a legacy culminating in Ben's last-chance quest to finally *arrive* in time for this birthday or else. (Once again, he conveniently blocked out the part about the not-so-good street and the directive to get out of town.)

All these discombobulated notions dissolved with the arrival of a perky nurse with a mole on her left cheek who barged in out of nowhere.

"How's my guy? Blood gasses look good, CO_2 level a bit high but let's see how you do. Objective is not to be admitted, right? Do not want to be a resident of this hospital. One blink for Yes, two blinks for No."

Though Ben didn't respond, she said, "That's the ticket. So how about some soothing drops? Good idea? You bet."

Still giving Ben no chance to reply, she tilted his head back and applied the drops with a cheery, "There you go, sweetie. Now for your temperature."

She stuck something in his ear but it was so fast he didn't feel it.

"Yes," said Perky, "holding steady. I'll be back in a bit with the nebulizer thingamabob. Cute as a button. Rolls in and out like a robot. Think of it as just hanging out here for a while. So, in a nutshell, no official admission and, before you know it, you can split."

"Split?" said Ben, realizing how hoarse his voice really was.

"Scoot, skip, scram. Listen, if you need anything, press the button. And don't pass out on me, you hear? Stay with it."

"Can't even doze off?"

"Not an option, heavens no. Not after what you've been through unless something's wrong."

"Like ... ?"

"Like you don't want to know."

"Blood pressure, right?"

"Which reminds me. The guy with the great bod and wild hair was asking about you. We sent him home for some shut-eye. Told him you're on a fast track long as you're not disturbed."

"Till when?"

"Morning at least. No close encounters, no worries is the order, understood?"

"Yes, ma'am."

"Repeat."

"Not to worry. And ..."

"Stay awake, calm and mellow."

"Mellow."

"That's it, sweetie. You got it."

With her departure came a break in the on-again off-again din from the nearby passing lanes. At first, Ben's dazed mind took in Perky's directive and considered what it would be like to be calm and mellow. To simply be: all banged up, under a cloud, letting others see to your needs.

This notion stayed with him till the din picked up again. Somewhere close by, a whiny voice filtered in. Ben assumed he was a floater. Nearby spots in the passing lane were a temporary stop for orderlies and their charges-- those lying on the gurneys, awaiting a signal to move on. At this point, the patients were free to exchange pleasantries, gripes, or lie quietly lost in thought. The whiner in the corridor, however, was not content to take any of this lying down.

"Somebody has got to do something about this," he snapped. "Think about it. All this crap about battered wives. What about battered husbands? Look at my arms, look at this face. I wait on her hand and foot. I do her bidding. And just because I ask where she's been and mention that her nice supper has been cold for hours, this is what I get. And this is not the first time. Oh no. Oh-oh-oh no."

"Too bad," rumbled the low voice that doubtless belonged to an orderly.

"Let me tell you, she was cute when I married her. But now she has become one tough mama."

During the time it took for this exchange to trail off, Ben wondered if the whiner on the gurney was rehearsing for a bit on a sitcom. In this town you never knew.

As more time passed, Ben came further out of the fuzzy abyss, his mind a bit sharper, grateful for the lull.

The lull, however, was short-lived as a new and louder voice drew closer and took the whiner's old spot. From the gist of his banter, Ben assumed the guy was a retired psychiatrist anxious to amuse the orderly or just plain anxious.

"Know what we say to each other? 'You're fine, how am I?'"

"Uh-huh," said the attendant.

"No good? Okay, here's another. The patient is lying on the couch. The analyst asks him to start from the beginning. The patient says, 'Okay, in the beginning I created the heavens and the earth.'"

"Uh-huh."

This hopeless routine really did it. No matter how hard the guy tried, he had nothing to show for it, not even a chuckle. Not unlike the prospect of everything Ben had been through amounting to zilch. Totally worthless.

Eyeing the closet, he was able to make out the scuffed edge of the cell phone protruding from his shirt pocket. Overhearing some problem here with reception due to the steel girders, he also recalled connecting with Portland information via the cowboy's speed dial. And other links, doubtless including one to Ray. Gazing up at the ceiling, his thoughts shifted to Molly and the hope she was safe and snug. Which led to a growing anxiety about when, exactly, C.J. would be popping in.

What followed was the abiding image of the cowboy yanking Molly's head back and flinging her around like a rag doll. He wished he'd rapped the guy over the head with something harder than Iris' can goods and done some real damage. It was all this unfinished business that got him going and kept him solidly in the here and now.

In the remaining hours before dawn, in between putting up with Perky's ministrations—inhaling the mist from the robot nebulizer, having his blood pressure and temperature checked, and other various and sundry interruptions—Ben spent the time sorting things out. With pen and a pad of paper provided by Perky, he made a list of provocative statements gleaned from C.J., Leo and the cowboy. He also noted the order of events, marked Molly down as eyewitness and victim, and added people who should be interrogated and/or anything else pertinent to an investigation. When he was finished, he had a concise summary all set to hand to C.J. and spare his vocal chords from any explanations. Plus he'd made Perky happy by limiting her frequent checks to see if he was still among the living.

But even so, second thoughts began to stream in. What did he know about any of this, save what he'd seen on the silver screen and TV and snatched from brainstorming sessions in a writers room? And of what value was a scribbled report from a fixture on the LAPD nuisance file?

If nothing else, he had to have C.J.'s assurance that the cowboy would be charged for arson and assault, was in some kind of holding pen, and eventually would be put away for good. And in some way Molly and her dubious dealings wouldn't come into play and she could rest easy.

This hoped-for outcome carried him through a meager breakfast of soothing Jell-O-like substances and the resumption of a heightened noise level throughout the ER.

Less than an hour later, the broad features and shaggy mane that belonged to Carlos Jose Rodriguez slipped into view.

"Oye, carnal, they told me to sleep because you were doing so good. And, calidad de gracias, I see they were right."

"Never mind. Let's have it."

"Let's have what?"

"Fill me in. Is the cowboy in shackles?"

"Whoa, tranquilizate. Olvidalo, man. Olvidalo."

"I *have* been sitting tight."

"Ai, Chihuahua. Que pasa contigo?"

"What's the matter? I'll tell you what's the matter ..." Ben pulled back. His throat couldn't take it.

C.J. rolled his eyes. He looked none the worse for his scuffle with the cowboy. Then again, he was one landing all the blows. In fact he looked totally refreshed, sporting a new shirt with a flaming red batik pattern to go with his smooth shave and a faint odor of lime cologne.

"Look, amigo, I only stopped by to see how you were, you know? But now when I hear that voice, so sore, we got to do something. Si, we must. When is your birthday? Tomorrow? Friday? Saturday? Ai, I must fix it with Chula. A little celebracion, not too big. But cold jars of tepache to wash down your throat. Something like that."

"Will you quit messing around?"

"Who's messing? Oh, and la musica of course. And some woman to get those juices flowing. Some chaparrita. No, you need two chaparritas after all this time."

Raising his hands, Ben said, "Knock it off."

"Why?" said C.J., obviously in one of his giddy moods. "We could start with cumbia and a beat like a clip-clopping horse. Then we segue to rancheros, corridos and nortenas. You hear that? *Segue* another word you gave me. I am so *fluent,* no?"

"No."

"Okay, you do not like my idea? Tell me your wish and I will honor it."

"Guess."

"Ah, you want to know. I will tell you. This cowboy of yours is in a holding cell."

"Great."

"Si. I go check with my Chicano troublemakers now. Two who are still recovering. I will show the cowboy's photo, take statements and wipe the smile from his face. Es loco. He has damage to his back and ribs and is coughing. But will accept nada, not even ask for his rights. Only points a finger at me. Like we are compadres. He points, smiles and rolls over on his cot."

"Is that it?"

"What?"

"Why you finally showed up last night? An outside chance for a little revenge?"

"Hey, he was clutching at you, I save your ass."

"And why was he clutching? Why was I there waiting for you?"

"Okay, I take my time. Because I say for you to keep out of trouble. But also tell Chula for you to keep your eyes open. And now you are here, sick, doliente, herido."

C.J. swaggered around not about to actually admit he was at fault.

"Si, okay. For you, for me I check on my two bandoleros and come right back."

"How soon?"

"One hour."

"And promise to see it through: arson, assault--the works." Waving his notes in the air, Ben said, "There's a lot more to this, C.J."

"Si, bueno. Tranquilizate."

"I mean it."

"Yo comprendo. Rest your throat, rest your brain. I come right back."

It would be more than an hour, Ben knew that. But at least he had made contact and would rouse C.J. to see to Molly and a lot more.

In the meantime, Perky took Ben off everything except the lozenges and eye drops. She even gave him permission to doze off and told him he might be able to split by late afternoon. That is, if he could get a relative to deliver some decent clothes. Which meant Iris. Someone Ben couldn't bear to think about after letting her down vis-à-vis her jungle mate Leo Orlov. Who, thanks to Ben, was now more manic than ever, given the immediate threat of deportation hanging over his head. Not to mention in trouble with Ray.

Not to mention the fallout from the whole subterfuge and scam.

Nevertheless, grogginess overtook all of these concerns. Unable to keep his eyes open a moment longer, he soon gave in and dozed off for a good thirty minutes.

He would have slept longer were it not for the arrival of the inimitable Mrs. Melnick. Barging through the fluttering partition with her squat body percolating beneath her tangerine muumuu, she unleashed her honking bark and woke Ben up.

"Not to worry," said Mrs. Melnick. "I told them I was a relative." Brandishing an *L.A. Times* she went on as if this were a running conversation. "Beautiful. Here's you above the fold and a hint of suspicious findings. So obviously you know what this means. Lucky you, crafty me."

Ben was still barely opening his sore eyes when she flashed the front page a second time right in his face. There he was, in the foreground with the EMTs lifting him on the stretcher and the billowing smoke in the background. The caption read: *This Is Not A Simulation*. The chances of Mrs. Melnick caring about his health were nil, but he did want to know where she was going with this.

Rambling on full tilt, Mrs. Melnick said, "Can you stand it? All these years a desert and now a fountain gushes. Anyways, I get a hold of Budd, my contact on *The Tonight Show* and said, 'What about Howie as not only the world's youngest oldest virgin but also a tie-in with an unlikely hero? In the papers and all over TV is Howie's sidekick, Ben. Another one with no sex life. Too pure like Howie and a throwback to Mickey Rooney and Judy Garland. Now who knows what you were doing there, Benjamin, but we can spin this sucker. How about 'They're one in a million, girls. Pure as the driven snow'? We'll get all kinds of broads worked up."

Ben strained to sit upright.

"Hey, Mr. Prine, are you getting my drift? I promised as soon as Howie's comet blasted off I would let you ride on his tail. So, am I coming through or what?"

Ben managed a hoarse, "Mrs. Melnick ..." but that was all.

"Shh, don't thank me and not to worry. I heard from Iris. Well not exactly heard, but when she cut me off, I knew. Whatever you had going, you blew it. So what? Misfortunes, who needs them? Spin City, like I said. By the way, Howie loves it. Always wanted to work with you since day one."

"Look, Mrs. Melnick ..."

"No no no, save your energy. But what's with the voice? Never mind, we can use it. Look, gotta run. Budd says there's a chance they can work us in tomorrow night due to multi cancellations from the A and B list, and the fact this back lot fire thing is so hot, no pun intended."

When Ben shook his head in disbelief while dabbing his sore eyelids, Mrs. Melnick honked a little louder. "You do know Budd, right? Oliver's significant other. I mentioned, I know I did. Oh, this is so great. And, before I forget, Oliver'll be back sometime after six. So you'd better call. Even though you're a mess, his Prelude is fine, tell him. Maybe get someone to drive it by, keep everything smooth like butter so there's no glitch."

"Look, Mrs. Melnick," said Ben, attempting to raise his voice.

"Shh, I said, save your strength. Read it and gloat and let me take care of the rest." She tossed the paper in his lap and barged out even faster than she'd barged in.

In her wake, Ben scanned the lead story as best he could. He wondered if Molly had seen it. Or caught the local news on Aunt June's TV? Was Molly even up yet, for that matter? Or still too scared to go out into the open?

Ben pressed the button. With a little effort, he managed to induce Perky to ring Aunt June's number. However, if no one picked up, Perky was not to leave a message on the machine. (What would June think when she returned? She would know Ben had broken his promise and let some footloose female into her sealed fortress.)

He sucked on another lozenge and awaited Perky's return. Alas, upon reentering all she could say was, "Sorry, sweetie, no answer."

By ten-thirty, Ben's anxiety level had risen another notch. Apart from his defining moment as a failure, nothing was clear, nothing was resolved. And of all the issues, the one constant was a concern over Molly's fate; a fear the psycho cowboy would somehow get out on bail and be on the loose. Disregarding any effect on his blood pressure, Ben anxiously awaited C.J.'s return.

Some twenty or so minutes later, he got his wish. However, C.J.'s agitation gave off a direct signal things hadn't gone as planned.

"What's wrong?" said Ben, as C.J. rapped his knuckles against the metal closet.

Letting up on the closet, C.J. said, "My boys they will not finger him. They say, Si, he did run them over. But if they tell, their companeros will come down hard on them. The barrio will come down hard on them because I am still a cop. Eso no lo creo."

"Eso no lo creo," C.J. repeated even louder. "I go back to the holding cell, the cowboy holding his ribs. And he says to me, 'Let me know when you are ready to deal. Because if I go down, you go down.' Still he has not talked to anybody. Nobody will talk to anybody. Dios mio, por favor."

C.J. used the side of his hand to abuse the tinny closet this time. "Eso no lo creo. Why does this cowboy look for me yesterday? Why does he smile and say these things?"

"I've been trying to tell you," said Ben, his voice a bit stronger.

"Hey, no me hagas esas jaladas."

"I am not jerking you around. Can you speak English?"

"Si. Como no? Advise me, mister Hollywood sell-out writer. What isn't there, you see. What is there, you don't see. What you know about anything?"

"I know when on duty, you have to follow-up leads."

"Ai, now he knows deployment periods. He knows ten hour shifts for four days. He knows about detaining and charging. You see, this Ben and I are the true and real mismatched cops."

"Ask me, dammit. Swallow your pendejo pride and ask me."

"Pendejo? You call me an idiot? You call me names?"

Perky stuck her head in and asked if there was some problem. She admonished C.J., declared in no uncertain terms that Ben needed absolute peace and quiet, smiled in that big-sisterly way of hers and scurried off.

C.J. moved away from the closet and said, "Okay, you got leads, mi consejero, my trusted advisor? Let me hear them."

Cutting it short for the sake of his throat, Ben told him the cowboy thinks C.J. is dirty. Pointing to his hanging, soiled dress shirt, Ben added that the cowboy came back for his cell phone because it contains incriminating, unlisted speed-dial numbers. Doubtless including one to Laurel Canyon to a mob guy named Ray who, also doubtless, linked a certain Pepe from the gym and his crew with a double cross over the sacks."

"Pepe from the gym?"

"Yes."

"A double cross over the sacks?"

"Yes."

"No," said C.J. "I take the sacks to the lockup."

"Tell that to the cowboy. Tell that to beak-nose Ray."

"Eso no lo creo."

"Will you stop saying that?" Ben popped another lozenge in his mouth and grabbed his homework. "Just check out my notes, will you? You need to do this. You have to do this."

"Where you get these ideas? What you know I need or have to do?"

"I know your mom is a good woman and your dad plays a sweet cornet. I know you can't shy away from the big breakers no matter how far out. I know you can't walk away from this. Especially 'cause you don't know what those sacks contain."

It may have been the words, it may have been the croak in Ben's voice. At any rate, C.J. snatched up the pieces of paper and sifted through them. When he questioned the part about the gun, Ben showed him the newspaper and the fire marshal's statement.

"Call and ask him," said Ben. "In the oil drum with the empty clip. Ask about the little wooden matches, the bullet holes in the barn doors. If it doesn't jibe, if the gun isn't registered or something, then forget about it. Forget the whole thing."

"I need to run this by my supervisor."

"So do it."

"So first I must read these words again. So first I need some caffeine or something."

He was gone only a few minutes. He returned complaining that he couldn't find a coffee machine anywhere. "Too many pieces," C.J. went on. "Not for your mind, a man who lives out of one suitcase, mixed up with Leo Orlov, crazy movie deals and smoking barns. My feet are on the ground, you know?"

Continuing to talk himself into it, C.J. tapped on Ben's notes as hard as he'd rapped on the closet. "All this maldito crap would have to be documented ... verified."

He stalled a while longer tapping on the closet door to a cumbia beat, stuck his head in the closet and retrieved the cell phone. "Hey, we got to get you some clothes, man. Somebody got to get you some clothes."

"Goodbye."

"Wait. This Ray, this could-be el jefe. He would want the sacks back you say? And this muchacha Molly. She can corroborate? She is not raro, not extrano, not a daydreamer like you?"

"Leave her out of it."

"Why? Because you are crazy for her and can not see straight?"

"I said, leave her be."

C.J. shook his head, added the newspaper to the collection and said, "I want you to swear esto es verdad."

For what it was worth, Ben raised his hand to the ceiling and swore it was all true.

"Remember, this is talvez. Maybe. The biggest *maybe* even you can imagine."

With that exit line, C.J. cut through the fluttering partition.

Left alone with only the static of wheeling gurneys and muffled voices in the corridor, Ben knew by telling C.J. to forget about Molly, C.J. might very well do just the opposite--flush Molly out, ask her to corroborate, even detain her. Giving Ben at least half a chance to see her again.

Chapter Twenty-eight

It was the third visit that morning to the holding cell that set C.J. in motion. This time the cowboy was up and about--bracing his back and rubbing his chest and ribs while, at the same time, giving C.J. a hard, cold look.

"About time," said the cowboy. "Okay, let's get it on."

"Oh?" said C.J., peering through the bars, talking over the usual mockery and swearing from the other four inmates. "You ready to talk?"

As if they were fellow conspirators, the cowboy shuffled forward till they were inches apart. "Cut the crap, Pepe. You had no business bein' there last night. Except to beat me to the goods."

"Oh?" C.J., repeated, taking his lead from the cowboy, staying just as cool. "And you had legitimate business there?"

"Ask Ray Shine. Ask the producer's woman."

"What producer?"

"I said cut the crap. Your cop buddies are itchin' for a statement. And that's what they're gonna get. Unless."

"Unless what?"

The cowboy coughed a few times into the back of his hand and said, "Unless you come through, honcho. Otherwise you and your little Hispanic creeps are all goin' down."

C.J. felt the muscles tighten around the back of his neck but kept on with the charade. "And that is what you think?"

"That's what I know."

"And you feel nothing? Not for what you did to them?"

The cowboy smirked, broke into a hacking laugh, dug his hands into his Levi jacket and came up empty. "I thought we were talkin' business."

"Ah, si. And what, my friend, do you offer?"

"Hook you up with the Outfit. Get you a share of the finder's fee. Plus you avoid a hassle for what you pulled last night. And you get to keep your cover."

"And this is it?"

"Look, I'm gonna walk. My way, you get some coin and don't have to watch your back. Options. I'm givin' you options."

Pretending to think it over, C.J. finally said, "I don't know. This is very difficult. Very difficult proposition."

"Easy. You assaulted me. I'm not gonna press charges. Any way you look at it, you're better off."

"And the barn, the smoke, the fire. What happened to this Ben and this girl?"

"Who knows? Who gives a goddamn?"

"I see. I will have to think about it."

"You will not think about it, wet back. You will spring me. I've rested up and I want out of this cage."

It was hard to resist reaching through the bars and grabbing this sadistic gringo by the neck. But C.J. burned some of the anger off by turning on his heels and taking the adjacent flight of stairs in half the time.

His supervisor was a standard-issue hard-nose. He had once been a Marine recruitment poster boy and was featured leading a crack drill team in the opening credits of a major motion picture. As expected, he'd kept the short haircut and trim body. In this same way, his speech was clipped, his suit neatly pressed, shoes shined, tie bright but not flashy. He insisted on being called Mac in deference to his glory days as a signal-caller at USC. And, again as might be expected, his main concern was image. Keeping a low profile, insisting the Hollywood Division hold the line so that nothing worrisome spooked the tourists. That recent ABC special on violence and the LAPD was about another world miles to the east. And his division's clean bill of health had better stay that way. Due to continuing Federal oversight, every move Mac's officers made was monitored.

"Well?" said Mac, sitting upright in his ice blue, air-conditioned office, all ten fingertips touching indicating rapt attention. "Did you play it the way I said? No Spanish, no emotion?"

"Yes."

"And?"

"This time he spoke to me."

"You see? What did I tell you?"

"Yes, but—"

"No buts. My understanding, Rodriguez, is that you people are brought up to be polite. It's only the loose cannons, the uneducated macho types that go off half-cocked."

C.J. shrugged. It was the fastest way to get past Mac's ignorance.

Palms down in his regulation-Corps pose, Mac went on. "Right. Now let me give you a heads-up. See if you can get something on this guy, you follow? In case somebody from the media gets wind of a muscular Latino beating up some civilian last night. That way we can spin it and run this character out of town. Or, if you get on to something, we can set up a file with eventual certificates of merit all around. But that would mean we'd have to increase the caseloads."

Fingertips touching again, Mac carried on. It took C.J. a good fifteen minutes to get a word in edgewise. To finally relay his exchange with the cowboy and the leads C.J. obtained from the smoke inhalation victim who wished to remain anonymous.

Before agreeing or disagreeing, Mac went into another song and dance. "All told, best play, Rodriguez, is keep the status quo. Five-and-dime burglaries and identity thefts you don't hear about. It's just entertainment, celebrity sightings —nothing sticking out or lingering. It's all hype, like that picture in the paper today."

For some reason Mac didn't get the connection between the newspaper photo and the smoke inhalation victim, which was just as well. C.J. just kept nodding, waiting him out. What he got was not what he wanted but better than nothing. He had half a shift to look into things. But he was not to holster his Smith and Wesson service weapon onto his ankle, blow his cover, or so much as ruffle a hair on this Ray from Vegas' head. Think of it as a fishing expedition, nothing more.

"But always keep in mind," Mac added, tapping his index finger on the stainless steel desk, "you are still on loan. I can always ship you back."

C.J. wanted to say that would be fine. He wanted to say he only accepted this posting because Chula couldn't take the gang wars and constant danger. The compromise was, he would not give up on his boys and would make sure they didn't shave their heads and die in a shootout before they were sixteen. He wanted to say all this, but kept it to himself.

"Also keep in mind," Mac said, coming to a close, "truth is, I'd hate to lose you. You're a great type. You keep fit and are one beautiful surfer."

Brushing off the compliments, C.J. said, "So what you are saying is, I have five hours to get somewhere but you are not counting on it. If the cowboy walks and makes no waves, that is fine with you. If he walks and does make waves, it is my ass."

"Something like that." Mac leaned back in his adjustable leather chair, hands clasped behind his neck. "Except, if it does turn out there was a weapon in the oil drum. If so, and other things turn up and we sit on our heels, then it's my ass. So be thorough while you're making no waves."

Mac rose from his chair and ushered C.J. out of his office. "Say, I hear you drilled the guy with a combo of jabs and a wicked right cross. What about a demo some time? Set up a ring, a decent opponent and afterwards, drinks all around."

C.J. let that one pass.

As an afterthought, Mac said, "Now you sure you got this all straight?"

"I must play it smart."

"Attaboy, Rodriguez. You got it."

C.J. hightailed it out of the station, donned his midnight-blue shirt-jacket with the mesh pockets, got what he needed out of his glove department and went to work. For the first time in a long time, he started his shift on the loose. His easygoing Korean partner would have go it alone:

snapping pictures of the former Grauman's Chinese and the handprints of the stars of yesterday; posing as a long lost tourist begging to have his money belt stolen and relieved of his passport. Poor Chan Ho Choo would miss fooling around with his flashy Mexican sidekick; the one with the wild hair who was even better at seeming lost and unable to speak a word of English.

Trying his luck as he tooled down Sunset into the stop-and-go, C.J. undid the flap on his top pocket, pulled out the cowboy's cell phone and hit the second speed dial. The early afternoon sun glinted through the brownish haze as he pulled his visor lower and waited through the beeps for somebody to pick up.

"Yeah?" the nasal voice droned over the howl of alternative rock in the background. "That you? What's the frickin' story here?"

"I got what you want," C.J. said over the noise. "I am coming by."

"Who is this? What happened to--?"

"You say no, I will turn around."

Hearing nothing, C.J. hung up and took a right heading up Laurel Canyon Boulevard. Thinking it was true; this cowboy, this cabron culero who ran over his boys and sent Ben to the E.R. could walk. Why? Because he, C.J. Rodriguez, did take his sweet time answering Ben's call for help. Because it was late and he and Chula were about to make love. Also, Ben could be imagining like always. And even if what he was saying—this cowboy had done things and driven away—Ben should file a complaint. It was only after he remembered he made Ben swear never to mention anything to do with a movie studio. So to call him, Ben must have been desesperado.

With this idea that would not go away, he'd gunned his supercharged six-speed Mustang and drove off. And only when he'd found no one manning the gate and smoke rising that he banged his horn. He'd arrived too late, yes, but just in time to give this cowboy some of what was coming to him. Now, the least he could do was to finish it, to make things right. Make it right for Ben, like he asked, and for C.J.'s own banda de locos, his Los Cobras clique. Make it right all way round.

Turning west onto Wonderland Avenue, C.J. settled on a simple plan. Connect enough dots to keep the cowboy under custody. Also see what spills over and how far this thing goes.

Snapping up the cell phone again, he hit the first number. It brought nothing, only an answering machine. The second and third try produced the same. On the fourth try, a low gravelly voice picked up, the kind you hear watching old gringo Westerns.

"What the hell, Deacon?"

C.J. drove on saying nothing.

"Come on, I got caller ID, I know it's you. You blew it, right? And find yourself between the ol' rock and a hard place."

Trying to imitate the cowboy's dry voice without giving himself away, C.J. faked a cough and said, "Uh-huh."

"Tell you what. Since you crossed me, I've half a mind to feed you to that accountant whose leg you busted. Oh, yeah, I found out all about that. And he's got pneumonia to boot. So, you call this number again and I'll put him on to you. Give anyone and everyone an anonymous tip where to find your sorry ass. You wanted to go it alone, well, pard, you got it. You are alone."

A sharp click and the old rancher was gone. C.J. pulled over, snatched out his mini-recorder, dictated some notes and squeezed back into the traffic. If nothing else, the cowboy now had a first name. And more than that. The accountant was not just another loco nuisance caller. He was the cowboy's victim numero three.

After a few minutes wait, this skinny Ray with the beak, blue goggles and silver pajamas, returned through the metal-mesh curtain. He was clutching a wire cutter and a handful of stainless steel strings. These he tossed by the dented Fender Stratocaster on the gaming table.

"Unzip that jacket thing all the way," said Ray, speaking through his nose. "How do I know you're not hiding a wire? The way things are shaking out, you could be working for anybody."

Going along to get things rolling, C.J. unzipped his shirt jacket, flung it open to reveal his bare skin and zipped it back halfway.

"That's just for openers, man. You need to know something," Ray said as he unwound the old strings off the posts. "And that something is this. True players are those who no one sees coming. But the downside is, they can screw you over faster than anybody."

"Like this Deacon fellow, this cowboy."

Ray didn't answer. He yanked at a thick string that wouldn't budge from the machine head, snipped it and tugged with the snub nose of the cutters.

C.J. drifted back to the aluminum cart in the near corner, pulled out the carafe and poured himself a cup of strong, hot coffee. While drinking it down, he realized there was no way he was going to bandy words with a toucan-nosed hustler with Vegas plates. Especially one who could abuse a white satin-lacquer Stratocaster. Simple truth, C.J. did not have fast enough English. He could not even bandy words with that mensa Angelique. He could still see her through the sliding glass door, hunched over on the bamboo-screened porch, scribbling. Wearing that puta lace bathrobe that covered up nothing; a lit cigarette dangling from her lipstick mouth. His only chance was to shake up this Ray, force a slip of the tongue and be gone.

"I see now," said C.J., setting down his cup, "this was a mistake. You are a person who breaks guitars and loses things. You are a poor judge of people who hired this Deacon."

"Oh yeah?" said Ray, flinging bits of guitar strings on the white Terrazzo floor. "If you weren't stuck in your barrio, if you hit the Vegas Strip and mentioned my name, mentioned Ray Shine, you'd eat those words. What I am saying is this. Ask anybody. Check the new slots at Bellagio, the pings and clinks that sound like cash falling. Check out the special effects that pull 'em in deeper and deeper, from quarters to dollars, dollars to five dollars, ba-da-bing ba-da-bing. My idea. The shadow-dancing hotties. The bimbos in the sinking pirate ship outside the fabulous —"

"Which has mierda to do with this business." Moving directly across from Ray at the edge of the gaming table, C.J. said, "This is about what I got and you want. This is about gran momento distribution."

"This is about a shakedown, you mean." Chewing on his tongue, Ray tried to thread the new strings, lining the first one through the chrome bridge to the headstock, through the hole in the machine head, looping it back underneath and tight against the post.

"Oye, cabron, you want to talk or play with your strings?"

"If I see some proof you took Deke out, plus got your hands on what I'm frickin' missing here."

C.J. pulled the Velcro-bound flap of his lower left jacket pocket, produced Deke's cell phone and slapped it on the plush-green felt table.

"Yeah, so, all right," said Ray, swearing at himself for wrapping the string over itself and jamming the machine head. "So okay, that's how you got my number."

"That is correct. Now my turn." Taking a guess, C.J. said, "Why do you send this Deacon with a gun?"

Twisting one of the knobs so hard his pinched face turned red, Ray said, "Listen, whatever he did to your Mexican losers is on his head. What he did at the frickin' studio last night is on his head. My play, my only play is the front. I had it in place. I had it in place good."

"You mean some maldito movie thing."

Ripping the string out of the post and starting over, Ray said, "Hold it. Whose shot is this? Let's see a sample or we got no business and I got no use for you or any of you Chicanos."

Still holding his temper and assuming Ray Shine had never laid eyes on the shipment, C.J. casually lifted the flap of a middle pocket, dug inside and rolled out a few fat pink-and-white capsules. Ray peeped under his blue goggles, examined them carefully, slipped them in a drawer under the side padding and said, "Yeah, pink and white, it figures. So all right, so now we're talking."

"Now I am talking. I want to know if you know how this is done."

"Right," said Ray, securing the string correctly this
time, plugging the guitar into a set of Super Reverb amps
and trying to tune it. "You want the name of the lab in
Toronto too? And how about how the goods travel down the
coast? Which leaves me where? Buried in the tar pits
under La Brea, that's where."

Making a twanging sound that would hurt anyone's
eardrums and twisting away, Ray strained to find an A,
fingering a fret on the lowest string.

Yanking out the drawer and retrieving the capsules,
C.J. yelled, "Then forget it. Es una perdida mi tiempo!"

Ray dropped the guitar. "What did you say?"

Hurrying toward the sliding glass door, C.J. yelled, "A
waste of my stinking time!"

Ray scurried in front of C.J. C.J. picked him up by his
bony elbows, swung him around in the air and set him
down on the gaming table as if he were a pesky child.

"Wait," said Ray, sliding back to the floor, tugging on
the back of C.J.'s shirt jacket. "You don't get what is riding
on this. Nerds horning-in strictly legal, palaces zotzed with
a wrecking ball, everything on shaky ground."

Brushing Ray aside, C.J. repeated, "Es una perdida mi
tiempo."

"Listen to me, will you? If you don't cough up my
collateral, there is no front, the pipeline is blown and I am
dead in this town, dead in Vegas, dead on this planet. I am
talking whacked."

"Then what is your proposition?"

Ray walked back to the table, located a thick rubber
band and began stretching and twirling it around his
hand. "Okay, we go back to square one. I will tell Leo we
got Pepe under wraps. No more cowboys, no more hired
guns. Just us three amigos."

"Leo? Orlov from the gym?"

"From the gym, from Odessa, from under a rock."

"He launders, si? This I can count on."

"Gets the front money and produces. But, seeing how
things have taken another U-turn, no more hack
screenwriter and whoever was running him. We go back to
the drawing board. You getting this?"

C.J. shook his head.

"No matter. Look, all you gotta do is fork over the high-jacked goods, so Leo cashes in, so his backers are no more the wiser."

"His backers?"

"Banks in Eastern Europe or something—who knows? The point is, Starshine's dummy operation looks solid and it's nothin' for you to worry your head."

"I see."

"It don't matter what you see. The smoky barn thing blows over, you get your cut, the front—whatever--gets back on track. That's it!"

C.J. stared at this cowering idiota and didn't know how to answer. By force of habit he ran his finger across the cross-hatched threads of the other pocket. With nothing better to say, he came up with this. "You go back to your drawing board. You come up with something much better."

"What are you saying?"

"I am saying, you will be called."

"When?"

"In a very few hours."

"Sooner. Much sooner. I can't take no more frickin' waiting."

"Lo siento, I am sorry. It is complicated. I must nail this down, comprende?"

Talking to himself again, Ray went back to his battle with the strings to find an A. Then cried out, "You have to cut a deal with me. You have to!"

C.J. slipped out through the glass doors and the sun porch, annoyed at himself for not sticking strictly to English. Then kept going past the bleached blond and the pool area.

She caught up with him a few yards before the high wooden gate leading out to the drive. Ordinarily he would have ignored her and kept going. There was something about her type--hard body, chewing gun, smoky cigarette butt between her fingers. But this time he noticed a look in her eyes and bruises on her face.

"What's the rush?" she said. "What happened? How'd it go?"

"Not good. People do not know what they are doing."

Hesitating, unsure whether to waste time with this ridiculo pop singer, C.J. reached for the latch.

"Hold it, like don't judge it by Ray."

"Oh?"

"You need reassurance? I mean, if it's like really important ..."

"I get this from you?"

"Who else?"

"And why would you give me reassurance?"

"'Cause I'm goin' outta my skull. 'Cause after my concert gigs tanked, I thought I had a ticket back. My own reality show on cable: *Sex Kitten Chronicles*. My own brand of breath mints and body-bath. An exercise video, a Christmas album for Burger King. And then they smack me with 'You're not girly enough'." For emphasis, she dropped the cigarette butt on the pink cement and mashed it with the heel of her sandals.

With nothing to lose, C.J. said, "So what are you that I should stand here and listen?"

"The only one who knows the score," she said, raising her voice over the racket Ray's tuning was making through the open sliding glass door.

"You know the score? I deal with you?"

"You bet your butt."

Pulling out the capsules from the middle pocket, C.J. said, "If this is so, tell me what are these?"

"What are you, kidding? I knew it, I knew it. You have no idea what you got hold of, do you?" She snatched one of the capsules and held it up high. "They're my very own Starshine special," she announced over the noise. "*Stardust*. My recreational drug, my design."

"And what is so special?"

"Euphoria, no more chronic fatigue. I am talking long-acting time-released thingamabobs."

Goading her on, C.J. rolled his eyes and reached for the latch again as the noise subsided.

"All right, all right. It's a 'unique combo of mescaline, amphetamines, ecstasy and synthetics that sets you rolling and never lets you down'." She said this as if answering an easy question on a quiz show. Instead of a drum roll, her answer was greeted by another blast from Ray's dented guitar.

"So," said Angelique, "you satisfied? You gonna fork over the shipment so's I can get back in gear?"

Pushing his luck, C.J. said, "Perhaps. But I would like also to know about this Molly person."

"What is that, a joke? Supposed to deliver like always, no questions asked. Then comes up with this pigeon idea. Can you believe it?"

"She is in on this operation?"

"She is in on nothing. Wants a free ride, break into movies—you know the type. But when push comes to shove, she gets cold feet, blows me off. That is so lame. I mean, what is this? Even that tall dude never got back to me."

Angelique threw her head back, popped the capsule in her mouth and swallowed. Then dug into her flimsy robe, chomped faster on her wad of gum and came up with a bent cigarette. "Hey, you got a lighter or something?"

"I do not smoke."

"Jeez, at least the tall dude had a box of matches."

Remembering Ben's story, C.J. couldn't help smiling.

"So," said Angelique, screwing up her face, "I say, hell with it, right? Hell with everybody and let's get this show on the road."

"But right now I must go." For the third time C.J. reached for the latch.

"What are you, crazy? You got to hear the smoke screen." Angelique flipped the bent cigarette into a hibiscus bush. Ray's electric guitar blasts resumed, sounding more and more like a jackhammer.

Angelique looked up into the brownish haze as if for divine inspiration, took a deep breath and said, "It's a kick-ass iPad video game for chicks. Gillian's idea."

The name Gillian rang a bell but, for now, he let it go.

"You listening?"

"I am listening," C.J. said, ready to cut her off but curious about the front Ray Shine had been talking about.

"The gamer becomes me, naturally. And there's lots of puzzles to solve. She has a hot bod like me, only better like before. And, hey, you got a hot bod too. You could be cloned-in for a bad guy or something. Ooh, awesome. Wait till I tell Leo."

"Orlov? The one who is in this with your boyfriend?"

"Boyfriend?"

"Ray."

"Oh, puh-lease. I am the star in Starshine. That scumbag is my business manager."

"But he is not happy. He is looking for a new way to hide."

"He is looking for a knuckle sandwich. I should've said former business manager. He has had it, he is through. Plus, if you see her, tell miss Molly, Who needs you? Same goes for the cowboy. Same goes for everybody who botched it. That was just a trial whatchamacallit."

"Balloon?"

"Righty-O, muchacho. Yeah yeah, wait, wait, it's coming to me. 'Stead of drug dealing on the side, you will cut way down on the cop thing and throw in with me. 'Cause, hunky, you'll be the draw, the candy that sucks the babes in. Hey hey, yeah yeah. And right after this hot-bod thing goes viral—I am jig-sawing myself back in with no bitchin' stand-in-- we follow with the chick-flick and ... oh my God, my gosh, my golly."

As her eyes started to cross, she blurted out for all the world to hear, "Hey there then now, my Stardust is kickin' in! Top of the world, Zorro! Top of the world!"

The jackhammer noise suddenly quit. Ray came tearing through the bamboo curtain demanding to know what she was blabbing about. Was she giving away more of her calling cards, "screwing him over with Pepe?"

Ray was on top of them before C.J. had a chance to slip away. Ray raised a fist aimed at C.J., thought better of it and shook Angelique so hard, her see-through robe flipped open revealing everything. C.J. backed out past the high wooden gate as she slapped Ray across the face, ordering Ray to get his bony ass off her property before she called the cops.

"Dios mio," said C.J. walking away. "The police? Que pasa?"

It began to dawn on him how many spin-offs there were. Drug trafficking. The front (unknown to too-hungry

Ben), banked by a blanqueo, an international laundering de dinero. This front up to its ears in fraud and cooking the books. Then, on the head of the cowboy, there was arson and many counts of assault. When you factor in all the links--cartels, the overseas banks and that Vegas crime syndicate ...

He tried not to get ahead of himself but it was hard to resist. He could see his life so different. No more the payaso on loan on the Hollywood tourist beat. A big promotion was in store for him, certificates of merit, his finger in a muy grande case load. The extra money to his mother for a dress shop in Sonora, and for him and Chula to start a new life.

Walking briskly alongside the curving, walled drive, C.J.'s face broke into a wider grin. Snapping his fingers to a cumbia beat, he made his way down to his flashy Mustang. What a break this was. Faster better English had not been necessary with those two idiota. What's more, even the few words of Spanish helped do the job.

Approaching the bottom of the drive, he poked a finger through the open weave of the lower pocket and shut the micro recorder off.

Returning to the stop-and-go on his way back to West Hollywood, he settled on a last gambit before handing over his findings. In the meantime, nearing Sunset, he made a call to the station. He learned from the desk sergeant that the cowboy's property bag contained two little boxes of wooden matches from a Durango Trading Post. No I.D., nothing else that would tell you who he was.

Swinging down Fairfax, he made another call. In short order, the fire chief's assistant told him used wooden matches were found on the livery stable floor and in different places around the loft, along with a charred handgun and an empty clip at the bottom of an oil drum. And one more thing: bullet casings on the plank flooring and bullet holes in the barn doors. The casings, clip and handgun had been turned over to Mac, C.J.'s super.

As C.J. reached Melrose, he knew he was much closer to nailing this Deacon but good.

Following another of Ben's leads, C.J. drove around the back of the studio till he spotted a parked mid-sized Ford, metallic-beige with rental plates.

After contacting Hertz at LAX, he got out some white cotton gloves and an evidence bag, got in through the unlocked driver's side and began poking around. When the first try got him nowhere, he took a timeout. With nothing better to do, he checked out what was going on close by. He found trucks grinding in an out of a back alley; workmen busy plastering, fitting in new glass and dragging panels of sheetrock. That was all. No tie-ins.

Back to the rental car. Working slowly and patiently, he came upon a spare magazine clip for a Walther handgun carefully hidden beneath the floor padding under the passenger seat-adjuster. He placed it into the evidence bag and zipped it shut.

Returning to his own car, he made two more calls. In twenty minutes time he was told two more things: The Ford was rented to Deacon James; a just-reported stolen Walther handgun was registered to Ray Shine, both residents of Las Vegas.

Next, C.J. popped the lid of the trunk. Unzipping the overnight bag he came across a silver attaché case, handwritten notes on a notepad and another cell, this one a smartphone with a bunch of messages. Most telling were voice mails from the SEC and the DEA. It seems the Feds had been trying to reach Elton Frick, the one sending crank calls to police stations in Hollywood, Vegas and San Francisco. This was his phone. They were not crank calls. They were legitimate.

Out came C.J.'s mini-recorder. As he added to his collection of leads and tangibles, he connected more dots and filled in the blanks about this Elton Frick. From the way things looked, the Feds were trying to reach this Frick hombre, as if Frick still had this cell but was afraid to answer. The latest message told Frick it was okay. They now knew he'd had a fever, loco in the cabeza when he made those calls. Up in some hunting and fishing lodge, suffering from a badly swollen ankle and pneumonia when he was found a day or so later near a mountain lake. Also nearsighted without his glasses to make things even worse.

How they'd traced the calls and why some agent was on his way this morning to a spot west of Montana's Glacier National Park was beyond C.J.'s imagination. Somehow it all figured and added to the charges the cowboy was up against. The testimony of the accountant alone was enough to do him in. All C.J. could do was submit his discoveries and let those higher up take it from here.

Checking back once more at the station, he got word that the cowboy had started banging a stool against the bars demanding to be turned loose. Pretty soon the other guys in the holding cell had to restrain him. It reminded C.J. of the time some hombre tried to keep a wild coyote. First the coyote gave him the evil eye, then it tore open the pen, then it howled and bayed so much they had to come and put it away.

"Dios mio," C.J. muttered. "First Frick, now the cowboy is going loco. What next? Lo que mas puede pasar?"

As the early afternoon wore on, C.J. became aware it had become very quiet. Returning to the narrow alley, curious as to why the cowboy had chosen this very spot to park his car, he saw that the workmen had quit. Then, moments later, he heard a squeak and a clang.

Presently, a muchacha bonita slipped through a hidden opening in the security fence. She was dragging what looked like a pigeon coop with handles. So busy she didn't look where she was going, tripped and stumbled but kept going and rushed down the alley heading toward the back of the building site. C.J. couldn't help thinking of the young women he'd seen many times since his Hollywood posting. Hopeful at first with that entusiasma look in the eye. But, like now, hurrying to cut their losses and leave it all behind.

Chapter Twenty-nine

Stuck in his daiquiri cubicle a while longer, Ben faked a smile and listened to Perky go on about what a lucky guy he was. She raved about the fact that in less than fifteen hours he had gone from smoke inhalation victim to a dude about to rejoin the living. He'd passed the latest battery of tests with flying colors and, like a tooth fairy, some lady had dropped off a change of clothes and a battered but still serviceable suitcase to boot.

"One lucky guy," Perky repeated, giving him a thumbs up.

Offering another fake smile, Ben sat up a bit straighter on the remade bed, wondering who the next floater would be. He also wondered how he would deal with Oliver's Prelude which was still in limbo at the Honda place. Good thing, of course, that Oliver didn't drive. Maybe the service department accepted Perky's plea that Ben was in no condition and could they please drop the car off on Oliver's driveway. Maybe they bought the idea, maybe they didn't. Be that as it may, slipping back to the forefront was the gist of Iris's note still clutched in his hand. That and a growing concern over what had become of Molly.

"No no no," Perky continued in a vain attempt to read his mind. "No heartfelt thank-yous, no cheesy goodbyes. My reward for playing nursemaid and errand boy comes from never seeing your backside again. Which means, the second the orderly pops in and wheels you out, you're no longer my concern."

She lingered at the fluted curtain and cocked her head. "Well there, kind of quiet out there right now, huh?"

"Yup."

"That's a break "

Ben nodded.

"Eyes better, throat okay?"

"Still a little sore."

"And your knee? Still ache? Not up to speed naturally, but you handled that long corridor real good."

"That I did."

"Yes, sir. Like a champion rodeo rider who might've taken a little fall."

"Yup, that's me."

"Oh, and don't forget the meds and stuff on the cart. Follow the directions."

"You bet."

In the ensuing silence, he knew the question was finally coming. To counter, he hung on to another fake smile.

"The lady who left the clothes and suitcase. A relative, huh?"

"Sort of."

"She coming back to pick you up?"

Waving the note, warding off any full blown query, Ben said, "Probably not. I haven't read this yet. I'll know more soon as I do."

"Sure, of course. But just in case, want me to ring somebody else? That number you gave me before?"

"No thanks. Thanks anyway."

Stalling some more, Perky said, "Pretty cool, having the L.A.P.D. pay your bill. Like I said, you are some lucky guy."

Ben had no idea what she was talking about. It occurred to him that he hadn't any medical insurance as well as car insurance, couldn't afford to keep up payments on anything. Perhaps C.J. had wangled something.

"Yup, I am some lucky guy," Ben said, hoping the well-meaning interrogation was now over.

"Right." Still doing her damnedest to end her stint on the upbeat, Perky said, "Tell me, those duds you're wearing. Button-down shirt, khaki pants, loafers—you're an actor right? Getting into your part for some old-timey flick. Like a take-off on stuff on Turner Classic Movies."

"Not really."

"A Hallmark TV thing?"

"Nope, sorry."

"Oh, don't hand me that. You are somebody in the entertainment business, I just know it. " Settling for this tag line, Perky blew Ben a kiss and dashed off.

Ben killed a few more minutes thinking again about Molly. Then, unable to put it off any longer, he unfolded the printout and scanned Iris' message:

Go figure. I send a cool, strictly business guy to straighten out your head. Next thing you know, the back lot is up in smoke and Leo has gone bananas. The last time I lay eyes on him, he's whining about his visa running out, sees immigration officers behind every bush. Not only that, he tells me some cockamamie balloon has burst and shekels to a bank in Bucharest are no longer in the bag. How anybody could understand any of this crap is beyond me. Anyways, thanks to you, he's flown the coop and my love life is down the toilet. So here's your stuff, enough to get by. Mrs. Melnick told me where to drop it off. She says you'll live and she's going to get you on TV to milk this, your latest screw-up. I told her if she even thinks about it, I will tear out her throat. So you can see from the way this message is going, it'll take a boatload of supplements and non-stop Yoga to even start to get my blood pressure down. And as far as your birthday goes, what do you say we do one of your let's pretend? You get lost and I'll tell June your mom finally came by and dragged you off, which she should've goddamn done in the first place.
Your used-to-be fake cousin,
Iris.

Ben crumpled up the note as the ache that had no name began to come over him. He tried to shake it off but to no avail, tossed the note into the waste-bin, returned to the bed and waited for the orderly.

In the meantime, the area around his knee began to throb and the noise level picked up. Some blowsy woman out in the corridor declared she had no idea who she was, how she got here and where she got the lump on her head. As usual, the attendant muttered a few uh-huhs and wheeled her off.

As the noise level abated, Ben forced his thoughts in another direction, still trying to get Iris' note out of his mind. The part about Mrs. Melnick took him to the dubious prospect of rejoining his fellow hacks. But try as he may, the old gang seemed like people he used to know. The coffee klatches, buzz sessions and rewrites, front pages of *Variety* and networking at the unemployment line--the whole industry began to fade like memories from a former life.

He shifted his focus to mundane immediate concerns. Where was he going to sleep tonight? Was Aunt June's vacant? It would be if Molly had taken off. But even if she was long gone, there was no way he could even think of going back to his old room. Aside from declaring he was definitely about to become solvent, the place was sold and June was skipping off to the Pacific Northwest. Like his ties to the industry, his link to Aunt June's place were at an end.

Absentmindedly, he snapped open the lid of his old suitcase and placed it on the bed. He gathered up the tube of prescription ointment, fresh dressings and tape, bottles of eye drops and packets of throat lozenges and tossed them on top of the rest of the stuff Iris had packed. He secured the latches, set the suitcase at the ready and resumed his waiting position.

Before long, the noise level picked up another notch. Adding to the din, a breathless female voice echoed up and down the corridor. Shutting it all out, Ben remained in limbo, biding his time.

Shortly, out of nowhere, Molly came bursting in.

"Oh, there you are. Man, this place is impossible: North Le Doux Road, North Carson Road, eight parking lots, George Burns Road, the Atrium Building, the Spielberg Building, the North Tower ... I mean, you could lose your mind."

At the moment, Ben couldn't bring himself to do anything but gaze at her. It wasn't the outfit, not the white peasant blouse over mauve jeans. And it wasn't the fresh-scrubbed look and her squeaky-clean honey-blond hair. As she clutched her ribs and caught her breath, it was her skittishness that made her seem so ephemeral.

Carrying on, Molly said, "Nice of you to give me away and put that cop buddy of yours onto me."

"Not true," said Ben, his voice as low-key as his washed-out feelings.

"Then how did he find me?"

"I don't know actually."

"Come on, you must have told him something."

When Ben shook his head, Molly gave him one of those get-off-it looks and said, "Hey, I didn't come all the way out here for nothing. I want an explanation."

"Look, it wasn't just me and some smoke. The guy threatened you with a gun and assaulted you."

"And?"

"And I was really worried."

"And now the guy—whose name is Deacon by the way— will be stalking me till he shuts me up for good."

"No."

"Oh, really?"

"Not if C.J. nails him."

"Great. Let's count on that. All I got going for me--after Angelique ratted on me too-- is no criminal trespass in return for a statement. Haven't I had enough? How much can a person take?"

More quick breathing on Molly's part. And no matter how much he tried to catch her eye, she wouldn't look directly at him. She played with her red hair band, shifted her weight back and forth and glanced up at the corners of the ceiling.

"So, anyways," Molly went on, "that also still leaves you and me. 'We'll settle up first thing,' was how it was left. But you didn't show up. And I didn't sleep much, let me tell you, figuring the angles."

Pointing to his throat, trying to indicate he was in no shape to banter with her, he said, "Please, can we just slow it down?"

"But no worries," Molly said, completely ignoring him. "I cleaned up, your auntie would never know I was there. Walked all the way to Larchmont and got a bite to eat so's not to open the frig and leave any traces. Or use the truck, of course, 'cause who knew where this Deacon creep was lurking. Drove here, the whole time with my eyes glued to the rearview mirror, which I had no intention of doing in the first place."

Going off on two more tangents, she revealed the pigeons weren't hers but Granny's and were now hidden in the bed of her truck. C.J. gave her Angelique's unlisted number after Molly "kinda begged him" and C.J. told her Ray was out of the picture. Plus Angelique might have some wiggle room, might be up on lesser charges if she too agreed to tell all. What C.J. didn't let on was Angelique had crossed her off her list. The second she got her on the phone, Angelique told her to "stick it in her ear" and hung up.

Looking straight at him now, Molly said, "Can you believe it? After all I've done. You want spunky, nice and eager—you got it. You want a no-questions-asked go-fer, personal delivery service—ditto again. And just 'cause I got antsy when Granny confiscated the keys to her wagon, just 'cause I figured something was fishy about this Hollywood run, what happens? What's my reward? I tell you, I was perfect for the part. It was my ticket, my big break, my foot in the door."

She tried to pace around but there was no place to go. She wound up at the fluted screen and turned on him again. "There was talk of going global, did you know that? And now it's shot. It is totally shot."

Ben tried to tell her it was all a crapshoot, always was, always will be. But she paid him no mind.

Another shuffle around the cramped space, then she rattled the fluted screen. "Oh, great, listen to me eating my heart out. I'll bet the whole hospital's getting a charge out of this."

"No, it's okay."

"Maybe for you. You're used to being a loser. But you're not dragging me down with you. Oh-oh-oh no. Nobody asked you to hole up in that barn and almost get choked to death. So I'm not falling for it, you hear me? You get it? I mean, how can anybody hook up with a guy who still reads Dr. Seuss?"

"I don't know."

"That's right. It's ridiculous. *You* are ridiculous!"

In the ensuing dead silence, tears welled up in his sore eyes. He faked one of those smiles, but it was no use. The tears trickled down his cheeks.

"Oh, man, what is it now?"

Ben turned his head and reached back for a Kleenex.

"Stop it, dammit."

But Ben couldn't stop it.

"Oh, why did you have to come along? Why did I have to run into you in the first place?"

Spinning around, she smacked into the orderly's wheelchair. Her momentum took her past the slight black figure in green scrubs and out of sight into the bustle of the corridor.

The orderly stooped down, retrieved his rimless spectacles and asked if he should give Ben some time to collect himself. But Ben was unable to reply, unable to do anything.

"That's what I'll do," said the orderly in a soft, nurturing tone. "I'll give you five minutes and come back for you."

Alone again, Ben's sensible side made an effort to step in, telling himself he hardly knew Molly. What was he thinking of? It was over. It never was.

But it was no use.

With nothing better to do, he set about dabbing his sore eyes, applied a few more drops and tried to get ready. The orderly certainly didn't deserve the added burden of a floater dragging his heels in an inconsolable funk. Ben got to his feet, gripped the suitcase handle, hobbled over to the wheelchair and flopped into position.

When the orderly reappeared, he gave Ben a wary look. When Ben told him it was okay, the orderly wavered a bit more. By rote, he reviewed what he called "decamping procedures" in that same coddling tone. Then did a last minute check, placed the suitcase on Ben's lap, and wanted to make absolutely sure Ben knew what he was doing. In response, Ben simply asked if they could please move on. Shrugging his bony shoulders, the orderly began wheeling Ben out.

Passing by the occupants of assorted gurneys and wheelchairs, the orderly was still unconvinced he was doing the right thing. Perhaps Ben needed to prolong his stay, request counseling, words like that? With a bit more conviction, Ben insisted that they proceed to the exit.

At the elevator, they encountered a couple consoling their little four-year-old whose right hand was covered with thick gauze and tape. They told him over and over what a brave little boy he was and that Mom and Dad would always be there for him. Ben couldn't help wondering what that would have been like. Having someone watching out for you, always making sure you're okay.

Before his spirits sank even lower, his whimsical side stepped in. How maudlin can it get? Wasn't the heartbroken battered failure enough? Did he have to toss in the lonely orphan too?

When the elevator doors parted at the ground floor, the little boy looked up and waved goodbye with his good hand. Ben waved back and watched the three of them taking their sweet time as they drifted out of sight.

Moments later, outside at the departure circle, Ben had to ward off the coddling attendant one last time. Yes, Ben assured him, he'd be fine. No, he didn't want him to call a cab. Yes, he, the kind aid to the gimpy and downcast should go and help others truly in need.

A few words of comfort, some time-honored homilies like, "Remember, this too shall pass," and Ben was alone and wheelchair-less.

He cast his gaze north. Suitcase in hand, he began hobbling along. Disregarding his throbbing knee, he threaded his way past the awaiting luxury cars that rimmed the massive North Tower and headed up George Burns Road. With a tint of sepia washing across the sky, he pictured himself in the last shot of a Chaplin classic: a poor but undaunted tramp, fading off into a slow dissolve. Another maudlin image to be sure, but easier to take than the shattered orphan.

The classic movie shot in his mind was cut off by a chorus of beeps. He waved the shiny black Mercedes on, and the white Porsche and the brace of cream colored luxury sedans. But the beeping didn't stop. It wasn't until the running board almost grazed his left side that Ben finally understood what was going on. Before he had a chance to speak, there was a squeal of brakes, an open door blocked his way, his suitcase was summarily taken out of his hands and tossed under the tarp of the truck bed next to the pigeon coop. With a traffic jam forming behind them, Molly yelled, "Hop in!" She helped lever him up and over the running board onto the passenger seat, scooted around and slid behind the wheel as they slammed their respective doors. To make more room, she tossed a Hollywood souvenir pillow and half-empty box of doughnuts under the dash by Ben's feet, worked the long wand of a gear shift hard, double-clutched and they were off.

As they hit Sunset, Molly said, "Guess I kinda lost it back there. I mean, after this whole stupid nightmare, fitful sleep and all. And your undercover buddy tells me about you and then you kinda lost it back there too. I'm saying, let's back up and give it another shot."

Quick translation: they could better conclude their unfinished business in the cab of the pickup. Now that she had simmered down, that is, and provided he was no longer teary.

At a loss, Ben simply nodded.

The ride was rough, the shocks, if there were any, probably leaking. But Ben hung in there. If she could ramrod this ancient crate with no qualms, he could sit still while riding shotgun and gird himself for a more definitive goodbye.

Maneuvering through the crush of five o'clock traffic and fending off the glare bleeding through the tinted smog, Molly eventually swung onto the Hollywood Freeway heading west. Above the growl of the tired old motor, Ben continued to wonder what she had in mind.

For openers, broaching the subject as she finally settled onto a right-hand lane, she offhandedly asked about his situation. Matching her tone, Ben told her that discounting Mrs. Melnick's latest gonzo scheme, and apart from some leftover cash and a dwindling amount he could draw from an ATM, his prospects for avoiding vagrancy were nil.

In turn, Molly admitted her own finances were in pretty rough shape. After Ray laid her off when the concert tours dried up, her only hope was getting paid for her deliveries and an advance on her upcoming role in Angelique's "new thing." A hope, like she already said, had been dashed forever more. In fact things were so bad, she had to give C.J. Granny's trailer as her home address.

All in all, the only good thing that came out of this exchange was the canceling of debt. As far as she was concerned, it was tit for tat and the subject was moot.

Continuing in this vein, Molly asked, "What about Aunt June and your birthday and all? What about that?"

Though he had no idea how she knew—perhaps he'd said something, perhaps she'd gotten it from C.J.—he told her it hinged on whether or not he'd at long last "arrived." As things stood, he had not only not arrived, he'd been tossed off the train.

"Tossed off the train—gotcha, right."

He turned away from her and looked out the open window at nothing in particular, still wondering when she would hit him with the wrap up. If she was through complaining how Ben had wrecked her life, what was it? Letting off steam, going for a long drive, pretending she was a typical Angelino? Hardly.

After an interval during which neither one of them spoke, she veered off somewhere in Camarillo. At first Ben thought this was where she was going to come out with it. But she simply pulled over by a seedy taco drive-through, left the motor running and said, "I really can't take any more of this. I have got to know where I'm at."

"Me too," said Ben, realizing he was miles from his old stamping ground, headed God-knows where.

"That's no help. I'm talking about my situation."

Ben thought for a moment and said, "Look, if it's still the stalking thing, by now maybe C.J. has enough on this pyro gunslinger to charge him and put him away."

"So you say. But what if the Vegas mob or whatever sprung him and he's right this minute on my trail."

"Not if he's double-crossed Ray, which he has," said Ben, surprised at how his voice and off-the-cuff style had suddenly revived. "He's obviously a loner and whoever was running him has hung him out to dry."

"In your dreams."

"Okay, I can check, if that's what you're driving at. I can make a call and find out."

"All right," said Molly, as she gunned the motor and took off again. "That's better. That would take care of problem number one."

Soon they were merging back on the Freeway bending north in the direction of Santa Barbara.

"What are you doing?" Ben finally hollered out.

"I'm thinking, I'm thinking. When it comes crashing down on you, you gotta keep rolling till you see your way clear."

"Terrific. And while you keep rolling, where does that leave me? What's the deal, Molly? I make the call, you're relieved and I limp around and flag a bus back? I could have made the call back in L.A."

"I don't want to be back in L.A. Don't you ever listen? Like I said, I am thinking."

Minutes later, with the old motor straining to keep it up at seventy, she said, "After problem one, there's still problem two. Bits and pieces, loose ends. You can fiddle and wangle. I mean, that's what you're good at."

"What are you saying?"

"I'm saying, okay, the call is a good idea. But that still leaves not knowing where I'm at. And how I'm supposed to face Granny."

"Ah, now we come down to it. Miss Molly's ulterior motives. Wangling Ben provides solutions and then she dumps him."

"Hey, stick with the program, will you? I've got issues."

More pressure on the gas pedal, more awkward silence. The hot air rushed through the open windows. As the pickup's motor groaned, the passing cars whooshed by. When they reached Ventura and merged close by the Coast Highway, the breeze from the ocean wafted in and the late afternoon sky settled into a powdery wash of blue.

"Pardon the interruption," said Ben, stifling a yawn, "when do we get the entire list?"

"I am just now breaking it down."

"Well, would you mind giving me a little hint before we run out of Southern California?"

"Fine. But don't interrupt till you hear me out."

For starters, Molly said, in addition to making the call, Ben could intercede a bit further. Even though she was a material witness and wasn't supposed to leave town, "because of the humongous fear thing," she needed to get clear away. Which meant Ben could also maybe work that out with C.J. Which, again, would still leave the problem of disarming Granny. Since Ben was so retro looking and harmless ... and since by the time they hit Castroville, Granny would've downed a tub of pricey wine and be totally sloshed "whipping out her guitar round the campfire and singing those folksy tunes. You know, like, *She's the queen of the Silver Dollar ... rules a smoky kingdom ... her scepter is a wine glass, a bar stool is her throne ...*"

In short, as Molly got that familiar distracted look, Ben could step in. Because if Molly showed up on her lonesome with the confiscated pigeons in tow, sloshed or not, Granny would let her have it and boot her off. "But if she saw Ben and he told her the story—wangled in the best way— Granny would be real happy and maybe even grateful for the male company. And for saving her granddaughter from a fall from grace. That way, everything would be forgiven."

And, Molly added, 'cause it was his birthday to boot, Ben would be offered all the barbeque and Cabernet Sauvignon he could handle. Plus a great outdoor tent and lots of peace and quiet to lick his wounds.

"Yeah," said Molly, loosening her grip on the wheel. "That could do it. For the time being that could do it just fine."

"I see," Ben said, finally getting a chance to speak. "Talk about wangling, I didn't have to say a word."

"Not bad, huh? I do amaze myself sometimes. Like the pigeon idea. Would've worked too, given half a chance."

"And enough rope, you could've hung yourself."

"Oh, really? Then forget it if that's the way you feel. Forget the whole thing."

Molly peeled out, passed a dozen cars in the right lane and kept the pedal tromped to the floor.

"That's not how I feel," Ben blurted out.

"If that's the way you treat a girl after all this."

Way too beat to keep this up and worried she might blow a gasket, Ben said, "Okay, all right ... use me, I give."

"I mean, what do you take me for? What do you think is going on here?"

"You tell me and we'll both know."

"Then why didn't you hop out while you had the chance?"

"Hey, let's just drop it, okay? Slow it down."

"No, let's have it, right now."

Feeling more and more woozy, Ben leaned his head back as the truck rolled on.

"Come on, Ben. It's a little late in the game to pretend to be tongue-tied."

Noticing a teasing tone in her voice, Ben rubbed his right knee, failed to stifle another yawn and said, "Cute. That's real cute. Will you slow down before we have an accident?"

Veering back into the right lane Molly said, "I would like an answer, please?"

Ben yawned a tad longer and deeper.

"I mean, what are you afraid of? What's really going on with you?"

"Me? What is this? The ol' pot calling the kettle black?"

"Come on, before you flake out on me."

"It's nothing. I can handle it."

"Talk to me."

"Look, missy, you don't spell things out for the planet's flightiest female."

"Oh, I see."

"That's right. You don't come out and tell her you'd like nothing better than to wind up around the ol' campfire with her and Granny. And no matter what, you just want to be with her. You don't leave yourself open like that. Not after all this."

After a long, palpable silence, almost imperceptibly, her features began to soften. There was a glint in her eyes and the most winning smile in the world. She eased off the gas pedal, stroked his left knee and said, "All right then ... good deal ... Let's just say we've got us a maybe for sure."

Ben smiled right back at her and said, "You're on."

He fought off a few more yawns. After receiving another pat, this one on the shoulder, he knew he was going under.

He reached down and retrieved the Hollywood souvenir pillow and curled up against the side panel.

With the ocean breeze wafting in, the curving roadway and horizon began to resemble the cover of Dr. Seuss's birthday book with its ribbons of candy cane in cinnamon, tangerine and grape. His right knee continued to throb. But, all in all, he had to admit he was having a good day.

Made in the USA
Lexington, KY
10 April 2013